UNSADDENED

Steel and Desire - Book Four

KENDRA GREENWOOD

Published by Blushing Books
An Imprint of
ABCD Graphics and Design, Inc.
A Virginia Corporation
977 Seminole Trail #233
Charlottesville, VA 22901

Kendra Greenwood
Unsaddened

eBook ISBN: 978-1-64563-806-3
Print ISBN: 978-1-64563-812-4
v1

Chapter 1

The door burst open, smacking the wall. "Mommy, Mommy!" Justice pried Molly's eyes open with her tiny fingers. "Wake up, Mommy, please wake up." Molly groaned and turned onto her back, focusing on the ceiling. She envied her daughter's enthusiasm for each new day. If she had even a tenth of that energy, she might make it out of bed.

"Sorry," the nanny said from the doorway. "I told her not to bother you but... should have locked your door." The nanny opened the blinds and Molly squinted, shielding her eyes from the morning.

Justice struggled to get on the bed and Molly grabbed her arm and helped. Justice straddled her waist. "Are you still sick, Mommy?"

"A little bit."

"You should go to the doctor. She can fix you."

If only. In the three months since Sam died, she'd been a hot mess. Her best pals and fellow FBI agents, Alyx, Jamie, and Laura had all visited, offering sympathy and encouragement. They begged her to go out to lunch, or a movie, anything to get her out of the house. The nanny came full-time now because she couldn't keep up with Justice, the poor kid would probably starve if it weren't for Colleen. "I'll be better soon," she said to Justice. "I just need to rest a little longer." She ran her fingers through her daughter's curly onyx locks.

"Okay, but feel better soon. Daddy's mad at you."

Molly's eyes stretched wide.

"He says time's up. Get outta bed."

What an odd thing for a four-year-old to say. But why couldn't an imaginary friend look like her father? Unless. Molly glanced at Colleen, who shrugged.

Molly searched the room for some sign of her husband's spirit. She'd heard children were more susceptible to *certain* influences and she didn't entirely reject that souls from the *other side* could reach across the divide, but… Children made up pretend friends and embraced worlds of fantasy. Justice insisted her furry unicorn, which she'd named Sparkle, was alive and Molly had made it a peanut butter sandwich more than once. Yeah, just a child's crazy imagination. Maybe that's why she was coping better than Molly.

"Come, honey," Colleen said, extending her hand. "We'll be late for school."

Justice put her hands on the sides of Molly's face and leaned in, nose-to-nose. Molly inhaled her sweet baby breath.

"Daddy means it. Get up."

Molly flinched. "Okay, baby, I'll try."

"I'm not a baby."

"Of course you're not."

Justice kissed her on the lips and smiled. "Bye, Mommy." She shimmied off the bed and ran to Colleen, circling the nanny's knees with her arms. "Mommy's getting up today," she said, gazing up.

"What day is it?" Molly asked.

"Wednesday," Colleen said.

Huh, *Hump Day* and Molly sorely wished she could get over the hump of her depression. Maybe today, perhaps tomorrow.

The nanny grasped Justice's tiny hand and turned toward the door. She glanced over her shoulder and said, "At least take a shower."

Ouch. But Colleen was accurate in her assessment. How long had it been?

With Colleen and Justice gone, she leaned back against the spindled headboard of the king-sized bed. A bed unbearably large for one person. Maybe she should get something smaller so she wouldn't feel so lonely. She remembered the nights she and Sam made love in this bed, especially the night they conceived Justice. What a perfect evening, what fire-tinged romance. Sam often joked they made a baby in one fell swoop because he set the mood so well. Candlelight dinner, dancing in the living room to Nina Simone. Molly sighed, her eyes welled and she pinched them shut, forcing back the never-ending deluge of tears. She had no idea a human body could manufacture that much water. Especially since she was probably deficient in every crucial nutrient known to mankind, since she barely ate. She feared stepping on the scale; she could already see her own ribs bulging out in the mirror, and her gaunt face.

The doorbell rang, followed by a pounding. Heavy footsteps trod the stairs. She'd surrendered her service revolver while on leave and her personal weapons were locked in the gun safe. Molly sat erect, pulling the covers up to her neck. His muscular body filled the doorframe. Molly exhaled slowly. "Jesus, you scared the piss out of me."

"You look like shit, how long is this going to continue?" said Rob Scarborough, Bureau Chief at the New York City FBI Office, and her boss. Alyx, Laura, and Jamie followed him into her bedroom dressed in their usual garb... dark suits paired with white or blue blouses.

She'd asked for a three-month bereavement leave and Rob agreed but she was nearing the end. "How did you get in?"

Alyx dangled her front door key. "We have each other's keys and alarm codes, remember?"

Molly didn't respond. Rob came to her bedside, hands on his hips. "I'm not walking in your shoes but people go through what you're going through every day. And they somehow find the damn strength to move on. Look, I'm starting a new task force and I want you to head it."

"If you ever get the chance to be a motivational speaker —*Don't.*" Molly ran her fingers through greasy hair. Never had Rob seen her in such a state.

"I'm not taking no for an answer. I'll expect you in the office." He turned to his agents. "How long will it take for you to make her presentable?"

"About an hour," Alyx said.

"Okay, then I'll expect you in the office before ten."

"I can't, I won't."

"Yes, you will," Jamie said. "With a little help from your friends."

Laura chimed in. "Think of your daughter. She needs you, and Sam wouldn't be happy if he saw you like this."

How profound. First Justice, now Laura. Was Sam sending her a message? More like shoving it down her throat. Strange coincidence that her fellow agents and boss show up at her door. Maybe.

"What's the task force charged with?" she said.

"We're targeting sextortion perps. We have several cases in Suffolk County. They've called us in. I've scheduled a meeting this morning at eleven so you can introduce yourself to the task force. You'll need to get up to speed yesterday because you have to go toe-to-toe with the Suffolk County Chief ADA later today at three."

Three? That didn't give her much time.

The term sextortion had recently been coined by the Bureau and agents had been volunteering to track perps when they were off duty. Pedophiles befriended kids on social media or gaming sites, pretending to be the same age and professing a sexual attraction. They got them to send naked pictures, then turned it into blackmail, threatening to expose them online and to their parents. Kids kept sending more pictures to prevent their discovery. Several suicides had been credited to the perverse practice.

Rob turned and mumbled, "Don't be late."

Her friends surrounded her bed with a collective don't-give-us-any-shit expression. Alyx tore back the bedcovers and yanked Molly toward the bathroom.

Showered, dressed and groomed, they shoved organic peanut butter toast and French roast coffee down her, then headed for the door. Molly snatched her purse from the hallway hook. A glint of gold stopped her mid-step. "Wait," she said. "I'll be right back."

"Don't you dare go back to bed," Alyx yelled as Molly sprinted upstairs. "Don't make us use our weapons."

Molly faced her dresser mirror. A pale replica of her old self stared back. Examining her hand, she considered the gold band. Her diamond engagement ring sat nestled in the velvet jewelry box on her dresser. She never wore it on the job. The wedding band either, only on the weekends, yet since Sam's death it had remained on her finger constantly, unwilling to sever their bond. Reminding herself... of what? She wasn't married anymore.

She opened the box, slipped the gold ring off her finger, and placed it beside her engagement ring. Snapping the box shut, she sighed, then started for the stairs.

"Good girl," Jamie said. "Good to know we still have some intimidation factor left."

Molly frowned. "Seriously? You three don't intimidate me in the slightest." They shared a laugh.

"The Four Horseman ride again," Alyx quipped.

Molly shook her head. "You're an idiot." Alyx stuck her tongue out. "One more thing, I need to text Colleen."

She glanced over her shoulder as she left. *Happy now, Sam?*

Chapter 2

Molly, accompanied by her liberation team, entered 26 Federal Plaza by nine in Laura's government-issued white Impala. Molly usually took the subway from her SoHo brownstone, her black Escalade currently garaged at Bureau headquarters. Perhaps they'd assigned it to someone else by now.

The security guards offered welcomes laden with a bushelful of sympathy. Ugh. Today would be long. Very, very long.

They traveled the elevator to the twenty-third floor and ran right into Matt Holloway. "Hey! You made it," he said, giving her a perfunctory hug. "So sorry about Sam. If I can do anything. You know I got you."

Molly closed her eyes, his scent sifting through the cologne. She hadn't smelled a man in months. Pinching her eyelids together, she fought back tears. *Not in the workplace, Goddamnit, not here.* "Thanks, Matt. That means a lot."

The embrace ended and she was reasonably sure her mascara and eyeliner were intact.

"I was thrilled to see Rob put you in charge of sextortion," Matt said. "You even got your own office."

"Corner window?"

"Yeah, I don't think so. Rob cleared out one of the old storage areas and gave it a name. Conference table and a ton of computers. It's like a war room."

Molly frowned. Rob Scarborough must have been hellishly confident his attempt to lure her back would work. Hmm.

A tsunami of good wishes hit. "Molly! Welcome back! We missed you! So sorry." So this, so that, so wonderful to be here and feel supported. Instead of crying – thank God – her smile widened nearly to the breaking point. Her daughter had been right. She needed to be with people, distracted by work, focusing on crises unrelated to her own life, fighting for the victims she'd sworn to protect.

A return to her Calling.

Or was Sam sending her that message? She shook her head, dislodging the absurd notion.

Rob Scarborough approached, his smile wider than hers.

"Glad you made it. The repercussions for disobeying a direct order from your superior would be quite painful."

"Well, I wouldn't want to be on your bad side."

"No, you wouldn't."

Matt informed her, "I'm on the task force so we'll be working together."

"Awesome," Molly said. "Get me up to speed."

"Matt will be your second in command," Rob added. "He's already given me a roster for your task force." Rob shoved his hands into his pants pockets. "And I've assigned you a NAT." He surveyed the room. "Lily?"

A tall, lanky woman stepped forward, her serious brown eyes focused on Rob. Molly figured her to be younger, maybe twenty-three or -four, a tad older if she went to law school as

Molly, Laura, Alyx and Jamie had. They were twenty-five as New-Agents-in-Training. After graduating college and grad school, the application process and training took anywhere from six to twelve months before you got to work in the field under the supervision of senior agents. Training that included over eight hundred hours of web-based courses in academics, case exercises, firearms training and operation skills, before the field training even began. In all, new agent training lasted about twenty weeks.

NATs could be a blessing and a curse. Their enthusiasm and need to impress, or prove themselves, could sometimes override their training, so you had to keep an eye—no, make that *both* eyes—on them. Getting your NAT killed would be a stain on your career, not that she ever remembered it happening and she certainly didn't want to be the first. Yet, their powers of observation and unjaded thinking could bring a fresh approach to an investigation and she hoped Lily would be just that.

Lily offered her hand. "Lily Blakely."

They shook. "Welcome aboard, Lily. Looking forward to working together."

Rob clapped. "All right, everybody, back to work." He told Matt, "Show Molly her office."

"This way," Matt said.

Molly and Lily followed Matt into the new war room, Alyx, Laura and Jamie bringing up the rear. He entered ahead, holding the door for them. "Geez," Molly said. "This is incredible." A huge improvement over her former cubicle.

"Nice digs," Alyx said.

"I'll say," Laura added.

"Impressive," Jamie said.

The four senior agents attended the same Quantico session for their training. Alyx and Laura were roommates and Molly bunked with Jamie. They graduated at the top of the class, ahead of every single one of the boys, and among them they held several records, Jamie for TEVOC and sharpshooting—training at the Naval academy and being a gold medal Olympian in skiing and shooting didn't hurt. Alyx was kick ass in hand-to-hand combat, particularly Krav Maga. Laura was an academic whiz kid and had a head for details no one could match. And her? Well, she didn't suck at anything, winning the top score in all the operational activities. Her powers of induction matched by no one, the ability to dissect a crime scene and identify suspects her super power. Their entire class had nicknamed them the Four Horseman of the Apocalypse, because if the world was about to end they wanted them at their side.

A man in maintenance coveralls knocked on the open door. "Agent Masterson?"

"Here," Molly said, raising her hand like a schoolgirl responding to roll call. She walked toward him.

"Okay if I put your name on the door? It's quick drying paint and I'll stay out of your way."

Her name on the door? What the–? "Ah… sure. Thank you."

He mimicked tipping his hat, without an actual hat and walked past her to a second door. Molly followed and peeked inside. The desk alone provided more space than her previous cubicle.

Alyx peered over Molly's shoulder. "I thought my task force on human-trafficking was a big deal, but I think you've outdone us."

Matt said, "We need a lot of computer personnel so we need space for the equipment."

"True," Alyx said.

Rob Scarborough appeared at her side. "Here," he said, presenting her service revolver. "You'll need this."

Accepting the holstered Glock 17M, it felt heavy in her hand. "Thanks."

Rob put a hand on her shoulder. "Glad to have you back, Agent Masterson."

"Feels like home. My second home. And thanks for this new opportunity. I won't let you down."

"I know."

Rob departed and Molly hooked the Kydex holster to her black trousers' waistband. A rush of satisfaction fueled her.

She strolled into the larger room, Lily on her heels. Twenty computer terminals, two massive printers, five large-screen video monitors, even their own mini-kitchen. She opened the frosted glass door labeled CONFERENCE ROOM and gawked at the space-age plexiglass table that could easily seat twenty people. The table's center held a video conference call center and two huge monitors hung on opposite walls. The chairs were covered in red leather pinned to the frame with half-inch studs. Okay, she was feeling really important... a little too VIP actually, and wondered if she was up to the task. What people didn't understand were self-doubt plagued over-achievers, too, perhaps on a whole other level.

Returning to the main stable, which would soon be filled with tenacious tech-savvy agents, she stopped in the middle and folded her arms over her chest. "I guess it's time to get to work. What time is the meeting again?" she asked Matt.

"Eleven. I've given everyone notice. We'll finish getting their gear installed by tomorrow morning. I'll stay back and supervise the equipment install and get everyone settled. Every trick we know to capture IP addresses is out of the hat. And these guys and gals are the best in the biz."

"Excellent."

"You and Lily meet with the Suffolk County DA's office this afternoon at three."

Alyx interjected, "We'll let you get to work. Let's the four of us do lunch soon."

Alone with Matt and Lily, Molly focused on the posters lining the walls. The first depicted a teenage boy in a white tee and jeans sitting on the bottom step of a stairway leading to the second floor of his home. Gazing at a phone, his hand on his forehead. The text said:

The internet connects your kids to the world

Do you know what type of world is connecting to them?

Another showed a closeup of a teen girl's face, holding her phone and looking alarmed, her eyes focused away from the screen. It said:

What is sextortion?

Sextortion is a crime that happens online when an adult convinces a person who is younger than eighteen to share sexual pictures or perform sexual acts on a webcam.

A third illustrated a teen-aged girl appearing despondent, her head down, peering at her phone. It offered an action plan:

How can I help someone else who is in this situation?

If you learn a friend, classmate, or family member is being victim-ized, listen to them with kindness and understanding. Tell them you are sorry this is happening to them and you want to help. Let them know that they are a victim of a crime and encourage them to ask for help. Each poster had contact info: #STOPSEXTORTION 1-800-CALL-FBI TIPS.FBI.GOV

"It's our nationwide sextortion awareness campaign. The posters have been distributed to schools, youth centers, churches and anywhere else we can target kids, their parents and teachers," Matt said. "Students will be walking by these posters warning them of a crime that begins on their smart-phones, computers, and game consoles."

"It's another level of tragic that most parents have no idea," Molly said.

"Both youth and caregivers must understand that a sexual predator can victimize children or teens in their own homes through the devices they use for fun and homework, even their security systems are at risk," Lily added. "Look at that case where the sicko hacked the home security system and taunted that girl in her bedroom, claiming he was Santa Clause, then enticing her to destroy property."

"These assholes better watch it," Molly said. "We're on the case now."

"Let's go kick some pedophile ass," Matt said.

Chapter 3

F lanked by Matt and Lily, Molly set her coffee on the conference table and surveyed the array of special agents, who'd been seated before she arrived. Lily would present the opening salvo, general information about their task and procedures.

"Morning, everyone," Molly said. "Welcome to the Sextortion Task Force. I will be the lead agent with Matt Holloway second in command and new-agent-in-training, Lily, working closely with me to get the task force up and running. My door is always open so do not hesitate to approach, I want to be in the loop at all times. Matt will run the war room so address him with any immediate concerns or questions. We have state of the art technology, which I assume you are familiar with." She sipped her coffee. "Lily disseminated a packet with general information regarding this newly coined term to each of you and I hope you've all read it thoroughly."

She and Matt took their seats and Lily began, gesturing to the posters on the wall. "The Bureau has initiated a media campaign targeting schools, youth centers, and other entities that service children. We've manned the hotline twenty-four, seven." The agents turned their heads, scanning the array of posters. "Before this task force, agents had been voluntarily aiding in tracking down these perps. I see several of you here today. These sexual predators manipulate their victims through gaming devices, social media sites and even online homework groups. They use money and gifts, threats, or feign romantic interest. A forty-year-old man will pose as a teenaged boy or girl and flirt with their mark. Many of these kids haven't experienced a sexual relationship and have very little savvy when it comes to the opposite sex. These perps are also adept at photoshopping images to make a victim think they already have compromising pictures of them. We recently investigated a case where the criminal offered money in exchange for explicit images. That man, Tyler Daniel Emineth, was recently sentenced to eighteen years in prison. One victim was a fourteen-year-old boy from West Virginia. Another victim from Michigan was only twelve. Yet another case involved a seventeen-year-old girl from Ohio who attempted suicide in a desperate try to escape the situation. In total, the FBI was able to identify twenty young people who were harassed, threatened, and sexually exploited online by an Indiana man who had served as a youth minister in his community. Forty-year-old Richard Finkbiner, in April 2012 had more than 22,000 videos of webcam feeds, much of it explicit content he had obtained from young people nation-wide. Investigators believe he had dozens more victims that they could not identify, perhaps hundreds."

Ian Turner recently moved from Detroit back to his home-town on Long Island. After graduating from University of Michigan's Law School, he'd joined the Detroit District

Attorney's Office as Assistant DA. He prosecuted homicide, rape, vehicular homicide and high-profile corruption cases. He went on to serve as Chief of the Rackets Bureau, Major Crime Bureau, and Training and Education Bureau before leaving the office in 2018. Now the Suffolk County Chief ADA, he headed a staff of 300, including prosecutors, investigators and support staff.

"Morning, Sylvia," he said, passing her desk. Sylvia was old enough to be his mother but you'd never guess. Her stylish gray bob and impeccable clothing gave her the appearance of a prestigious CEO. And she acted the part. It didn't take long for him to embrace that her thirty-year career in the DA's office was a gift to be savored. She knew the ropes, the people, *everything.* They agreed he'd call her Sylvia and she'd call him Ian. No formalities between them—she didn't fetch coffee or food—and she had no problem telling him what to do or to speak up when he was heading for trouble. This was the complete opposite from his role at the St. Andrew's Club as supervisor of new submissives and dungeon master. His dominant behavior with women only existed at the club and never seeped into his professional life. Women were his equal and, on many occasions, superior. He thought women the stronger gender. Because if men had to go through childbirth, the population would diminish to dystopian levels fast.

"Morning, Ian. I'll be right in."

He stuffed a pod into the coffee maker and perused the stacks of papers organized on his desk, deciding on the day's priorities. The coffee maker grunted its last few drops and Ian added cream and sugar, settling behind his desk.

"I have a confirmation from the FBI bureau chief in Manhattan. He's making his voluntary task force on sextortion official. He's charged Special Agent Molly Masterson with heading the task force and she'll be here at three." Sylvia sat and crossed her twenty-year-old legs.

"Excellent. How many cases do we have so far?"

"Three. One in Sayville, another in Babylon and the third in Bellport. I've given you all the paperwork."

Ian picked up the pile labeled Sextortion Cases and leafed through the first pages. Pictures of the young victims squeezed his heart. Fresh-faced school photos, just children, barely through puberty. Next came images sent to the perps. What made a person a pedophile? He never understood how someone embraced a sexual attraction to children and that modern medicine couldn't cure it.

"Rough stuff," Sylvia said.

"Truly." Ian placed three fingers over his lips, exhaling through his nose.

"You've got a meeting with DA Hendrickson at ten, then the weekly meeting with staff at eleven. You should get lunch early, before meeting Agent Masterson." Sylvia rose. "Make sure you read the entire file before she gets here."

"Understood. Thanks Sylvia. You should probably sit in on the meeting with the FBI."

"Of course."

Ian sifted through more pages, his frown intensifying with each new victim.

Meetings done, Ian munched a Cobb salad, finishing around 1:30. He leafed through the files and made some notes, in preparation for meeting Agent Masterson. She arrived early and Sylvia ushered her in.

"Special Agent Molly Masterson." Molly extended her hand.

Ian hesitated, mesmerized by her big brown eyes and jet-black hair—messy, but it looked like she'd done it on purpose, the irregular waves nipping the collar of the black suit jacket she wore over a soft white blouse. His mouth went dry, but he managed a response. He took her hand, her grip firm. "Chief ADA Ian Turner. Nice to meet you, although the circumstances are less then desirable." He'd love to meet with her somewhere else, anywhere else, and especially at the club.

"And this is Special Agent Lily Blakely," Agent Masterson said.

Lily appeared younger than Agent Masterson, her fresh face, soft brown eyes, and long chestnut locks more appropriate for a fashion model. Were all FBI agents this attractive? "Pleasure," he said, shaking her hand.

Sylvia cleared her throat, pulling Ian from his musings. "Please, have a seat," he instructed. They gathered around his conference table, Sylvia to his right and the agents to his left. "I assume you're up to speed on our cases."

"We are," Agent Masterson said. Agent Blakely pulled a file from a briefcase and laid it in front of Molly.

Ian continued, "We have three cases reported to the Suffolk County DA's office. We heard about the FBI's involvement on a voluntary basis and urged Agent Scarborough to make it official and include our cases."

"Understood, "Molly said. "We've got nearly twenty reports, including yours. The task force is comprised of twelve agents, most with IT expertise. My boss has authorized unlimited resources as needed. Currently, we're trolling game sites for additional victims and trying to trace computer footprints. Needless to say, these guys are savvy at camouflaging themselves."

"We don't have the manpower to do that amount of computer forensics so help from the FBI is sorely needed."

Molly opened the file in front of her and referenced the first victim. "Let's review the particulars of each case, all in Suffolk County, correct?"

"Yes. But I have a feeling that once the new task force

comes across police personnel it's going to explode. Hope you're ready."

Agent Masterson widened her eyes, her lips taut. "Me too."

They reviewed each case and Sylvia typed on her laptop. Sylvia had been a stenographer back in the day when secretaries used it for notetaking and transcripts. She had some magical way of combining her prior skills with a laptop. It looked like gibberish to him but she always had a legible summary on his desk within an hour of any meeting.

"He's major-league hot," Lily said as she slipped behind the wheel of the black Escalade.

Molly stared at her, wide-eyed. "Inappropriate. But accurate." She paused. "Tomorrow morning we'll review all the cases with the task force and plan our attack. Send copies of the Suffolk County files to everyone so they'll be up to speed."

"Yes, ma'am."

"And don't call me ma'am it makes me feel old. Molly will do just fine."

Molly drove her re-issued black Escalade to her Soho brownstone, arriving home around six. Colleen loaded the dishwasher, the leftovers from dinner on the counter. The aroma of food pinged hunger pains.

Justice sat on the counter while Colleen worked. She stretched her arms outward. "Mommy, Mommy, you're up. Better?"

Molly smiled and scooped her tiny daughter into her arms. "I do feel better. You were right, it was time to get out of bed."

Justice frowned. "It wasn't my idea, it was Daddy's."

Molly hugged her daughter tightly, inhaling her sweet scent. "Well Daddy was right."

Colleen said, "There's leftover chicken and broccoli. Do you feel like eating?"

"I'm starved. Thanks."

Colleen spooned food onto a plate and stuck it into the microwave. She pressed the two-minute express cook button. "How was work?"

"Good. The Bureau put me in charge of a new task force. I feel like I have a purpose again."

"I'm glad." Colleen put the last glass in the dishwasher and added a soap pellet. "I won't turn it on so you can add your dishes." She leaned her back against the sink and crossed her arms. "You had me worried."

"I know. Thanks for sticking by me. I'm forever in your debt. And I'm sorry for being so neglectful. If it wasn't for you, Justice would have suffered."

Colleen scrutinized Molly with her dark eyes. "She did suffer. But I'm sure she'll forget once things get back to normal."

"Not sure normal is ever going to happen, but I'm going to do my best."

"Good to hear."

Justice secured Molly's face with her small hands, forcing Molly to look at her. "Daddy says 'good job,' Mommy, but he's keeping his eye on you."

Molly pulled back and frowned. "Okaaay..." She scanned the room for ghostly signs. Nothing. But she couldn't help wondering if Sam was really here, there. Somewhere. *Of course not, you shouldn't take a child's musings seriously—file them under unicorns, fairies, and monsters under the bed.*

Right?

Chapter 4

I an awoke to a message from Sylvia. "Six new sextortion cases."

"Shit." He headed for the shower. He spent Friday and Saturday nights at the club, occasionally adding a Thursday or Sunday based on his schedule and available personnel to work the dungeon. The club was seriously understaffed lately and they'd had a surge of new clients. Jack, the club owner, had requested all the Masters to reach out to potential new Masters. Since Ian was new to the area, he didn't know many people. He'd attended high school in Bayport yet hadn't kept in touch with anyone from the old days. His parents moved to Michigan after he graduated. His father, a corporate attorney, left a prestigious Manhattan investment firm to take a new position at Long Point Capital, a private equity firm in Royal Oak. His mother, also an attorney, worked for the public defender's office in Manhattan and the Detroit office welcomed her with open arms.

Showered, shaved and dressed in a white shirt and navy-blue suit trousers, he fastened his silver cufflinks embossed with the letters IT, which the computer techs constantly taunted him about. He added a lavender and white striped tie and slipped into his suit jacket. He'd rented a condo in East Islip near the water, only a twenty-minute drive to work, until he could find something more permanent.

Sylvia met him in his office with new files. They agreed on his daily agenda when his office phone rang. "Chief ADA Turner's office. How can I help?" Sylvia handed the receiver to Ian. "Special Agent Masterson."

Molly's authoritative voice came across like a news bulletin. "My IT guys identified a new victim, a minor. Jonathan Ogburn, at 27 Johnson Avenue, Bohemia. Give me your cell number and I'll send pics to your phone. We're on our way there now."

Ian complied, texting his number. "The perp?"

"Nothing yet. I'll keep you posted."

"I'll meet you there—" The connection abruptly ended. "Sylvia, get me a district car and a police officer to drive me. The FBI identified a new victim and we're going to interview him. He's in Bohemia."

Sylvia made the calls and hugged her tablet to her chest. "You haven't even had your coffee."

Ian went to the coffeemaker, to-go cups were stored in the cabinet underneath. He filled the paper cup, fastened the lid and whooshed out the door in seconds.

Molly knocked on the front entrance of a two-story colonial, probably built in the sixties. One black vinyl shutter hung precariously and the lawn needed mowing. "The kid's probably in school," she said to Lily. She knocked again.

"Then that's our next stop?" Lily asked.

"Yup."

The door opened, a screen door separating them, and a

disheveled woman stared out. She wore sweats, her dirty-blonde hair cinched in a haphazard pony. "Yes?"

They flashed their credentials. "Special Agent Molly Masterson and this is Special Agent Lily Blakely. Are you Mrs. Ogburn?"

"I am."

"And you have a fourteen-year-old son named Jonathan?"

"Yes. What's this about? Is he in trouble?"

"We have a warrant to search the house. I assume he has a phone, computer, and a gaming system?"

Mrs. Ogburn hugged her chest. "A warrant? What's he done?"

"He's not in trouble. We believe someone is targeting him," Molly said.

"Targeting him? For what?"

"Is your son home, Mrs. Ogburn? We need to speak to him."

"Agents, you're freaking me out. Please tell me what's going on!"

Lily interjected, "We will, Mrs. Ogburn. As soon as we know more."

Molly grabbed the screen door handle. "This is the last time I'll ask nicely. Is your *son home*, Mrs. Ogburn?"

"He said he didn't feel well and asked if he could stay home from school. He went back to bed."

A loud crash startled the threesome. Mrs. Ogburn turned and focused on the top of the stairs. "Jon?" she yelled.

Pulling the door open wide, Molly pushed past Mrs. Ogburn and bolted up the stairs, Lily on her heels. "Which room is his?"

"Last one on the left."

Molly knocked on the door. "Jonathan, FBI, open the door." Molly turned the knob but the door wouldn't budge.

"Jonathan? Let me in," Mrs. Ogburn cried. She attempted to open the door but something blocked the way.

"Let us," Molly said, moving the mother out of the way. She and Lily put their shoulders into it and the door budged. Fuck that hurt. Again, and it opened enough for them to enter sideways.

The teen lay flat on his back on the gray carpeting, clad only in boxers, his eyes closed. Lily and Molly knelt on either side of him, Lily felt his neck for a pulse. She shook her head at Molly, put her ear to his face. "Not breathing." Lily started CPR.

Mrs. Ogburn shrieked her son's name and knelt near his head. She placed both hands on either side and shook him. "Jonathan, what's wrong? Wake up!"

Molly surveyed the room and spotted a medicine bottle on his desk. She grabbed it and read the label. "OxyContin," she said to his mother. "How did he get these?"

"Oh God. They're mine. Left over from some dental work I had done."

"How many pills were left?" The bottle was empty.

"I'm not sure. I didn't take more than two. They made me woozy."

"The prescription was for thirty." She squinted at Lily. "Get the Narcan. I'll call 911." Molly took over CPR while making the call, the phone tucked between her chin and shoulder. "This is FBI Special Agent Molly Masterson. I'm at 27 Johnson Avenue in Bohemia. A fourteen-year-old male has overdosed on OxyContin. Possibly 28 pills. We're performing CPR and will administer Narcan. Send an ambo." A pause. "No, not breathing and no pulse." She passed the phone to Mrs. Ogburn. "Stay on the line with them until the ambulance arrives. Mrs. Ogburn nodded numbly and Molly feared she was going into shock. She resumed compressions.

"Yes, I'm here. I'm his mother," she said into the phone.

Lily returned with the auto-injector and Ian Turner, accompanied by his cop cohort. She knelt near the teen's leg and plunged the syringe into his outer thigh.

"What happened?" Ian Turner said.

"Looks like he OD'd. OxyContin. We're administering Narcan and 911 is on the line."

The teen gagged. Molly turned him away from her. "Everyone move back." Jonathan coughed and then vomited. She held him steady as he retched. "It's okay, Jonathan. We've got you. Try to stay calm."

Sirens pierced the warm spring air. "I'll go down and direct them in," Ian's partner said.

Mrs. Ogburn peppered Molly with questions. "Are you telling me he tried to kill himself? That's impossible. He's a happy well-adjusted kid. He'd never do something like this."

"Unfortunately, there was something he wasn't telling you."

"What?" she said, gaping into thin air. "We are super close, talk all the time."

"Is Jonathan's father available?"

"He works in the city. I'll call him and have him meet us as the hospital."

"Great thinking."

Jonathan opened his eyes and Lily took his pulse again. "Thready and slow, but there."

"Lucky break," Ian said. "If you hadn't identified him and raced out to interview him, this could've been another tragedy."

"What are you doing here?" Molly said.

"If you stayed on the phone another second you would have heard me say I was going to meet you at the kid's address."

Lily said, "When Agent Masterson is in laser-focus mode she's sort of deaf."

Molly frowned at Lily. "I am not."

Lily didn't respond.

The EMTs filled the small bedroom, checking Jonathan's vitals, then transferring him to the gurney. "Can I go with him?" Mrs. Ogburn asked the blond EMT.

"Of course."

The posse followed the gurney down the stairs, watching as the teen and his mother boarded the ambulance, the flashing red lights dancing on their frowning faces. "What hospital?" Molly asked.

"Good Samaritan."

She turned to Ian. "We have a warrant for the kid's computer, phone and gaming system. Lily and I will gather the equipment and meet you at the hospital."

———

Ian approached the emergency room doors while his police escort parked the car. The attendants helped Mrs. Ogburn depart the ambulance and steadied her, then unloaded the gurney. She wailed, inconsolable, reaching for her son's hand. Ian ran to her side and tucked her arm under his. "Let the professionals do their job, Mrs. Ogburn. I'll stay with you until we know he's out of danger."

"Who are you?" she asked.

"My name is Ian Turner and I'm with the Suffolk County DA's office."

The deep furrow lining Mrs. Ogburn's forehead and red eyes tightened his chest. She leaned her head against his shoulder, tears wetting the blue fabric. He held her tight against him and led her through the automated doors. The entrance flooded with medical personnel shouting questions, giving stats, and barking orders as they wheeled Jonathan into a curtained bay. Ian settled Mrs. Ogburn on a black plastic seat.

"Please," she begged, "can you tell me what's going on?"

Ian hesitated, holding his breath and letting it out slowly. "Perhaps we should go somewhere more private." He surveyed the surroundings and spied a cozy nook with cushioned seating. "Come," he urged. Mrs. Ogburn followed and they sat at a right angle to each other. "Agent Masterson and I have formed a new task force targeting sextortion cases."

"What is that? It sounds bad."

He placed a reassuring hand on her arm. "It's when pedophiles target teens online. They present as boys or girls around the same age as the mark, professing attraction and seducing them into sending naked pictures of themselves."

Mrs. Ogburn's hands flew to her mouth, eyes like saucers. She muttered, "You think a pedophile has been in contact with my son?"

"I don't think, I know."

"Jesus, Mary, and Joseph. That can't be." She buried her reddened face in her hands, her sobs making others look on.

Ian kept his voice low and calm. "It's very difficult to hear such news. But these perps are quite adept at manipulating young teens. The number of cases has escalated by three hundred percent in the last year. Thus, the new task force."

"He didn't… he didn't… send… pictures, did he?"

"I'm afraid so."

"And you've seen them?"

"Yes."

She stood and stamped her sneaker-clad feet. "No! No! That's impossible. He'd never do something like that. He'd have told me what was happening. I would have helped him. Reported it to the police."

Ian stood and placed both hands on her shoulders. "I know this is terrifying, but staying composed is paramount. We need all the information you can give us. All our resources are focused on catching this guy."

A middle-aged woman in scrubs approached, stethoscope around her neck. "Mrs. Ogburn?"

Chapter 5

Jonathan's mother turned, her hands prayer-like under her chin. "Over here," she said, raising her hand. "My boy?"

The woman beelined forward. "Out of the woods. If he hadn't received CPR and Narcan I fear the outcome would have been quite different."

Ian outstretched his hand. "Ian Turner, Chief ADA for Suffolk County."

"Dr. Melanie Baker." She shook his hand, eyes narrowed. "Is the kid in trouble? Do we need to collect evidence?"

"Not at this time. He's a victim of an online crime, which resulted in his failure to see a positive resolution."

"Have the police been contacted?"

"Special Agent Molly Masterson," came a voice from behind.

Dr. Baker faced the two agents and introduced herself. "Are you the ones who administered the Narcan?"

"I am," Lily said, "at Agent Masterson's direction. Agent Blakely." They shook hands. "Agent Masterson performed

CPR and turned him on his side when he gained consciousness so he wouldn't aspirate his vomit."

"Well done, agents. I was just telling Mrs. Ogburn that without your intervention we'd probably be having a very different discussion."

A six-foot burly man barreled into the emergency room lobby, wearing a dark pinstriped suit, his red tie dangling from his suit-coat pocket. "Where's my son?" he demanded. "I need to see my son."

A nurse approached, speaking softly. "Of course, sir. Tell me your son's name."

"Jonathan, Jonathan Ogburn. I'm his father."

"Brett!" Mrs. Ogburn screamed.

He ran to her, grabbing her by the forearms. "What in hell happened?"

"Sit," his wife said. "I'll explain."

"I don't want to sit. I want to see Jonathan."

"I'm Dr. Baker. Your son is doing well, thanks to these two special agents."

"Special Agents? What does the FBI have to do with this?"

Molly approached. "This is complicated, let's sit and talk."

"Are you deaf? I want to see my son. Now!"

"Your son attempted suicide," Dr. Baker said. "These agents saved his life."

Mr. Ogburn's eyes darted, everyone got a stab. "That's impossible. My son would never do something so asinine." He clenched his jaw, his fists balled at his sides. "Mary, when did you know about this?"

Mrs. Ogburn sunk into a chair, her eyes focused on the floor. "The agents came to the door this morning. They wanted to see Jonathan, they had warrants."

The husband targeted Molly and Lily. "What the hell for?"

Molly decided hitting Mr. Ogburn with the facts was the only remedy to get him to calm down. She faced him, he towered over her. "He's been targeted by a pedophile, sending nude pictures of himself, then the guy tried to blackmail him."

Mr. Ogburn's jaw dropped. "I'll kill him with my bare hands."

Molly had no doubt the man could be lethal. She would've guessed him to be some sort of military dude, or a martial arts expert. Maybe a weightlifter. "We just got this case this morning. Our investigation is in the initial stages."

"Find the guy before I do."

Ian intervened. "Sir, I know this is very painful to hear, but we will do our best to find the perpetrator. You'll get your day in court."

"Who the hell are you?"

"Ian Turner, Suffolk County DA's office. The FBI identified your son as a possible victim, but he's under my jurisdiction and they notified my office."

Mr. Ogburn's body seemed to deflate, his head dropping. He pinched his eyes and his shoulders heaved. His wife stood and clutched him in her arms. He openly wept on her shoulder.

"Why? Why our son?" Mr. Ogburn released his grip on his wife and Molly neared. Mr. Ogburn rubbed his temples, heaving a sigh. "This world is fucked up."

"I can take you to see Jonathan," Dr. Baker said. "I suggest you stay calm. No judgments, no interrogation." Mr. Ogburn nodded.

"Can we hold off on questions for the moment?" the doctor asked Molly and Ian. "He needs rest. I can let you know when I think he's ready."

"Of course," Molly said. "The sooner the better of course." Molly offered her card to the doctor who tucked it into the breast pocket of her scrubs.

"We do have to refer him to a social worker. He'll be required to get counseling."

Nobody responded and the doctor led Jonathan's parents to the bay, their hands entwined lovingly.

Molly rubbed her temples, her mind drifting to her daughter. What if something like this happened to Justice? The thought terrified her. Children should be protected from such horrors and she was determined to catch as many of these perverts as she could. To save other families from a similar nightmare.

"What's next?" Ian said.

"Let's head back to your office and review what we have so far. Lily, check in with Matt, maybe we have a lead."

Sylvia met Ian at his office door, speaking quietly, tablet in hand. Molly and Lily sat at the conference table, eyeing the coffee pot.

"Caffeine?" he said.

"That would be great," Molly said.

"Same," Lily added.

Ian commenced his usual coffee-making routine and handed two steaming mugs to his colleagues, placing the creamer and sugar in the center of the table. He sat across from the women and sipped.

"You make your own coffee?" Molly inquired.

"Of course. In this day and age I don't think anyone should be waited on. I mean, unless you pay them for that specific service, like a server, or cleaning personnel."

"I like your attitude," Molly said.

Ian smiled. "My mother is a no-nonsense woman. She believes people should take care of themselves." Neither Molly or Lily responded and he gulped more coffee but for some reason he felt compelled to continue. "When I was a kid, if I came inside bleeding, she'd take a quick look to make sure it wasn't life threatening then send me upstairs to clean and bandage it. One time, I called down and said, 'It's a lot of blood, Mom!' You know what she said? 'Use two band aids.'"

Molly laughed. "That's one tough woman."

"Tell me."

Lily placed the evidence file the FBI had collected for Jonathan's case on the dark wood table, providing Ian with a copy.

He leafed through the cache of unnerving pictures. Not a good day when nude photos of kids were involved. Ian's stomach clenched and he pinched the bridge of his nose.

"The perp identified as a teenage male, which suggests the kid is exploring homosexuality. My first impression of the father makes me think that inclination might not go down well in the Ogburn house."

"I think your assessment is accurate," Ian said.

Lily added, "The techs had an IP address, but it vanished quickly, leaving no trail."

"How can I help?" Ian said.

"We have to interview Jonathan and I'll send you a report. We'll let you know when we're ready to make an arrest."

"I'd like to be there when you interview the kid."

"Of course, I'll let you know when I nail things down."

The agents rose, packing their files into Lily's briefcase. "I'll be in touch," Molly said.

The briefcase fell to the floor as Lily attempted to hitch it on her shoulder and missed. Ian and Molly reached for it, bumping heads, his hand atop hers as they both grasped the handle. They stared into each other's eyes for the briefest of moments, his breath on her lips, then quickly rose, Ian holding the case. Molly rubbed her forehead. *Awkward.*

"Sorry," Ian said.

"My mistake." Molly extended her hand and Ian relinquished the case, his fingers brushing hers again. His touch... what was the word for it? Warm? No. Hot. "Talk soon." She left with Lily in tow, her face aflame, praying Ian hadn't noticed.

Ian shut the door, his pulse throbbing. He couldn't deny his attraction to Agent Molly Masterson. She had spunk and when he stared into her brown Bambi eyes for an endless second, every part of his body came alive. Every damn inch.

He rarely went to the club on Thursdays but Jack had called an emergency meeting of the Masters tonight, before the club opened to the clientele. Hopefully, he could release the sexual tension that had been building since he first laid eyes on Molly Masterson.

Ian arrived back at his rental condo around 5:30 and quickly donned his club shirt and black jeans. He'd have to hustle as it took about an hour to make it to Montauk and that was without traffic. The summer tourist season was just beginning, but Thursday should be safe. On a Friday night after July 4th, drive time could easily take two hours.

He entered the club a little after six-thirty and ran right into Zach. Really, they almost knocked each other over. What happened to his body radar, he couldn't maneuver around a human body all of a sudden?

"Sorry, Sir," Zach said, "didn't see you there."

"Really?" Ian said. "I'm not exactly a small guy."

"Neither am I." They both laughed. "Evening, Master Ian. How are you this evening?"

"Considering I almost got bowled over by a bruiser like you, fairly well, thank you."

"Master Jack has delayed the opening tonight until eight because of the Masters meeting."

"Any idea what's up?"

"Not a clue."

Ian exited the sumptuous foyer, with its black and white wallpaper and gleaming black tiled floor, passing through the ominous onyx door and into the bowels of the St. Andrews Club.

The club felt weird, no pulsing music or bodies grinding on the dance floor. Even the tiny blue lights embedded in the glass bar were out. No bartender either. The darkened club imbued an ominous vibe. Ian's mind wandered: Was it shutting down? Had the membership suddenly waned? Were more Doms fleeing the scene, like Daniel, Steve and now Colin?

Jack exited his office along with several other Masters, all had drinks in hand. "Ian," Jack said. "Make yourself a drink. We're meeting in the Masters' lounge."

"Everything okay?" Ian asked.

Chapter 6

Molly returned home to the predictable enthusiasm of a four-year-old. "Mommy! Mommy! Look what I made in school today." Molly struggled out of her suit jacket as Justice clutched at her legs, pumping up and down on her toes. Colleen came to her rescue, grabbing the coat and hanging it on the hook.

Molly crouched, knees on the floor. "Let me see." She studied the picture: A stick figure had 'Mommy' written above with an arrow pointing over her head. Alongside Molly's image was obviously Justice, holding her hand, the accompanying arrow labeled Me. Behind them was a gray figure, a man. "Who's this?" Molly asked, pointing to the ghostly shadow.

"Daddy," she said.

Molly scrunched her eyebrows together. "Do you... do you *see* Daddy?" She feared Justice's response. Maybe she needed to consult a therapist... or... did she dare think it? A *psychic*. Molly shook her head. When did she start believing in ghosts and such?

"No, silly," Justice said, "he died. I just hear him."

Oh God. "Does Daddy talk to you a lot?"

Justice shrugged her tiny shoulders.

Molly focused on the image of Minnie Mouse on Justice's pajamas, a knot in her stomach. She glanced up at Colleen who shrugged her shoulders too. "It's a wonderful picture, sweetie. Let's hang it on the fridge." She handed over the drawing to Colleen who attached it to the front of the stainless-steel appliance with a magnetic goldfish.

Molly glanced at the kitchen clock: 7:10. "Time for bed," she said.

"Will you read me a story?"

"Of course."

Colleen grabbed Justice by the hand. "Teeth first."

"Okay," Justice said and Colleen led her to the bathroom.

Molly stood over the kitchen sink, leaning heavily on the counter. What to do?

Ian mixed himself a scotch on the rocks with a splash of water. He swirled it a few times and sipped.

He sauntered over to the cordoned off area where the Masters congregated, a series of throne-like chairs of dark wood accessorized with purple velvet and beveled studs. They were usually arranged in smaller circles but tonight they made one giant one. A vacant seat next to Jack, he descended into it. Jack handed him a sealed manila envelope, which the other Masters already had in their possession. A pink slip? Although Ian didn't receive a paycheck, his remuneration in the form of free dues, dues which were astronomical compared to other clubs, thus the elite clientele.

"I'll make this quick," Jack said, "since we open in about forty-five minutes." He slugged his drink, setting the glass down on a side table. All the Masters had their Dom faces on: stoic, intimidating, threatening.

Ian girded his loins, expecting bad news. The St. Andrews Club had fit his needs like a glove. Since the death of his fiancée two years ago he'd shunned the dating scene, and moved back to Long Island to escape the usual haunts where he and Rebecca had fallen in love. His emotions still raw, his interest in women had dampened. No one could compare to Rebecca.

"I'm planning on renovating the club," Jack announced. "Please open your envelopes."

Ian let out the breath he'd been holding and released the clasp, removing the contents. A three-page document with floor plans and a list of new amenities.

"I plan to leave the private rooms available during the overhaul, mostly for your use and for training new submissives as most of the work will be in the main area. We will have limited availability on the weekends and I will put everyone's dues on hold until the renovation is complete. I anticipate it taking about two months. Of course, we all know these projects usually don't come in on time. But I'm hoping. I've offered a hefty bonus to the project manager if it does."

The Masters perused the handouts, their serious faces scrutinizing the plans.

Master Mark asked, "I assume this will result in our schedules being curtailed."

"Somewhat, but as I said the private rooms will be available and I will still schedule submissive training. I'll send you the new schedule Monday morning. Tonight, and the rest of the weekend, will be business as usual. We'll start ripping things down Monday morning after the Fourth of July weekend. Any more questions?"

"I'm liking what I see on paper," Master Shadow said. "You're constructing an outdoor play area I see."

"Yes," Jack said. "Sort of a Grecian Garden with lots of hidden areas for shackles, swings and such. I've got a bunch of surprises and hope to hold some innovative events. There's even a maze where you can chase your little subbies and have your way with them."

The Masters nodded their heads or grunted approval and Shadow said, "I'm liking that idea."

"I'm throwing a party on Sunday, the fifth, for all the members as a sign off. Six o'clock. Food and open bar. Hope you can all make it."

A round of: "Thanks, Great, I'll be there," dotted the air.

The group dispersed slowly, conversations lingering over the proposed improvements. Masters Edward and William approached Ian. Master Edward slapped Ian on the back. "I guess you'll still be busy managing the submissives. I'm here for whatever you need."

"Same here," Master William said. "I need to keep my groove on."

"I'll see what Jack has outlined and will definitely need your attendance on the weekends. I hope enough equipment will be available. The atmosphere will be different. Not sure how that will fare with clients."

"It might be fun," Master Edward said. "Like having sex in a haunted house."

"Huh," Master William said. "We could definitely play with that theme."

Ian considered their comments. Yeah, he could work with that, a more ominous setting. Could be a thrill ride.

Master Shadow joined them. Most thought the ominous moniker a nickname, but it was actually his legal surname, as in John Thomas Shadow. To the staff he was JT but to the subs he was Master Shadow. He insisted it heightened his intimidation factor.

"Hey, JT, we were just saying that even though we have limited access to the club during the renovations it might be a ton of fun. More like an abandoned building, all shadows and plastic sheeting, dark corners and absent ceilings. You'd fit in perfect. Master Shadow's domain."

A laugh circled the crowd, several more Masters having overheard.

Shadow stripped off his shirt and flexed his muscles, his tattoos on full display—flames on his forearms and shoulders, his ladder company number over his heart. "I'm scary enough, not sure how much more menace our little subbies can handle."

Justice tucked in for the night, Molly poured a glass of Pinot Noir, sat at the kitchen table and ate leftover lasagna as Colleen donned her jean jacket. "This is delicious," she said.

"Thanks." Colleen picked up her bag and headed for the door. She turned. "I know you're worried about all this ghost stuff. But she's a little kid with a wild imagination. I wouldn't overreact. It'll be okay."

Sipping her wine, Molly glanced at Colleen. "I know. It's just a little unsettling. First, Justice tells me Sam is telling me to get back to work and then my boss and three buddies show up and force me back. It just feels a little too coincidental. And in my world there are no coincidences. Ever." She forked another piece of lasagna, hesitating in front of her lips before plunging it in.

"See you tomorrow, noon, right?" Colleen said.

"Yes. I have to interview a victim at three. I should be home by six."

"Whatever you need. I have no plans for the night so if you need me to stay longer I can. I have a paper to write. English lit, my fave." Colleen rolled her eyes, then made her escape.

Molly scraped her plate and placed it into the dishwasher along with her utensils. She swallowed the last of her wine and added the glass. After spending months doing absolutely nothing, getting back to work had exhausted her. What a slug. What had happened to the person she used to be? Never waning energy, focus, attention to detail, managing a home, a child and a husband? She did have cleaning help and Colleen carried a lot of the burden yet Molly still managed to cook dinner on the nights she was home and always on the weekend. Of course, Sam had been a big part of her efficiency, offering to pitch in with chores and child-care, without her having to ask.

Molly entered her bedroom, stripped off her clothes and tossed them on the bedside chair. She showered and climbed into bed early, intent on watching crappy TV. She received a message from Dr. Baker, confirming her meeting with Jonathan. She'd given Lily the day off. She texted Ian: *Interviewing Jonathan tomorrow around three. Join if you want.* The image of his handsome face invaded her thoughts, his chestnut brown hair and piercing blue eyes. Lily had been completely accurate in her assessment. He was major league hot, but he had a kind and caring demeanor. Protective.

An immediate response came from Ian. *Did you get permission from his parents?*

I did.

Great, meet you there. Her pulse spiked and she slid deeper under the covers. She scanned the room, like a timid tortoise peeking out its shell. "Sam, you better not be lurking in the shadows. That would be creepy." She seized the remote control and pressed ON. The light on the bedside table exploded, shards of glass blanketing the tabletop.

Covering her head with her arms, she gasped, then peeked out slowly, obscuring the O of her mouth with her hand. Eyes wide, she studied the room for anything untoward. Nothing. She waited, half expecting her dead husband to materialize.

"Sam?"

Heavy metal music blared, the dance floor was overcrowded, and a line at the bar. The club nearly exceeding its legal maximum. Jack had sent out an email blast announcing the renovation project would start the Monday after Independence Day weekend. Ian figured since there'd be a dearth of dead time when the club partially shut down, the clientele was getting its licks in now. He'd finished inspecting the submissives and assigned them all to Doms for the night and prepared to walk through the dungeon to see what members played there tonight.

"Ian," Jack said, placing a hand on Ian's shoulder. Jack faced him, a file under his arm. "I have a special assignment for you." He handed him the file. "Her name is Kelly Ryan. Some serious abuse, rape, major injuries, hospitalized for ten days. Happened in college."

Ian clasped the file. "How old now?"

"She's twenty-five, been in therapy for years, but still unable to engage in any sexual activity. Sensitive to the touch, to the extreme." Ian had worked with major abuse victims before with a good success record. "A friend referred her, Alyssa Downey."

"Oh, the physicist. She's acclimating well."

"Apparently they work together and she sang our praises."

"Good to hear. Is she on premises tonight?"

"In my office. I've reserved a private room for you upstairs. Take a minute and read her file and then I'll bring her up to meet you." He handed Ian a key to room four.

"Glad to help." Ian took the key and the file upstairs and settled himself in the recliner, usually used for aftercare, or sometimes other festivities.

The details of Kelly's abuse turned his stomach, his jaw involuntarily clenched, one fist balled at his side. "Jesus, what kind of man could treat another human being like that?"

His phone pinged an incoming text from Molly. *Interviewing Jonathan tomorrow around three. Join if you want.* His heartbeat quickened. Any excuse to see Molly was a good one. He was already counting the hours. He affirmed his attendance immediately. The feisty brunette invaded his psyche, her tousled hair falling into those soft brown eyes, her pert pink lips and rosy cheeks. He wanted to ask her out but… she was a colleague and she lived in the city. Not exactly a recipe for success. Maybe he should wait until the case was done, but there was the distinct possibility there would be more cases and the work relationship would continue indefinitely.

A knock on the door and Jack entered, ushering in a petite blonde in a short violet wraparound dress. Her hair was secured in a tight ponytail accenting her high cheekbones. Quite a stunner. He saddened, imagining the rapist attacking her in some dark alley, helpless to defend herself and succumbing to such unbearable violence. He gritted his teeth wishing he had access to the asshole, he'd pummel him into next Tuesday.

"Master Ian, this is Kelly Ryan."

He tucked the file into the chair's crease and rose to meet her, her eyes cast downward. But he didn't think she was in protocol, she was afraid, shy, withdrawn. "Kelly, pleased to meet you. Jack has explained your background and I want you to know I'm here to help." She didn't move. He offered his hand, and she ignored him, or she didn't see him, her eyes suddenly closed. "Eyes on mine, please," he said, then extended his hand again.

Kelly slowly raised her gaze, peering out under feathery black lashes. She hesitated before finally shaking his hand, her grip soft, gentle, not really a grip at all.

"I'll leave you now," Jack said. "You're in excellent hands, pet." He exited, quietly shutting the door. Kelly's eyes widened, her lips tight. Terrified.

Chapter 7

Molly's heart pounded, her palms damp. She slithered to the left side of the bed, hopeful no glass shards had reached that far, and turned on the other lamp. She searched the room for a shadow, a glow or white light, fog or a faint image? Nothing, although the room had turned frigid. Was she losing her mind? No such thing as a ghost, no such thing. Her crippling grief had perverted her thinking.

Exiting on the other side of the bed, she tiptoed gingerly to the far wall and flicked on the overhead lights, bringing them all the way up, the brightness momentarily blinding her. She hugged herself tightly, protecting herself from… what?

She scampered to the closet and slipped her toes into a pair of fur-lined moccasins, then stripped the bed and rolled the throw rug into a ball, attempting to keep the splinters contained. She deposited everything in the laundry room. Colleen had stopped sleeping over unless work dictated otherwise and could finish the cleanup tomorrow morning.

She vacuumed the hard wood floor praying, lost in her disjointed contemplations.

"Why you up?"

Molly jumped. A beat passed. She exhaled.

Justice stood in the doorway clutching Sparkle to her chest, her pink Minnie Mouse pajamas twisted every which way, just like her hair. Molly switched off the vacuum.

"Stay back," Molly said, her hand stretched out like a crossing-guard. "There's glass everywhere."

"What happened?"

"A light bulb exploded."

"Uh-oh."

"Go back to bed, sweetie. I'll come and tuck you in when I'm finished."

"Daddy says, sorry."

Molly dropped the vacuum hose and kneeled in front of Justice, her vision once again furtively scanning the room. "Sweetheart, this has to stop. Daddy isn't here anymore. I explained to you he's in heaven and maybe one day we'll see him again."

"I remember, but Daddy says he has stuff to do here before he can go to heaven."

Molly grasped her daughter's delicate upper arms. "Honey, you have to stop saying things like that. It's just your imagination." Okay, attempting to influence a four-year-old with her logical and rational FBI brain was actually not logical or rational. She heaved a sigh. "It's late, sweetie, let's get you back to bed and we can talk more about this in the morning. Okay?"

"Okay, Mommy, but Daddy is still sorry. He got a little mad."

Molly wanted to ask what Daddy was mad about, but refrained and then commiserated. "Tell Daddy it's okay. I forgive him."

46

Justice scampered back to her room, Molly still on her knees. She held her head in her hands, her heart in her throat. The flood came. Tears streamed down her cheeks dampening her tee shirt. "Why did this happen to us?" A breeze fluttered at her back, sending a shiver through her. An abrupt warmth seized her shoulder. She gazed upward, half expecting to see Sam's smiling face.

Ian made his way to an upholstered loveseat where many a new submissive had pleasured him. His dick came to attention. But there'd be no sex tonight, Kelly wasn't ready, not even close.

He sat, patting the cushion next to him. Kelly accepted his offer, making sure sufficient space remained between them, folded her hands in her lap and crossed her legs at the ankles, her butt on the edge of the cushion. Eyes still focused on the floor.

He laid his arm along the loveseat's back and crossed one leg over the other. "Eyes on me," he ordered. Kelly turned his way, her enormous chocolate irises fixated on his. "I will not touch you until you give permission. Understood?"

"Understood."

"Do you understand if we take this association to conclusion it means I will fuck you. You will be mine for the duration of the training. I will do my best but I demand total honesty and total obedience and I will punish you if you stray or lie. I will explore every last inch of you, Kelly, inside and out, and you will hide nothing. Do you understand and agree?"

"Yes, Sir."

"You've never participated in any BDSM behaviors before, correct?"

"Correct."

"No blindfolds, restraints?"

"No."

"How much has Alyssa told you about what goes on here?"

"Nothing. She said it would be more of a thrill to find out on my own. And what she likes isn't necessarily what I would like."

"Excellent advice." He pivoted his body toward her. "Let's go over submissive protocol. You will call me, Sir, or Master, and you must always use my title when addressing me. You are not to speak unless I ask you a direct question and your safe words are red, yellow and green. Just like a traffic signal. Red means stop immediately and we'll talk about how you feel, both physically and emotionally. Yellow is a warning you're uncomfortable and to slow down. It's the most important word because it means you are testing your limits and that's how you learn what new things excite and satisfy you, so use it sparingly, hold out as long as you can." He paused allowing his message to sink in. "Green means go, you're fine and hopefully enjoying yourself."

Kelly nodded yet kept silent.

"Excellent. Already in protocol." He smiled and she mirrored him with a hint of a grin. "Now, let's try the slave position. You can keep your clothes for now." She blanched, as most women did when they heard the word slave, so he offered his usual defense. "You're not a slave. It's a protocol position symbolizing your submissiveness." He allowed a moment to pass. "Stand and face me." Kelly complied, hands at her sides, eyes on him. He uncrossed his legs and sat forward. "Kneel." She sank to her knees. "Sit on your heels and place your hands on your thighs, palms up. Eyes on the floor." Perfect.

Ian rose, unbuckled his belt and pulled it through the loops, opened the top button of his jeans, then tugged his black polo shirt over his head. He tossed them on the bed. "Please stand. Time to lose the clothes." He stood alongside her as she slowly rose, facing him. "Green?" he asked.

"Yes."

"Yes what?"

Kelly frowned, her eyes darting sideways.

"Use my title," he prompted.

"Oh, yes, yes, Sir."

"Excellent."

She slipped out of her heels, then untied the wrap on her dress and let if fall to the ground in a soft heap. She wore a lacey black bra, her full breasts forming a line of cleavage, and a black satin thong. Focusing on her magnificent full breasts, his eyes drifted to a scar near the inside of her right thigh. He gritted his teeth… a *bite mark*. Not sure if he should acknowledge it or ignore it.

There were other scars, many scars. The bastard.

"You see them…" Kelly blurted, her face flushing.

He silenced her with three fingers on her lips. "Shush… it doesn't matter. You're a beautiful woman and any man would be lucky to be with you. But a man must earn it, not take it." He swallowed hard after uttering words he truly believed, words every man should heed.

"Color?" he asked.

"Ah… green, Sir."

He decided not to linger on her disfigurement. "Good. In the future you will arrive without underwear, just a short skirt and a top. Club rules for submissives-in-training." She remained silent and appeared calm but then again he wasn't sure if it was compliance to protocol or… *terror*.

He secured his hands behind his back. "Underwear off."

She didn't move.

"Color?"

"Ah, yellow." She shook her head. "No, I mean green, Sir. Green."

"Then please follow my order." Kelly reached behind to open the fastener, slipping the straps down her shoulders and depositing the garment on the red carpet. One finger slid inside the thong and she glided it down, stepping out, and with a flick of her toe, it shot sideways. She was damn cute like this and he struggled not to smile. "Hands clasped behind your back. Eyes on me, darling." Ian studied her body, his gaze landing on her face, surprised at her apparent serenity. Perhaps she was adjusting, comfortable even. "That pubic hair has to go. Wax everything smooth for next time."

"Yes, sir."

"Permission to touch?" he asked. Kelly nodded. "Use your words please."

"Yes, yes, Sir."

He'd go slow, nothing too intimate until he fully assessed her state of being. Placing both hands on her shoulders, he gently squeezed, then let his hands drift down to her elbows. His fingers migrated to her waist, his firm grip holding her in place.

Kelly's eyes floated up, lingering on his chest before landing on his face. His hands wandered upward until they surrounded her neck, the staccato beat of her heart in his hands. His thumbs massaged her shoulders. She closed her eyes and he let her.

"On the bed," he ordered, "face down, hands over your head."

He tugged her to the bedside and stripped down the slate-gray comforter and top sheet. She crawled onto the mattress and assumed the designated position. He clambered on top, straddling her thighs, his hands settling on her back.

He rubbed the knots from her shoulders, running his fingers down her vertebrae with firm pressure. Kelly moaned.

"Quiet, little one." She bit her lips, but couldn't hide her smile. He slung his leg over, unburdening her from his weight and knelt beside her. "Turn over," he said, "I'm going to restrain you."

Molly slept in the spare bedroom of her four-bedroom brownstone, the room she and Sam had planned to use for the new baby. The new baby who would never be born. They'd planned on three kids, but now, Justice was destined to be an only child, just like Molly. Her parents had met in Paris while her mother, a native Parisian, attended Ecole Nationale Superieure des Beauz-Arts to study sculpture, her days spent in the studio, evenings and weekends in the city with its incredible wealth of culture and inspiration.

Molly's American-born father studied at the Cordon Bleu, perfecting his culinary skills. They met at the Louvre one sunny summer afternoon, sharing a glass of wine – or three – then dinner and talking into the wee hours. Both her parents claimed it was love at first sight. They married while her father worked under the famed French chef Paul Bocuse while her mother spent hours sculpting, pitching to galleries in the hopes of having her work presented to the public.

Her parents found fame and fortune in their careers and Molly lived in Paris until she was ten, when her parents decided to return to the states. She missed her parents, not having seen them since Sam's funeral. Semi-retired, they'd opened a small farm-to-table restaurant in Montauk, Long Island, but the restaurant still kept her father busy, especially in tourist season, and her mother often traveled the world, lecturing and teaching. It was nearly July 4th and she'd agreed to visit her parents for the weekend where she and Justice could enjoy the beach and lovely summer weather. Colleen would be gone for two weeks and Molly couldn't take more time off since she'd already been on leave for several months. Maybe Justice could stay with her parents for a week or two, if her mother's schedule permitted.

Life went on, inexorably. But memories thrived in the mind and heart, and could make it so that nothing truly died. Her six-year-old self drifted into dreamland on the banks of the Champs-Élysées, tossing bread to the ducks.

Ian secured one slim wrist into the restraint, tethering it to the headboard. He studied Kelly's face for signs of distress. "Still green?" he asked.

"Yes, Sir."

He walked to the other side of the bed and repeated the action with her second arm, pulling the leather tight, both her hands gripping the brass spindles. He straddled her, laying his full weight on her pelvis, his hands resting on his thighs. "I want you to keep your eyes open. Keep your focus on my face. I do not want you imagining the rapist. You're with me and I won't hurt you. I'm only here to give you pleasure. You can trust me and you will use your safe words if you get uncomfortable, but not too quickly. Make sure you're really in distress. Maybe count to ten first."

Kelly nodded.

"Good girl." Ian laid his hands on her belly, massaging with his thumbs, circling her waist then drifting upwards. A breast in hand, he moved slowly, kneading, rubbing the taut nipple. Kelly closed her eyes. "Eyes open, darling." She flashed him a broad-eyed stare. "Give me a color, Kelly."

"Green, Sir, bright green."

He continued massaging her breast with both hands, then leaned over and took a nipple into his mouth. Kelly moaned. He laved the tiny bud, sucking it against the roof of his mouth. Kelly pushed her chest higher, tighter against his mouth. He smiled inside, this was going exceptionally well, so far.

Chapter 8

Molly arrived at the hospital around 2:30 p.m., intending to review Jonathan's status with his doctor before interviewing the teen. The nurse paged Dr. Baker who ambled into the ER about ten minutes later.

"Agent Masterson," she said, extending her hand.

"Dr. Baker. Thanks for getting in touch."

"Of course."

"How's he doing?"

"Better. Physically he's fine, psychologically not so much. He'll be on a thirty-day hold at Sagamore Children's hospital where he can receive counseling, along with his parents. I believe the boy is homosexual but was in denial until this happened."

"The perp did come on to him as a gay teen and I think for the first time he allowed himself to come to terms with his sexuality."

"I agree, however his first venture into that community had a dreadful outcome. And I'm not sure about the parents. They could make this worse."

"I hear you."

"Molly?"

Ian Turner walked through the automatic doors. "Ian. Just catching up with Dr. Baker for an update on the kid's condition." Ian shook Dr. Baker's hand. "Dr. Baker indicates Jonathan is doing well physically. Mentally is another issue."

"To be expected," Ian said. "How are the parents handling this?" he asked the doctor.

"They're calm, but I don't think anyone has dealt with the reality yet. Probably a good thing for now. We'll be moving him to Sagamore later today and hopefully they can sort this all out with therapy."

"Are the parents here now?" Molly asked Dr. Baker.

"They were here all morning but just went down to get coffee."

"Good. Ready to interview him?" Molly asked Ian.

"I'll let you take the lead," Ian said.

Jonathan had been moved to the fourth floor and Molly and Ian rode the elevator up. They entered room 422 and found the teen watching baseball on TV. His eyes widened when he saw them. "Hi Jonathan," Molly said. "How are you feeling?"

"Okay," Jonathan said.

"I'm Special Agent Molly Masterson and this is Ian Turner with the Suffolk County DA's office."

"Hi," Jonathan said.

"We'd like to ask you some questions. You up for that?"

Jonathan pulled his knees up and smoothed the covers. He crossed his hands over his hospital-gowned chest. "Guess so… do my parents have to know what we talk about?"

"Not for now. We'll figure out what to tell them together."

Molly pulled up a bedside chair and withdrew her

notepad and pen from her purse. Ian sat a few yards away. "When did this person first contact you?"

"About a month ago. Actually, exactly a month ago. I remember because it was my birthday, May 24th and I couldn't believe I'd met such a hot guy who seemed interested in me."

"So, you identify as gay."

"Lose the labels. If you have to use a word, we prefer queer."

"Got it. But you haven't told your parents?"

"No. I think my mom would be okay with it, but not so sure about my dad. He's a former Navy Seal, a tough guy, you know… I think he's trying to be more tolerant in general but it's a struggle for him. Not sure a queer son fits into his life."

"I totally understand. It takes time." Molly uncrossed and recrossed her legs, jotting notes in her notepad. "How did this guy approach you?"

"I was gaming, and I play a lot of opponents I don't personally know. But this guy asked if I wanted to talk off the site and we exchanged emails. He sent me pictures, said he was only an hour away and maybe we could meet sometime."

"We were able to access the pictures he sent…"

"Not the pictures _I_ sent!"

"We also have those."

Jonathan pounded his forehead against his bent knees. "No, no, no…" His head jerked up. "Please, tell me my parents haven't seen them. Please, please…"

"No, but they know they exist," Ian offered. "I explained what we knew to your mom. Before your dad arrived. I don't know what she shared with him."

Jonathan slammed his head back against the pillow. "I'm fucked."

Molly and Ian exchanged glances. Molly said, "I know it's difficult to see past the moment, but it will get better. I plan on catching this guy and sending him to prison for a good long time." Molly's phone vibrated and she pulled it from her pocket. *Matt: We got the guy's location—Ronkonkoma, we're on our way."*

Excellent. Interviewing the kid now. Let me know if you make an arrest.

Matt sent the thumbs-up emoji.

"We have a lead on the guy," Molly told Ian. "Address is in Ronkonkoma."

"Excellent, that's my jurisdiction."

"My agents will let me know as soon as they make an arrest. Jonathan," she said. "Good chance we'll get this guy. We'll let you know as soon as we do."

Jonathan glared at Molly, then Ian. "Do I have to go to court? Testify?"

"Depends," Ian said, sitting forward, forearms on his thighs. "If he confesses, then no. If he retains counsel and fights the charges then we'll need evidence to bring the case. That would include all communications and pictures, along with your testimony."

"Fuck," Jonathan said. "Fuck me."

"Jonathan…" Mrs. Ogburn entered, coffee cup in hand, her husband at her side. "Watch your mouth."

"Son, I don't want to hear that language from you. Ever." He faced Molly. "Sorry we're late, Agent, have you caught this pervert yet?"

"We're close. I just heard from my partner. We have an address and they're on the way. Hoping for an arrest shortly."

"I want to face this guy. Man to man. I expect you to make that happen."

Ian said, "Let's take this one step at a time. Once we have him we will see how the case plays out."

"Will my son have to testify?" Mrs. Ogburn said.

"It's a possibility but I will try to keep him off the stand. Depends on what the guy pleads and how much evidence we need."

"I don't want the kid to testify," Mr. Ogburn added. "I won't allow him to be embarrassed in public." He settled on the edge of the bed and squeezed his son's knee. "I'll protect you," he said. "Nobody is going to hurt you again."

Jonathan jerked his knee away. "I'm not a little kid."

"I think we have all we need for now," Molly said. "We'll be in touch."

Molly and Ian excused themselves and headed toward the parking lot. "How about a drink?" Ian suggested.

Molly checked her phone. "It's only four-thirty."

"It's five o'clock somewhere." Ian smiled, delivering a wink.

Molly's heart hammered as if she'd just sprinted after a runaway felon. Was this simply a drink with a coworker? Or something else? Ian wore no jewelry other than a watch, a Tag. Definitely no wedding ring. But she never wore one on the job either, so maybe he… yet his job didn't require sparring with or tackling thieves and killers. Getting caught on a fence or some other dangerous object. Nor did it let a criminal know you had family, loved ones who could be targeted. Hmm… Colleen did say she could stay late.

"It's just a drink," Ian said. Although he hoped it would lead to more.

Molly ran her hands through her messy bob. "I should probably get home in time to put my daughter to bed."

Ian's eyebrows lifted. "You have a daughter?"

"Yes, she's four."

"I see." Yet he had *not* seen that coming. "I guess your husband expects you home then."

Molly hesitated, her eyes tight. "No husband."

"Divorced?"

"Widowed."

Ian drew his eyebrows together. Damn, he'd stepped into a quagmire he hadn't anticipated. "I'm so sorry. I didn't know."

"It's fine." Molly rubbed her forehead. "I guess one drink to celebrate an imminent arrest would be okay."

"Great. We'll go to the Bayside Bar and Grill. It's right around the corner from me. 300 Bayview Avenue, East Islip."

Molly punched the address into her GPS. "Got it, meet you there."

Twenty minutes later, Ian held the door for Molly and they entered the local seafood restaurant, requesting an outside table by the bay. The day had turned sunny, the breeze warm for early July. It was always chilly by the water on Long Island, the ocean and bay winds a cooling zephyr.

The waitress seated them and offered menus. "Can I get you something to drink?"

"Lady's first," Ian said, deferring to Molly.

"Vodka gimlet," she said. "On the rocks."

"Any special vodka?" The waitress poised her pen over pad.

"Tito's, if you have it."

"No problem." She scribbled the order. "And for you, sir?"

"Martini, Tanqueray, rocks and a twist of lemon."

"You got it."

"Not going back to the office?" Molly asked.

"Nah. I have enough staff to handle whatever comes up. Plus, I have a commitment tonight."

"A date?"

Ian smiled. "Not exactly." He'd agreed to work with Kelly again, however he'd rather spend time with Molly.

"What does that mean?"

"I'm not exactly a man of tradition."

Chapter 9

M olly frowned. "Why not? A handsome guy like you with a prestigious job, seemingly sane, I'd even add kind and empathetic."

Ian's eyebrows arched, his hands laced together on the starched white tablecloth. "Wow, that's pretty high praise. Thank you."

"Just stating the facts, counselor." Molly leaned forward, elbows on the table, her chin perched on her entwined fingers. "So, why no dating?"

Ian hesitated. It was a place he never ventured. The waitress returned and placed drinks in front of them.

"Thank you," Molly said.

Ian twirled his glass a few times then sipped. That first crisp swallow always the best. "It's complicated." He had no intention of revealing his role at the St. Andrews Club.

"Bullshit. Give it to me straight."

He grinned. Molly pulled no punches, getting right to the point, although he was pretty sure she could level a real punch—to the jaw—and it would hurt. He took another sip, the cool cocktail chilling his throat. Ian twirled his glass again, focusing on the lemon strip floating in the icy gin. "Like you, the one I loved died. Two years ago."

"Oh, Ian, I'm so sorry."

"I don't like to talk about it. I've talked it to death. Literally. And I'm done with that. Nothing I say or do will change the situation."

"I get it, I really do."

Ian gazed into Molly's russet orbs. She probably did. Maybe he should share.

"Was she sick?"

"No. She was murdered. For twenty-four dollars, her engagement ring, and the diamond solitaire I gave her for Valentine's Day. It was a month before the wedding."

Molly covered her gasp with her hands, then mumbled, "Oh God, that's horrible. Did they catch the guy?"

"They did and that's when I abandoned being a defense attorney and switched to the DA's office."

"Understandable."

"My parents were pissed."

The waitress returned and asked if they wished to order something.

"How about a snack?" Ian said. "Their baked clams are outstanding as is the fried calamari. And all the raw seafood is fresh."

Molly hesitated, she probably needed to get home to her daughter, but... "Sounds good, I like all of that, whatever you want."

Ian addressed the waitress. "We'll do an order of the baked clams and calamari, and some clams on the half shell. Bring those first."

"You betcha, coming right up, sir." And she sashayed away in her short jean cutoffs and checkered tank top, scribbling as she went.

"Why were your parents pissed?"

"Because they're legal aid lawyers. My dad started out as a corporate attorney and made a shit-load of money, but my mom was always fighting for the poor and downtrodden. She turned around some big convictions for innocent guys who were sentenced to life and even the death penalty. DNA evidence helped vacate a lot of convictions and my mother was on it, big-time."

"Huh," Molly said. "How did your dad feel about that?"

"My house was the house of arguments, heated debate the daily fare. But it never got out of control or personal. Eventually she wore him down and he quit corporate and joined her. They run their own firm taking on cases where people can't afford an adequate defense. Luckily, they're set for life with the money he made *working for the man.*"

"Wow, that an amazing story, like a movie."

Ian laughed. "I never thought about that, but I kind of agree."

The waitress returned with a dozen clams on the half shell, accompanied by cocktail and mignonette sauces, served on a bed of rock salt and shaved ice.

"Yum," Molly said. "I can't remember the last time I had these." She selected one, added a spoonful of mignonette and slurped it down. "Fabulous."

Ian followed suit, the salty liquor tantalizing his tongue and sliding down his throat. He sipped his martini. Raw seafood and a martini the perfect pair.

"What about your parents?" he asked.

"Hmm," Molly said before imbibing another mouthful of gimlet. "Nothing like yours. My mom is French and she met my father in Paris. He grew up in New York City and was on a culinary scholarship at Cordon Bleu. She was in art school studying sculpture. They met at the Louvre and swear it was love at first sight. I lived there until I was ten, then they decided to move to the states."

"Talk about a movie…"

"Right?" Molly sucked down another clam.

"Are they still working?"

"Yes and no. My dad left a very famous restaurant in the city, tired of the madhouse and opened a small seafood place in Montauk. My mother still travels the world, lecturing and teaching. I think she's working on a new collection but she never shares her work until she's completed it. She's pretty famous."

"What's her name?"

"Alyene Bouchard. She kept her maiden name for her work. But I have my father's name, Masterson. I never officially took my husband's name."

"No way! Alyene Bouchard, the famous sculptor? Love her stuff."

Molly frowned. "You've seen her work?"

"I took art history as one of my required electives. Your mother had that exhibit at the Met and we got extra credit if we went, so a buddy and I took a field trip to New York City. I was blown away. Her knack for details, facial expressions… it really moved me."

"Get out, you're serious?"

"I am." The calamari and baked clams arrived and they both indulged, savoring the delectable bites.

"I love this place," Molly exclaimed. "I'd eat here every night."

"I pretty much do."

As if on cue, a broad-shouldered man with a lush head of gray hair stood at the table. "Ian, my man, how you doing tonight?"

"Great, Fred, how are you?"

"Awesome, as always." He turned to Molly. "And who is the lovely young woman?"

"Molly Masterson, she's a colleague. Molly this is Fred

Mancini, the owner."

"Pleasure to meet you, Mr. Mancini. I love your place, the food is scrumptious."

"I aim to please," he said, "and Fred will do just fine."

He said to Ian, "Glad to see you out with a woman." Then addressed Molly, "This guy spends too much time by himself. He needs a good woman."

Molly choked on her gimlet and Ian blanched.

"A colleague, Fred," Ian reminded. "Just a colleague."

"Oh, sure. Too bad." He winked at Molly. "He's a good catch and I know a good catch when I see it."

Fred slapped Ian on the back. "Nice to meet you, Molly. Please come back soon." He winked again before moving to another table to make his nightly rounds.

Ian leaned in, his elbows on the table. "What's your story? I shared mine, your turn."

Molly popped a crispy piece of calamari into her mouth and chewed slowly. Ian was right, he'd shared private painful moments and the least she could do was tell her tale. "We were on our way to a friend's engagement party last April. We were traveling east on Northern State Parkway, just before the entrance onto 347. A tractor-trailer entered illegally and hit an overpass. It rolled onto our car, crushing it. Sam was killed instantly, the driver also, I survived with minor injuries. Justice was home with the nanny, thank God." She swore Ian could see right through her, into her heart, the open wound still bleeding. Her throat constricted. She wanted to share her story but she didn't want his pity.

Ian stared at his empty glass, then gazed up, yet his baby blues didn't appear sad, more... thoughtful, resolute, indomitable. "Pretty horrible. Looks like we've both taken our lumps from the Fates." One corner of his mouth turned up. "Your daughter's name is Justice? A little too on the nose for a federal agent." His full smile washed over her like a warm waterfall. He might have the most beautiful smile she'd ever seen on a man.

Molly beamed in return. "I know, my parents didn't care much for it at first, but they're over it."

"I like it, it's a strong name."

"Thanks."

"What's it like having a four-year-old?"

"Exhausting, but the best thing that ever happened to me, and way better than a three-year-old. She just turned four. Her birthday was the week before my husband's accident."

Ian rested his seafood fork on the square white plate. "I wanted a big family. I have three older sisters and they put me through the ringer. Dressing me up, sometimes I got to be the king, but mostly I was the baby. But as they got older they treated me like one of them and I learned to talk about my feelings, to express emotion. I think overall they made me a better man."

"From what I've seen, I would have to agree."

"First you tell me I'm handsome, with a prestigious job, seemingly sane, even add kind and empathetic and now you add more praise. I think I'm blushing."

"On that note," Molly said, "let's call it a night." She pushed back from her chair and deposited the cloth napkin on the table. She slung her purse over her shoulder and rose.

Ian stood and faced her. "Molly, I know you're still in mourning and I would never want to intrude or be presumptuous, but I'd really like to see you again."

Molly fumbled with the strap on her purse, her eyes cast downward. What the hell was she doing? This was a mistake.

She'd worried Ian would read something into this and her fears had been accurate. Stupid, stupid, stupid.

She liked Ian, liked him a lot but she'd only been widowed three months. Too soon to even consider dating. "I enjoyed having a drink with you but I'm not ready to date anyone. I'm not sure I ever will. And besides, I thought you said you don't date."

"I'm thinking of changing my ways, but I understand. There's no rush." He walked her to her car, holding the door open. "I'll let you know what's going on with the case as soon as I hear something."

"Awesome. And thanks for the drink."

He shut the door and she exited the parking lot as he stood there, eyes still on her. Stopped at a light, she thrust her forehead onto the steering wheel. *Idiot.*

Ian got behind the wheel of his black, series 750i BMW and pushed the ignition button. He leaned his head back against the headrest and sighed forcefully. Holy shit... she was *that* Molly. He'd attended Colin's engagement party and recalled the report of the tragic accident. She was close friends with his Dom buddies' wives, so maybe she wouldn't be too freaked when she found out he worked at the St. Andrews Club... that's if she knew the truth about their husbands.

Chapter 10

Ian entered the Masters' lounge around seven, heading for the locker room. He'd committed to working with Kelly again and hoped to continue her excellent progress. Although what he really wanted was to be with Molly. Did he dare consider her submitting to him as a Dom? Something he only embraced in the bedroom, role-playing, a game for adults only.

His phone rang. "Colin."

"Hey buddy, you working at the club tonight?"

"Guilty."

"Making some new subbie find nirvana."

"Hoping to, she's suffered some traumatic abuse so I feel like I'm sitting on a powder keg. Could go either way."

"I know that drill. Good luck. Listen, the reason I called is Daniel, Steve, and I are playing golf tomorrow then going back to Daniel's house for a barbecue. Up for the links, some cocktails and a little chow?"

"Sounds great. What time?"

"Tee-off is at one so meet us around 12:30. We're playing at Southampton. Daniel's a member."

"Okay, meet you there."

Ian would be proximate to Southampton after his shift at the club, and his golf gear was always in the trunk. He often stayed at the local motel when working consecutive nights at the club. He'd been checking out summer rentals, as the East End of Long Island was a fun playground in the summer, and the surfing great, but the traffic could be an epic battle.

"Ian, my man, how are you?" Master Shadow said. He threw his phone, keys, and wallet into his locker and spun the combination lock, then gave the handle a tug for good measure.

"Fine, you?"

"Most excellent. Looking forward to a night of hard play. What's your schedule?"

"Working with Kelly, the new trainee again." Ian locked his personal items away, but kept his phone in case there was a break in the case. He faced Shadow.

"How's she doing? Some bad shit for that chick."

"The worst, but she made significant progress the first time we worked together. Hoping to move her along further tonight."

"When do you think you'll set her loose, would love to play with her."

Ian smirked. "Your reputation precedes you so I think it will be a while before she's up to your demands."

Shadow slapped Ian on the shoulder. "You're not exactly an easy Dom either. I bet she's ready sooner than you think."

Master Shadow exited the lounge and Ian sat heavily on the wooden bench, his head in his hands. What was Molly doing at this very minute? Was she reading her daughter a bedtime story then tucking her into bed, then smothering her with a hundred kisses like his mother used to?

Only three months since her husband died, no way was she ready to move on... to give him a chance. He was barely seeing straight after Rebecca got killed and that was two years ago. But he couldn't deny the pull Molly had on him, his desire for her, his need to love a woman and for her to love him back.

Justice already asleep, Molly bid Colleen goodnight and told her she wouldn't be needed again until Monday morning. Colleen had finished cleaning up the debris from the exploding light bulb and remade the bed. Molly unbuttoned her blouse slowly, thinking of Ian sitting across the table, sipping his drink, his icy blue eyes studying her, no pity, just empathy. And he certainly understood her state of mind. She threw her shirt in the hamper and stowed her suit in the closet, along with her simple black shoes. If the circumstances had been different she would have worn something more feminine, a flowered dress or a shoulder-less top, with strappy sandals, dangly earrings, and a flouncy skirt. She would have taken more time with her make-up... a smoky eye and a brighter lipstick. Good God, she hadn't thought about her appearance in a long time. Sam liked her as a no-muss, no-fuss woman, and often remarked that her natural beauty was all he wanted. Yet she sometimes missed playing dress-up, a little color or frill, perhaps some lace? And for some reason she wanted to dress up for Ian, flirt a little, be coy and have him chase until he caught her, then he'd throw her on the bed and ravish her. Oh. My. God. Such salacious thoughts. What the hell was wrong with her? She searched the room, waiting for a phantomlike chill, or something to explode.

Her cell rang, startling her half out of her wits. "Hey Alyx, how are you?" She stared at her underwear-clad body in the mirror, rubbing her forehead.

"Good. How is it being back at work?"

"You guys were right, I needed to have a purpose again. Outside of the home."

"I knew it. So happy you're in the world with the rest of us. Listen, the guys are playing golf Sunday and we decided to have a little barbecue after. Come, and bring Justice, say about one, the guys should be home by six. The pool is open and heated. Of course there's the beach and the ocean, although the water is still a little cold for swimming. I have tons of beach toys so you don't need to bring paraphernalia or towels."

"That sounds great. School just finished and I need to think about what to do with Justice. She's too young for summer camp and I don't want to put her in school all summer. I'm thinking of leaving her with my parents for a few weeks. Hopefully, I'll come up with plan B by then. What can I bring?"

"How about dessert? Laura, Jamie and I have the rest covered and of course Lydia is helping us, or should I say, acting as Master Chef."

Molly chuckled. Lydia had been Daniel's housekeeper before he met Alyx and now she'd become a second mother to Alyx. Or maybe the only mother, as Alyx's had vanished when she was a child and presumed dead. "Great, see you about one."

Molly pressed her phone to her chest and smiled. Getting back into the groove felt good. She needed to build a new life, a different life. Her thoughts drifted to Ian again, his incredible good looks turned her into putty. He had a certain swagger, like a surfer who'd just conquered the biggest of waves. That dark brown hair, and a tan that made it seem like he'd just stepped off the beach after a long day on the water. His blue eyes like cerulean eddies in a turbulent ocean. A warmth spread over her, her pulse a pounding rhythm.

She pictured his arms around her, undressing her, stroking her, kissing her. Good God... Sam had only been gone three months. She couldn't... she just wouldn't.

———

Ian walked onto the floor, deciding to skip his usual drink, he'd already had a martini. Kelly waited in the submissive's pen, shackled to the metal bar waiting for her Dom... for him. He waved and nodded to other Masters as he approached the pen, submissives in tow in one way or another—leashes, firm hands clutching wrists or necks—dragging them into the carnal depths of the throbbing club. The beat of the music melded with his heartbeat, excitement spiking, the thrill of the conquest. Or was it?

Normally he'd be psyched to play with a new submissive, even one like Kelly who wasn't even close to letting him fuck her. Something felt different tonight. Molly. He still wanted Molly. He shook his head. No chance of that.

Kelly's eyes followed him as he took each step closer. She smiled as he reached over the pen's fence and unshackled her. He widened the gate for her exit. "Evening, Sir. Excited to see you again."

"Are you?" Ian slipped two fingers into a furry red manacle and tugged her toward him.

"Yes, Sir. Very."

"I'm glad. So. We'll try some new things tonight. Do you prefer a private room or would you like to play in public?"

"Whatever pleases Sir. I'm not afraid."

Ian's eyebrows shot up. That quickly? She was over her fears? He doubted it. Doubted it very seriously. "Hmm," he said. "I'm surprised to hear you say that. I thought this would take longer."

"Me too, Sir. But I feel different with you, safe, and excited to explore my new sexuality."

Normally a statement of this nature would thrill him, to see a new submissive embrace her role, to want to be dominated by him, a gift he never took lightly. He was flummoxed, his burgeoning feelings for Molly and the attention of a beautiful young woman like Kelly scrambling his emotions.

"Then we'll play on the floor so other Masters can get a look at you and offer to work with you in the future."

"What?" Kelly said. "Others? I thought I'd only work with you."

"I'm just getting you back into the saddle, darling. Lots more studs to ride. Besides, other Masters have different likes and may be able to take you someplace I don't."

"But I only want you!"

Ian struggled not to smile. Every Master knew letting a sub get too involved emotionally was something to avoid. Emotions led to entanglements and the only entanglement a Master desired was one with rope or leather.

"We're done talking. You're in protocol, no talking unless I allow it." He secured a wrist and pulled her forward. "Let's find a restraining bench. I think you need to be spanked."

Molly switched on the TV, snuggled in bed, her navy-blue FBI tee shirt her bedclothes. The phone vibrated on the nightstand, she reached for it. Matt. "News?"

"We got him. He was actually home but tried to make a run for it. We nabbed him in the woods behind his house, in a tree house. Crazy, right?"

"For sure. That's excellent news. Where is he?"

"In the Suffolk County jail. Isolation, twenty-four-hour surveillance. Not taking any chances."

"Good. Has anyone notified Ian? I can call him."

"The Suffolk County detectives filed their report but it wouldn't hurt to reach out to him personally."

"Glad to do it. We'll touch base Monday morning, get our ducks in a row with the DA's office. Nice work, Matt."

"You too, if you hadn't gotten to that kid when you did, well… I hate to think."

"Back atcha. Have Lily collect all the reports and set up a meeting at the DA's office for Monday. I'd like to arraign this guy before the holiday."

"Already on it. See you Monday morning." She dialed Ian.

Chapter 11

I an buckled the last strap on the restraining bench around Kelly's ankle, then stuck a finger between her soft flesh and the leather making sure it wasn't too tight. No bruises on his watch. Her lush ass teased him, he wanted to touch it, rub it, spank it and he intended to take his time. He removed his shirt and draped it on a nearby chair and stood between her legs. The first swat was gentle and he rubbed the flesh afterward. Kelly didn't utter a peep. Good girl. The second slap came harder and her body flinched, still silent. He moved around to her side so he could see her face. Her eyes were closed, lips pressed tight. He slapped her pink flesh again, then twice more, massaging the skin afterwards.

His phone vibrated in his pocket. He shouldn't check it, Kelly needed his undivided attention. However, it could be Molly about the case, or maybe she'd changed her mind and wanted to see him again. He continued spanking his little subbie until she finally yelped. "Quiet, ouch is not a safe word so I will continue until I'm satisfied. Or... she was satis-

KENDRA GREENWOOD

fied. He probed the wetness between her legs, definitely aroused.

The phone continued to vibrate and his curiosity bested him. He pulled his cell from his pocket. Molly. His pulse accelerated, his breathing quickened. He shouldn't answer it, but he desperately wanted to hear Molly's voice. He shoved it back in his pocket because it would be poor protocol to do otherwise.

He spanked Kelly until her ass flamed, then probed her vagina with two fingers. "Are you close? Do you want to come?"

"Oh, yes, yes, Sir."

He smiled, maybe she had progressed, however he wasn't sure the emotional rush that comes with an orgasm would be desirable. It could go either way, breaking her free or plummeting her further downward. Risky at best. He decided against it. "Not yet, little subbie. The longer you hold out the better your orgasm will be. And we have much more exploring to do."

Ian unshackled his new subbie and led her to a flogging cross. "Kneel, in the slave position." Kelly immediately complied. The phone call from Molly niggled at him. Maybe it was the case and she needed him for something important. He thought of tying Kelly to the giant X while he returned the call, but Masters never left a tied-up subbie alone.

Master Shadow walked by and Ian almost asked for help but thought better of it. Shadow might freak her out. A slap on his back and he turned to face Master Edward, his dirty blond buzz cut and corded neck identifying his former Marine status. Now he worked for Homeland Security. "How's our new subbie doing?"

"Well, she's coming along nicely." Ian immediately knew he'd made a pun and rephrased. "Actually, she wants to come but I haven't allowed it. I don't think she's ready."

"Need some help?"

"I do, would you mind taking over for a few minutes? I'll be right back."

"No problem. A flogging is in order then?"

"Yes. You know her background?"

"Absolutely."

"Her safe words are red, yellow and green. And remind her 'ouch' isn't a safe word."

They both chuckled. "Pretty common mistake," Master Edward said. "I'll break her of that bad habit pronto."

"Thanks. I'll be right back." To Kelly, he said, "Master Edward is going to take a turn. I'll be back to check on you in a few minutes."

Kelly turned her head, straining to see his face. She didn't speak although he was sure she wanted to protest. "Be good for Master Edward or you'll earn another spanking." He winked.

He ventured into the Master's Lounge where music wasn't pounding walls and dialed Molly.

"Hey."

"What's up? Change your mind about seeing me again?" He hoped.

"What? No. It's about the case. We caught the guy and he's in the Suffolk County lockup. Solitary, suicide watch, monitored twenty-four, seven."

"Great news."

"I want him arraigned as soon as possible. Can you make that happen?"

Alone in the lounge, Ian paced. "I'll have to look over the evidence. Has he confessed?"

"No. Matt and Lily are interrogating him now."

"I'll go over everything first thing Monday morning and let you know."

"Thanks, Ian. Night."

Molly plugged her phone into the charger and buried herself under the covers. She perused the DVR filled with all the shows she used to watch, none of which interested her lately. She surfed the channels and settled on a repeat of Real Time. Bill Maher's usual rants would take her mind off her personal trials and focus it on the country's tribulations. Perfect.

Chapter 12

J ustice screamed and splashed, bobbing up and down in her self-made waves. "Look Mommy, I'm Dory!" She wiggled on the surface, thrusting her tiny butt back and forth like a slithering eel. Molly stood waist-high in the water, watching with pure glee. The kid proved a natural in the water, under, or on top. She jumped off the diving board with abandon. No fear of the deep. The blow-up water wings had vanished over a year ago.

Alyx and Laura sat in blue-cushioned lounges catching rays, both babies asleep inside, monitors at the ready in case they woke. However, they needn't worry, Lydia would have babes in arms before tears got real.

Jamie sat at a table and rattled off completed tasks then peppered them with questions. "I just went over everything with the wedding planner: the venue's set, flowers, menu, limos… all check. The guys have their tuxedoes and my dress will be in next week." She sighed, crossing items off her list. "I can't believe the wedding is next month."

"Me either," Alyx said.

"The only thing left is to agree on your dresses. We've put if off too long already."

Laura and Alyx removed their sunglasses and stared at each other. Alyx offered, "Ain't gonna be easy finding a time when we can all make it."

"I know, I know…" Jamie exhaled again. "Maybe we should pick a color and agree on style elements then everyone can get their own. I don't really want identical dresses."

"Hallelujah," Alyx said. "I vote for black. The guys are wearing black and white tuxedos and I think a black and white wedding is really classy."

"Agreed," Laura said.

"Love that," Molly said.

"All right. I want all black, no trimmings, tea-length hems. Send pics to all of us when you find something."

Justice landed a cannonball two feet in front of Molly. "Justice!" she screamed, wiping water from her face and fingering wet hair off her forehead.

Justice popped up in front of her and squealed. "Gotcha, Mommy."

"You certainly did, little munchkin." Molly hugged Justice to her chest. "Let's take a break. How about a snack?"

"Okay, Mommy." Molly carried her to the shallow end and they walked up the steps hand-in-hand.

A baby monitor squeaked. "Impeccable timing," Alyx said. "The guys should be home in an hour. Let's get babies fed and freshen up. I'll check with Lydia about helping in *her* kitchen."

They gathered inside and changed out of bathing suits. Jamie helped Lydia plate hors d'oeuvres and pull salads from the fridge, while Alyx and Laura nursed their babes. Everything set, Lydia left for the day. Molly settled in the corner chair and toweled off Justice.

"You know what, Mommy?"

"What, honey?"

"I'm going to the 'lympics."

"Excuse me?"

"You know, the 'lympics?"

Molly frowned. "How do you know about the Olympics?" She tugged a sunflower motif sundress over Justice's tangled dark locks and tied the back string into a bow.

"It was on TV and Colleen told me."

She turned Justice to face her. "What did she tell you?"

"She said people do races, even girls, and they win medals, gold ones and silver."

"Wow, that's amazing. What sport do you want to race in?"

Justice tapped Molly on the nose. "Silly Mommy, swimming. I'm a really good swimmer."

"You are," Molly agreed. She looked up. Justice had Alyx, Laura, and Jamie's undivided attention.

"Aunt Jamie went to the Olympics," Laura said. "She won a gold medal."

Molly struggled to brush Justice's hair into a long pony secured by a yellow scrunchie. Justice was already on the move. She wriggled away from Molly and stood near Jamie plating stuffed celery. She tugged on the hem of Jamie's pink tee shirt. "Really?" Justice said. "Can I see it?"

Jamie dropped to her knees. "It's home. Next time you come over I'll show it to you."

"What race did you do?"

"I did the Winter Olympic Games, and I won for skiing." Molly was happy Jamie left off the shooting part. Guns were part of her life but Justice was too young to understand.

"Skiing? Like on a snowy mountain?"

"Yup."

"How did you get so good?"

"My daddy taught me." As soon as the words left Jamie's lips, everyone knew she'd made a grave error.

Justice curled her lip and dropped her head. "My daddy died." They all stopped what they were doing, like a game of freeze tag, and waited for someone to rescue the moment.

Jamie grabbed Justice by her shoulders and chucked her chin up with her knuckle. "That's why we have coaches. Lots of people don't have daddies yet it doesn't mean they can't be winners. We'll find you a coach." A collective sigh of relief filled the room.

Justice ran to Molly. "Can we, Mommy, can we get a coach?"

"Of course, sweetie. Whatever you need, we'll find a way."

Justice pumped up and down on her toes, her tiny hands clasped under her chin. "Thank you, Mommy." She threw her arms around Molly's neck and squeezed.

"You didn't tell us he was a ringer," came a male voice from the foyer. Daniel.

"Seriously, a handicap of two? Some of the guys on the pro tour don't have a two," Steve said.

Colin added, "He was a scratch player in college, almost went pro but Lady Justice came a-calling."

"I can't believe you guys are beating on my handicap." That voice, Molly thought she recognized it, but… no way.

"Well, next time, he's my partner," Daniel said, entering the kitchen. Colin stood behind him and removed his cap, running his fingers through his matted hair. Daniel pointed his thumb over his shoulder where Ian stood shaking his head. "Do you believe this guy is a two handicap?" he announced to the women.

"Leave the poor guy alone," Colin said.

Molly stood, her hand tethered to Justice. Her eyes met

Ian's, his eyebrows nearly reaching his hairline when he sighted her.

"Molly," he said.

Molly couldn't deny it, his physical presence was simply breathtaking. The power of his lean muscular body unmistakable. She shivered and tried to breathe normally. Those eyes, blue as the Caribbean, piercing, hopefully undressing her. She'd been captivated the moment she'd set eyes on him. The sculpted planes of his face, the glossy chocolate-brown hair that brushed his collar. But his sharp intelligence, wit, and relentless energy coupled with a heart so tender, made her pulse skip to another beat altogether. She craved him.

"Ian," she sputtered. Great, her best friends had set her up on a blind date. She clenched her teeth. She'd kill them. However, it seemed Ian was just as surprised as she.

"You two know each other?" Laura said.

"We're working a case together," Molly said.

"I-I- didn't know you'd be here," Ian mumbled.

"Apparently," Molly offered.

"Seriously? You guys set us up?" Ian queried.

"Guilty," Alyx said, "but it was Laura and me. The others are off the hook. We just thought maybe you'd enjoy our company, and perhaps each other's, too."

"Besides, you're both in the wedding party," Jamie announced.

Molly pinched the bridge of her nose. "Sam's only been dead three months." An awkward silence chilled the room.

"I know. I'm sorry," Laura finally said. "It's just we hate seeing you alone."

"I'm fine."

Daniel clapped his hands. "How about cocktails?" he said, changing the subject, to Molly's relief. "Guys, follow me to the bar, I'll need your assistance."

Before anyone moved, Justice marched toward Ian and

tugged on the edge of his black and white plaid shorts. "Is this Justice?" he asked Molly.

"It is."

"Hi, Justice." He extended his hand. "I'm Ian. Nice to meet you."

Justice stared up, studying his face, then perched her hands on her hips. "Are you a daddy?"

"Ah, no I'm not."

Justice frowned as she considered his answer with adult-like intensity. Molly could only imagine what was about to come out of her mouth next. She held her breath.

Justice said, "Hmm." She made them wait. Her face brightened. "Wanna be my coach?"

The women gasped.

The men frowned.

Molly smacked her forehead.

Chapter 13

Ian raised his eyebrows. "A little help here?"

"Justice, come here," Molly said, extending her hand. Justice remained still, her eyes focused on Ian's like a sniper rifle's laser. Molly sighed, dropping her hand. "She wants to be in the Olympics, like her Aunt Jamie. The summer Olympics, for swimming."

Ian scanned the room, landing on Jamie. "You're an Olympian?"

Colin answered, "Gold medalist—skiing and shooting biathlon. She doesn't like to talk about it."

Ian squeezed the back of his neck and exhaled slowly. He squatted, eye-to-eye with Justice, forearms on his thighs. "I'd love to be your coach, if your Mommy says it's okay. And when you get too good for me we'll find you a better coach."

Justice smiled, her eyes alight. "Thank you, Ian. Thanks a lot." She threw her arms around his neck. His heart melted at the unexpected affection.

Daniel clapped his hands together. "Drinks? Cosmos, Gimlets, Martinis, Margaritas? I always aim to please the ladies," he said breaking the tension again.

"Margaritas," came the unified response.

The gentlemen exited to the bar. Justice followed and Steve picked her up and perched her on his shoulders. "Gonna be our helper?"

"Yes, Uncle Steve. I'm a good helper."

Molly turned on her best friends. Laura put up both hands. "I already apologized. Let's not make any more recriminations. It won't happen again."

"Setting me up was bad enough but now I want to know how you guys know Ian."

Her three pals exchanged clandestine glances but remained silent. Finally, Alyx said, "Would you believe golf?"

"No, I wouldn't." Damn it. What did the other three men have in common? The St. Andrews Club. Good God. He was one of them, one of those Doms. Molly considered the man she'd just met, a caring, kind soul, not intimidating or demanding, not an alpha type like so many other men she'd worked with. But Steve, Daniel, and Colin didn't seem that way either. She'd never have suspected them to be Dominants at a sex club. Still... she had no interest in that kind of sexual relationship. She'd definitely been the aggressor in her sex life with Sam. Like that time in college when he asked her how to give oral sex to his then girlfriend. He was chicken to go down there. The next day they talked about how it went and it made her so hot, she jumped him right on her bottom bunk. They both broke off their relationships and had been together ever since. And she had no idea how her three best friends found that submissive role satisfying. None of it fit.

The silence lingered, then Molly finally declared, "He knows them from that sex club... he's one of them."

Alyx threw her hands on her hips. "Well, don't make it sound like they're a pack of werewolves or a vampire coven."

Laura chuckled, followed by Jamie and Alyx. "Yeah," Jamie said, "don't knock it until you've tried it."

Molly shook her head, then dragged her hands down her face. "I swear, the three of you have lost your minds."

"Guilty as charged," Laura said. "Our sanity has been compromised by too much great sex and mind-blowing orgasms."

"Seriously? Getting tied up and spanked? And God only knows what other things you guys do together." Molly slapped her mouth, slowly dropping her hand. "Do you… do you guys… have group sex?"

The three women laughed again. "Of course not," Alyx said, "we keep our bedroom antics to ourselves. We do go to the club on occasion but mostly it's for a party. Like the one they're having for Fourth of July. The owner, Jack, is starting a renovation project the following Monday and wants to go out with a bang before the grand re-opening." She grimaced. "I know, I know, I can't believe I actually said that."

"Good God," Molly said, sinking into a chair. "I can't believe Ian is into that stuff. I thought he was just a regular nice guy. Kind, caring, empathetic…"

Alyx stepped closer to Molly. "Oh my God. You like him?"

Molly widened her eyes, eyebrows as far up as they could go. "What? No! Of course not."

Laura chimed in. "Have you been out with him?"

"No. Not really. We just had a drink after work yesterday."

The trio surrounded her, hovering over her like an expert interrogation team, which, of course, they were. "There's nothing wrong with having a drink with a guy," Jamie said. "A really hot guy, I might add."

"I wholeheartedly agree," Laura said. "You've been holed up in that apartment like a nun for months now."

"Sam wouldn't want you to live like that for the rest of your life," Alyx added.

Molly crossed her arms over her chest. "Oh my God. Stop."

Steve plopped Justice on a barstool, while Daniel filled the ice bucket from the under-counter refrigerator. "What do you guys want?" Daniel said.

"Sticking with beer," Steve said and Ian and Colin agreed.

"I've got a great new IPA," Daniel said. He placed margarita glasses on the counter and asked Justice to put ice in the pitcher. He handed her tongs and she kneeled up on the stool so she could reach, but after three slippery misses, he said, "Just use your hands, sweetie."

"I think you guys are in hot water," Ian said, settling on the stool next to Justice. He studied her petite features, a smaller version of Molly, big brown eyes, her hair longer but the exact same onyx luster.

"I didn't know it was a set-up," Colin said. "In fact, I didn't think about it at all. Molly and Sam often joined us and I was just glad Molly agreed to hang with us."

"Same here," Steve said, "although I don't know how anyone moves on after something like that. I don't know how I'd cope if anything happened to Laura."

A pall descended over them, as each appeared to consider a life alone after finding the loves of their life. But of course, Ian knew exactly how she felt. Daniel placed four beers on the bar and popped the tops.

Colin took a swig, then said, "Actually, Ian might be the perfect guy for Molly." The men studied Colin quizzically.

"I'm right here," Ian said.

"I don't mean to put you on the spot if you don't want to talk about it," Colin said.

Ian took a long sip of the icy beverage. "Maybe you're right, but I'm not sure she's ready. It's been two years and I haven't even considered dating until I met Molly."

Ian had avoided talking about Rebecca's death for a long time, tired of the pity and bumbling comments when he did share. Yet he felt a new camaraderie with these guys, a group he wanted to join. He'd left his friends behind but formed a quick bond with Colin at the club, who'd invited him to his engagement party and now as a groomsman in his wedding.

"Not in front of the kid," Ian said.

Daniel intervened. "Good job on the ice cubes, honey. Would you do me a favor and go ask Aunt Alyx if she wants to have drinks on the deck?"

"Okay," Justice said. Steve helped her off the bar stool and she scurried away. The three men waited for Ian to continue.

Ian twirled his beer bottle on the granite bar top. "Rebecca, my fiancé was killed, murdered for a few dollars and some jewelry. It happened a little over two years ago, and eventually I decided to move back to Long Island. Too many hauntings where we worked and lived."

"Jesus," Steve said. "That's horrible."

Daniel shook his head. "So sorry, man. I can't even imagine how I'd function."

"I thought it would be easier if I just moved and tried to pretend it never happened. Not sure that's a great plan, however. I can't deny I was attracted to Molly the minute I saw her. We had a drink after work yesterday and I felt we might be kindred spirits." Ian laughed. He stared at Colin.

"After she told me about Sam I realized they were the couple from your engagement party."

"Shit," Colin said, "that's right, they never made it to the party so you never met her before."

Justice bounded into the room. "On the deck, Uncle Daniel."

Drinks were served and appetizers passed, the conversation turning light and casual, laughter replacing the seriousness of the prior interlude.

Ian smiled at Justice as she nibbled on a tiny wiener dipped in ketchup. The dimples on her cheeks deepened and she came toward him. "Want a bite?" she asked, offering the half-eaten morsel.

"Sure," Ian said, opening his mouth.

Justice popped the tidbit in and he made like a shark, nipping her fingers. Justice squealed and jumped back, garnering everyone's attention. She came close again, wedging herself between Ian's legs, landing her hands on his thighs. They were nose-to-nose. "You know what?"

"What?"

"My daddy says he likes you."

Chapter 14

S hock hung in the air like an odor. Open mouths, hiked up eyebrows, hand-covered lips. Molly closed her eyes and held her breath. Should she admit this had been happening all too often? That she'd begun to suspect something supernatural might be at hand? She opened her eyes, scrutinizing the reactions of her best friends... and *Ian*.

He gaped at Molly, tight lines between his eyes. Good God, what should she say? She could brush it off with her usual excuse, a child's imagination. That would be the sanest response, yet on the other hand they might be able to help her figure out what to do. A therapist... Or was she merely overreacting?

Then again, these people all dealt in reality, evidence, what the eye could see: Steve a detective, Daniel a doctor, Colin a tech guy and of course, her fellow agents. Supernatural explanations wouldn't cut it. But what about the exploding lightbulb? And Justice's uncanny messages that she insisted were coming from Sam?

"Justice, sweetie, come here." Molly extended her arms

and her daughter ran into them. She hugged Justice to her chest, kissing the top of her head. "Why don't you go and get your pajamas from our bag and bring them back to me?"

"Okay, Mommy." And Justice disappeared through the sliding glass doors.

"I'm sorry," Molly said. "She keeps saying things like this. I told her Daddy is in heaven and he can't talk to her but she insists."

"Does she claim to see him?" Alyx said.

"No. She just hears him."

"She's processing her dad's death the only way she knows how," Daniel began.

"I know, it's what I keep telling myself, but strange things keep happening. She says things before they occur. Like, the morning you guys arrived with Rob, she said Sam told her it was time to get back to work."

"That doesn't necessarily mean…" Alyx said.

"Coincidence," Jamie added.

Molly ignored them. She focused on Ian. "And then the other night, after we'd had drinks…" Molly sighed, wrapping her arms around her chest. "I was getting ready for bed and I was thinking about what a nice time we'd had and the light-bulb next to my bed suddenly exploded. Honestly, I freaked and then Justice was in my room saying, 'Daddy says he's sorry, he got mad, but he's okay now.' I even looked around wondering if Sam was somewhere in the room. Justice insisted again that she couldn't see him, yet his voice called out."

Silence was the collective response. Molly snorted. "I must be losing my mind. I don't know whether to ignore it, see a shrink, or consult a psychic."

Ian rose and took the adjacent spot on the dark green loveseat. "Hey, take a breath." He placed a hand over hers.

"Don't overreact. She's a little kid. Let her think whatever makes her comfortable."

"Does she seem upset?" Jamie said. "Afraid?"

"No. She acts like it's perfectly normal."

"Then give it some time," Jamie said. "As far as Sam actually trying to speak to you? I say the jury is out. Who really knows what happens after death?"

Daniel added, "I've seen some weird things in my medical practice over the years. Death experiences give me pause."

Ian squeezed Molly's hand. "I agree. It's hard to explain death to a child. Hell, it's hard for us grownups. I often felt Rebecca's presence after she died. I can't say how much was wishful thinking or if something else was at work. Energy has to go somewhere. Does it stay sentient and find its way to someone? Who knows?"

Justice bounded onto the deck, PJs in hand.

"Let's get dinner ready," Alyx said.

Daniel manned the grill, flipping skewers of colossal shrimp and hangar steaks. They set the table and plated potato salad, sautéed asparagus, tomato and red onions with a lemon-balsamic dressing, and crusty rolls with ghee. Justice sat on a booster seat between Molly and Ian. He cut her food and buttered a roll for her. Conversation turned to work laments and accomplishments, and eventually to Jamie and Colin's upcoming nuptials.

They served Molly's dessert, tiny petite fours, from her corner bakery along with fresh brewed coffee. A crackling blaze in the copper fire pit ended the evening, Justice snuggled in Molly's lap, as she munched a s'more, chocolate and marshmallow smooshing her lips. Goodbyes were levied, each couple returning to their nearby beach houses, and Ian to his condo in East Islip. Molly intended to sleep over then travel back to the city in the morning.

"Justice, ask Aunt Alyx to help you brush your teeth. I'll be up in a minute to tuck you in."

"Okay," Justice said. "Bye, Ian, don't forget to be my coach."

"I won't." He picked Justice up in his arms. "You let me know when you're ready and I'll be there."

"Thanks." She wrapped her tiny arms around his neck and kissed his cheek. Ian held her for an extra moment before returning her to the ground.

Justice grabbed Alyx's outstretched hand and mounted the stairs.

Guests departing, they waved goodbye from the front porch. Daniel excused himself to the kitchen, yet Ian lingered. "I feel like we should talk," he said to Molly.

"About Justice?"

"No, about us."

Molly fiddled with the hem of her tee shirt, eyes cast down. He wanted to take her in his arms and tell her everything would be fine. He'd protect her, cherish her, bring happiness to her life. And Justice, he was already smitten with the little imp.

"Did you really have a good time Friday night? I know I did," he said.

Her chestnut brown eyes peered up, glistening in the waning moonlight. "Ian, I just can't. I mean, yes, I did enjoy our evening together. It was a respite from the sadness for a while. And I laughed. I haven't laughed in the longest. I know I'm sounding like a broken record, but Sam's only been gone three months. I couldn't possibly…"

Ian grabbed both her hands. "You can't think away emotions, Molly. I've at least learned that much by now. Your head can't change how you feel. I'm not putting any pressure on you. No rush. We can take it slow."

———

Molly resisted the urge to throw herself at the handsome ADA. Maybe they could have a physical relationship, a best friend with benefits kind of thing. He had to be into casual sex since he played at that club. She wouldn't mind having sex again. Although, she wasn't sure she was the kind of sexual partner he desired. And she could never play the submissive role. Should she suggest such a relationship? Ask about his role at the club?

She focused on his warm hands holding hers, his grip firm. She wanted those hands on her body, everywhere, stroking, massaging, caressing. The dampness between her legs affirmed the truth, her undeniable attraction to this man, to this *Dominant*. Maybe her sex life needed a little shaking up, more excitement, someone to test her limits, bring her places she'd never gone before. Good God, her mind was in the gutter but she seriously wanted to stay there.

"What's going on in that pretty little head of yours? I can see the smoke coming out of your ears."

He laced his fingers through hers and pulled her close, her hands pinned behind his back, their chests pressed together. Molly couldn't breathe, his physical presence consuming her. She wanted him, wanted him badly. Eyes met and she swore he could see right into her psyche. Smell the pheromones wafting off her body, the dampness between her legs. Her eyes drifted to his sumptuous lips, she wanted those lips on her skin. Every inch of it. The need to kiss him irrefutable.

Ian leaned in and Molly closed her eyes. Their lips touched, his lips firm yet soft. She struggled not to moan. He released her hands and she wrapped them around his waist. He took her with his kiss, his strength, his command. She imagined him tying her to the bed and doing evil things. Her pulse spiked. His tongue probed deep and she responded eagerly, too eagerly. God. She wanted to strip her clothes off, throw herself at him. Give him all the pleasure she could summon. He had her in an erotic vice, unable to move except for her mouth. Cocooned in a web of blistering passion. No doubt he controlled every move and in that instant could do anything he wanted. Because, heaven forgive her, she'd let him.

Molly pulled back slowly, savoring the heat of the moment, the thrill of kissing the incredibly handsome, dare she say it? *Dominant.*

Ian ran his thumb over her wet lips. "I don't think you can refute our attraction. I felt it the moment I saw you."

Molly's face flushed. Her body already aflame. "I can't deny it, but I must. It's wrong for me to feel this way." She put her hands up. "I know, feelings can't be wished away, but I must. I can't act on them. What would people think?"

Ian huffed. "You care what people think?"

"Let's just say I prefer not to be called the widow whore."

"I promise I won't tell anyone at the office, if that's got you worried."

"Maybe we could just be friends, with... you know... benefits?"

"You want to fuck me and make like I'm your friend but not fall in love with me?"

"Well, when you say it like that it sounds terrible." She bit her lip before continuing, "But you're into casual sex, right? I mean, you belong to that club, St. Andrews, like Daniel, Colin, and Steve? You're a Dominant, right?" She shook her head. "I'll admit having sex with a Dominant sounds exotic, tempting even, but I could never play the submissive role."

"Don't be so sure. Seems your gal pals all got into it. It's just a game, none of us would want that dynamic in the other aspects of our lives."

Molly swallowed hard. She needed to end this conversation, pronto. "I can't talk about this anymore." Dropping her head, she closed her eyes and hugged herself. "Good night, Ian. I'll call you in the morning so we can proceed with Jonathan's case."

She turned toward the front door but Ian grabbed her hand and pulled her into him. He fixed her against his chest, her arms pinned to her sides, and plundered her mouth. She was imprisoned, unable to move. Her shoulders deflated, her body turned to jelly, and she feared she'd swoon.

The kiss slowly ended, Ian nibbling on her bottom lip before releasing her. His eyes seared her, like he could devour her right there on the porch. "Hmm," he whispered near her ear, sending a delicious shiver down her spine. "There just might be a few submissive bones in this delectable body of yours after all."

"No way…" she mumbled. And yet she had turned to putty in his arms. He could mold her into anything he wanted at this exact moment. Which was… *absolutely ridiculous. When had she ever considered letting anyone have control?*

Ian pressed his forehead against hers, his breath warm on her face. "The lady doth protest too much."

Chapter 15

Traffic back to the city Monday morning had been light, mostly because they'd left the Taylors at the crack of dawn. Not that sleeping in was an option, as Justice usually woke by six.

Molly called her mother from the car. "*Ma chérie*," her mother said. "Will we see you for the Fourth of July weekend?"

"Yes, Mom, and I don't know your schedule but wondered if I could leave Justice with you until the fourteenth? Colleen needs two weeks off and I have to work. Sam used to, used to—"

"Of course, chérie, we'd love to have her."

"You're a life-saver. Thanks, Mom."

"We'll see you Thursday, then?"

"Yes, we should be there in time for dinner."

"Wonderful."

"Thanks again, Mom. Love you."

"Love you, too."

Colleen arrived at seven-thirty and Justice jumped into her arms and kissed her cheek. Molly smiled at the affectionate welcome, knowing Colleen had been a godsend. She and Sam often commented on how lucky they were to have found her, but after Sam's death Molly knew that without Colleen she and Justice wouldn't have fared well. Colleen reminded Molly of her mother—no nonsense, no whining, with just the tiniest allusion of compassion.

Colleen hung her backpack on the peg next to the entrance and proceeded to make coffee. "I'm taking Justice to the Children's Museum today and probably have lunch in the park. Do you need us back by any special time?"

Molly spread peanut butter on toast, licking the excess off the knife and tossing it in the sink. "It might be a long day. I'll be out on the island, we're hoping for an arraignment but court schedules can be unpredictable, so I might be late."

"No problem. I can stay over if you need me to. Has Justice had breakfast?"

"She had a yogurt pouch and some apple slices in the car. See if she wants anything else. I've got to run." Molly pressed the two slices of toast together and took a bite.

Colleen pulled cream from the refrigerator and placed it alongside the coffee maker as it hissed its last drop. "My vacation time still solid?"

"Definitely. Justice will be with my parents until the fourteenth. See you back Monday, the fifteenth." She poured coffee into a travel mug and added cream and sugar.

"Perfect," Colleen said.

"Do you have plans? Going anywhere fun?"

"I wish. I'm taking a two-week seminar on addiction. Should be fun." Colleen rolled her eyes.

"Yeah… no," Molly agreed. She knelt and gave Justice a smooch. "Have fun at the museum and park today."

Justice ignored her and asked Colleen, "Can we get ice cream at the park?"

"Of course, munchkin."

Thirty minutes later, Molly arrived at her office where Matt and Lily commiserated with other members of the task force. Matt followed her into her office. "We've got six new cases."

"Damn," Molly said, dropping her purse on her desk.

"One in Brooklyn, two on the upper East Side, another in Tudor City and two more in Tribeca. I've sent agents out to interview the victims. Should start getting reports soon."

"How about the tech side, any hits on the perps?"

"Not yet. These guys are good. As soon as we trace something it disappears. The technology is frustrating."

"I'm going to check in with the Suffolk DA's office to see if the guy in the Ogburn case will be arraigned today."

"I expected you'd be out of the office most of the day, so not to worry. Lily and I have everything covered. She's doing great, by the way. Smart, quick on the uptake and assertive in just the right quantity. I like."

Molly had her phone in hand. "Sometimes the universe does you a solid."

ADA Alicia Lopez, a petite black woman with stylish dread-locks, sat in the chair in front of Ian's desk. Her diminutive physical appearance could disarm you however she proved to be a fierce and tenacious adversary. Intimidating even.

"Since we've got solid evidence linking this perp to the charges, he's pleading guilty, so I filed last night," she said. "The clerk assured me the case is on the docket for three. We drew Judge Smoot."

"Good. She's tough on sex offenders. Should go smoothly."

ADA Lopez rose. "I'm meeting with the kid and his

parents at noon. He won't have to testify but I'll explain everything to the family so they'll be prepared for what they see in court."

Ian sipped his tepid coffee. "The father is a bit of a hothead so keep your antennae up. I don't want the dad bolting over the railing and going after this guy."

"Understood."

"See you in court."

ADA Lopez left, passing Sylvia on the way out. They reviewed his calendar for the day and Ian made sure she blocked out time for the arraignment. Sylvia exited and he swallowed the last of his coffee, which somehow always managed to be cold. His phone rang.

"Molly, good morning."

"Hi, Ian. Is the arraignment set for today?"

"Yes, it should be smooth sailing. The guy confessed, the kid won't have to testify and we drew a good judge."

"I'd like to attend if that's okay."

"That's a definite. We might need your testimony. One of my ADAs is handling the proceedings and you should touch base with her beforehand. I know she's meeting with the family at noon, would that work?"

"I've cleared my calendar. See you then." The line went dead and Ian stared at the screen. Neither had mentioned last night. He'd wanted to say something more personal when he said hello but the conversation had immediately turned to business and he couldn't find a segue. He wondered if she would pretend like they'd never kissed, never talked about venturing into relationship territory. The idea of a casual sexual relationship had caught him off guard, rebuffing sex not usually in his repertoire. But he'd finally left that all behind after a string of robotic encounters with strange women, which he now understood was a futile attempt to assuage his pain and loneliness and—dare he admit it?— anger, after Rebecca's death. Angry sex only ended well in the movies.

Judge Vera Smoot banged her gavel. "Next case," she said. Her clerk read the docket number and description of the charges against Charles Stanton.

ADA Lopez addressed the judge, Jonathan Ogburn seated alongside, Molly and Ian directly behind her. "Your Honor, the State filed felony charges against Mr. Stanton for the sextortion of a minor boy on a gaming site, pretending to be a teen of similar age and feigning attraction. The boy was enticed to send nude pictures of himself, then once Mr. Stanton had these pictures he threatened to expose said minor on social media if he did not send additional pictures, some of which demanded sexual performance images."

"Mr. Stanton, how do you plead?" Judge Vera Smoot said.

Mr. Stanton stood along with his attorney. "Guilty, Your Honor."

"Very well. I sentence you to twenty years in federal penitentiary and you will be listed on the sex offender registry for life." Stanton hung his head, but remained silent. "Bailiff, Mr. Stanton is remanded into your custody."

The bailiff led the handcuffed prisoner out the side door. "That was quick," Molly said to Ian, "I thought this was just an arraignment."

Stanton's public defender voiced her exact sentiments. "Your Honor, I was under the impression this was an arraignment today, and sentencing would be at a later date."

"No need to waste the court's time, Mr. Keegan."

Ian and Molly rose and she whispered, "Smooth, just like you said."

"Jonathan Ogburn, please stand," Judge Smoot said.

The teen's eyes widened and he looked to Ms. Lopez for

direction. Ms. Lopez stood, urging Jonathan upward with a nudge under his arm.

"Do you admit to sending nude pictures over the internet to Mr. Stanton?"

"Your Honor," Ms. Lopez said. "The boy is not on trial here."

"Answer my question, young man. Did you send nude pictures of yourself over the internet?"

Ms. Lopez answered, "It's in our filing, he did, Your Honor. But he is the victim here."

"Ms. Lopez if you say another word I will hold you in contempt. I want an answer from this young man."

Ms. Lopez whispered to Jonathan, "Go ahead."

"Yes, I did."

"Then I find you guilty of felony charges for a sexual performance with the intent to produce and distribute child pornography. I sentence you to one year in a secure juvenile correctional facility in Bay Pointe, Massachusetts and you will be listed on the sex offender registry for life. Bailiff, the defendant is remanded into your custody." She banged her gavel.

"What the hell?" Jonathan's father yelled from the gallery. "You can't send my kid to jail for something this pervert did to him." He turned to Molly. "You lied to me, you promised he'd be safe, that you'd help him and now he's going to jail?"

Molly placed a hand on his forearm. "I'm sorry, Mr. Ogburn. This doesn't make any sense. Try not to worry, we'll fix it."

Mr. Ogburn rushed the judge's bench and was immediately restrained and handcuffed.

Ian bolted through the wooden gate and confronted the judge. "Your Honor, the County has filed no charges against this child. He is a victim and he didn't attempt to distribute pornography, there was no intent."

"Mr. Turner, sit down or I'll hold you in contempt."

"I will not sit down, Your Honor. There's been no trial, no arguments from counsel. You're over-stepping your authority by about a mile."

"I'm not required to hear arguments when the defendant has admitted guilt."

"He's not a defendant!"

"One more word, Counselor, and you'll be spending a night in the courthouse lockup."

"I will report you to the bar for this," Ian said.

Judge Smoot banged her gavel. "Bailiff, escort Chief ADA Turner to lockup. A night in jail and a five-thousand-dollar fine should teach him some respect for the court."

The bailiff took Ian's arm and turned him around, slapping cuffs on his wrists behind his back. The entire courtroom stood slack-jawed.

To Ian, ADA Lopez said in a loud desperate whisper, "What do you want me to do?

Chapter 16

Molly followed Ian to the holding room where court officers demanded he empty his pockets. "Sorry about this, sir," the shorter one said. As Molly entered the taller one said, "Ma'am, you can't be in here."

"I'm his attorney," Molly said, "and I want to speak with my client." She pulled a business card from her pocket and handed it to the officer. She always carried her attorney cards in the event of just such an emergency.

The guard perused the card and returned it. "Of course, Ms. Masterson."

"And remove the cuffs." The officer's cohort unshackled Ian and returned the manacles to his belt.

"We'll wait outside," he said.

Ian stared as Molly pulled out a chair from the metal table and seated herself while he sat across from her.

"You're an attorney?"

"I am."

Ian folded his hands on the table. "Lucky me."

"So, what the hell happened in there. Is that woman insane?"

"I'm not sure. She has a reputation for being tough on sex offenders. I thought that was a good thing, but that crap she pulled on the kid was way out of line."

Molly sat back and folded her arms over her chest. "Even if she decided he was guilty, he's a first-time, nonviolent, juvenile offender and would normally get probation."

"Agreed."

"And sentencing the kid out of state? That sets off an alarm. There are plenty of juvenile facilities in New York, plus, his parents will have undue hardship getting to see him."

"Don't worry, I'm going to investigate this fully. I won't tolerate that kind of shotgun justice in my office."

"How can I help?"

Ian removed his watch and handed it to Molly. "Take this and my wallet and phone, my keys are in my desk, take those too. Ask Sylvia."

Molly palmed the pricey timepiece as Ian shoved his valuables in her direction. She said, "I can stay at a local motel and I'll be here first thing in the morning. My nanny can stay with Justice."

"Thanks, but why don't you stay at my place. It's close by and I have a guest room. Sylvia will give you my address."

"That's not necessary, I can stay in a motel."

"I insist. The alarm code is 7335#. Case closed. Now, go see Sylvia and tell her what happened, although I'm sure it's hit the office by now."

"I'll pay the fine so you're out first thing in the morning."

"Can you manage that? I'll write you a check tomorrow."

"Not a problem." Molly's financial status had multiplied exponentially since the accident. First, there was the million-dollar insurance policy and then the truck that hit them belonged to a major corporation and they forked over the obscene amount of ninety million dollars without even the hint of a lawsuit. Her attorney wanted to sue for more but no amount of money would bring Sam back and the dollar figure was irrelevant. The money was sitting in her savings account. She really needed to do something with it.

Ian leaned back in his chair and ran his fingers through his glossy dark hair. "Tell Lopez we'll review Judge Smoot's records first thing tomorrow morning. All her decisions, sentencing, the works."

Molly stood, gathering Ian's valuables. Ian rose and came close. "I wanted to talk about last night but this day went to shit before I could get there."

Molly couldn't look away from his piercing blue eyes. Yeah, she wanted to kiss him again. "The timing is just off Ian. We will talk, eventually, just not now."

She turned to exit but glanced over her shoulder. She felt like she'd just kicked a puppy.

Sylvia nearly tackled Molly as she entered Ian's office. "What happened?" she said.

"I'm not sure, but something stinks."

"Ms. Lopez gave me the thumbnail sketch but I'm not sure I understand."

"The judge found the kid guilty of felony child pornography charges and sentenced him to one year in an out-of-state juvenile facility. Why would she do that? There are plenty of places in state."

"Agreed," Sylvia said. "Must Ian stay in the lockup all night?"

"Afraid so. I'm going down to pay the fine now so he should be out bright and early. In the meantime, where is ADA Lopez?"

"She went to inform the DA."

"Can you point me in that direction?"

"Down the hall to the left. You can't miss it."

Molly took a step then stopped. "Oh, and I have Ian's valuables plus he told me to take his keys from his desk."

Sylvia moved Ian's chair and opened the middle drawer, handing keys to Molly. "Anything else?"

"I need his address. I'm going to stay at his place tonight rather than drive home to the city and back again." Sylvia scribbled on a note pad and handed the slip to Molly. "What about a change of clothes for Ian?"

"He always has one in his office bathroom, he can shower as well."

"Good. How early will you be in? It may take a while to go through all the paperwork and the more eyes the better."

"I'm usually here by eight but I can come in earlier if need be."

"Eight is fine. See you then."

Molly neared the frosted glass door labeled Suffolk County District Attorney Brian Hendrickson. She knocked. "Enter," a male voice said. ADA Lopez sat in the chair to the left, the DA behind his desk. "I'm Special Agent Molly Masterson," she said, approaching and extending her hand.

The DA rose and shook her hand, directing her into the seat beside Ms. Lopez.

"I've volunteered as Mr. Turner's attorney. I've spoken with him and will pay the fine straightaway."

"You're an attorney, Agent Masterson?" DA Hendrickson said.

"Yes, sir."

"Excellent. Ms. Lopez explained the proceedings and I'm very concerned."

Molly turned to Ms. Lopez. "Ian said to meet him tomorrow morning at the Court Clerk's Office so we can obtain Judge Smoot's records and review them for anything untoward. Eight okay?"

"I'm there," Ms. Lopez said.

Molly rose. "We'll keep you informed, sir. As soon as we know anything."

Hendrickson stood. "Very well. I'll wait to hear from you."

Molly and Ms. Lopez exited, shutting the door behind them. "Is Ian all right?" Ms. Lopez said.

"I think so, more pissed than anything."

Molly left her black Escalade in the courthouse parking lot and drove Ian's BMW back to his place. Up ahead, she spied the restaurant where they'd had drinks and an unexpected smile formed. She wanted to do that night over again. Or just *again. And again and again and again…* She'd spent the night with him… in her dreams… but she must ignore her subconscious yearnings, just like she did when she had a mad crush on John Shadow in high school. Besides, in high school, she was sort of the nerdy smart girl. A good athlete, yet didn't exactly turn heads. When she got to college everything changed. Her new roommate was from New York City and a beauty and fashion maven. In a week she'd transformed Molly into the 'hot chick on campus' and guys were knocking down her door. She laughed aloud, by the time she met Sam sophomore year she found herself coaching him through sex with his first real girlfriend. They soon went from mentor and student to couple-of-the year. She chuckled again.

Molly steered the BMW into the restaurant's parking lot to get something for dinner. She sat at the bar where Fred Mancini arranged orange, lemon and lime slices in a three-pocket container near the end of the counter. He looked her way and she gave a small wave. "Ah, Agent Masterson, you're back." He sauntered toward her, resting his forearms on the bar top. "Where's Ian?"

Molly couldn't suppress her smile. She knew Fred would

get a laugh out of her response. "In jail." She wasn't disappointed.

"What?" Fred said, his eyes humongous, his bushy white eyebrows lifted nearly to his scalp.

"It's a long story, but he's okay. Gave some ornery judge a little bit too much lip. She fined him for contempt and sent him to the courthouse lockup for the night."

Fred ran his stubby fingers through his thick white hair. "Jesus, that sucks."

"Yeah, it does. I'm acting as his attorney and staying at his place tonight so I can be there first thing in the morning. When I passed your restaurant I realized I'd better get some dinner. The chances of a single guy having any food in his house is probably nil."

"I see, so you're an attorney," Fred said, narrowing his gaze. "And you're staying at his place but you're not dating?"

"It's just a convenience, so I don't have to stay at a motel. He insisted."

"Ah-huh…" He smirked, one eyebrow arched.

"Really, he's a great guy but I'm just not able to date right now." Fred continued to scrutinize her. "My husband died a few months ago. And I have a young daughter. It would be inappropriate for me to date anyone. No matter how amazing he is." Good God. Why did she feel compelled to tell Fred her life story? He was a total stranger.

Fred's eyes softened, he smiled. "I think it would be good for both of you. I'm sure he told you he's had a rough time of it too."

"He did, but it's complicated." Like the club, she thought, that pretty much nixed a relationship with Chief ADA Ian Turner, *the Dominant*.

"It's Molly, right?" Fred said. She nodded. "Molly, my wife died twenty years ago. We had two small kids and I was a zombie for months. I had to go to school for a conference one afternoon because my son was acting out. His teacher was sympathetic but told me I had to pick myself up by my bootstraps and get right, for my kids. At first, I was appalled she was taking that tone with me, but we wound up talking for a long time and she helped me see I had to move on. There's no time limit for that. There are no rules. We don't live in an archaic society where we're required to mourn for a specific time period anymore. It's lonely out there and in my book the sooner we can find someone to share our life with, the better. Give yourself a break."

Molly pressed her hands to her lips and closed her eyes.

"Sorry," Fred said, "my wife tells me I should keep my opinions to myself more often."

"Your wife?"

"Yeah, I married that school teacher and she's still the love of my life. No disrespect to my first wife."

Chapter 17

I an sat on the bench of the grimy jail cell, hoping he wouldn't catch some awful disease. He'd give anything for a gallon of hand sanitizer. Maybe he should ask Sylvia...

A guard approached, unlocked the cell, a metal tray in his blue latex-gloved hand. "Sorry, sir, the food ain't exactly gourmet here."

Ian recognized the officer from the time an unruly suspect tried to punch him. The guard had the guy in handcuffs before Ian could even duck. "Bill, right?" he said.

"Yes, sir. It seems like this time *the judge* punched you. Sorry I couldn't help out."

Ian laughed. "Me too."

Bill set the tray on the bench. Ian eyed the white bread encasing orange cheese and, he couldn't believe it, they still made bologna? Who ate that shit anymore? Wasn't it made from pigs' lips and toes or something? Wait... pigs didn't have toes. Did they have lips? Wasn't there a saying about lipstick and pigs? Jesus. At least there was a bag of chips, a pickle, an apple and a bottle of water. What he wouldn't give for a cold one right now, and maybe the fish sandwich from Fred's place. His stomach growled.

Bill tucked his thumbs into the massive belt adorned with protective apparatus. "Anything else I can get you, sir?"

"Maybe some plastic wrap. I'd like to wrap myself in it so I don't get the plague."

"I hear you." Bill smiled. "Seriously, I'm here all night so call if you need anything."

"Will do."

Bill departed, the bang of the cell door shutting sending a shiver though Ian's bones. It would be a long night. Maybe he'd spend it fantasizing about Molly.

Molly perused the menu. "What do you recommend for takeout?" she asked Fred.

"I'm famous for my lobster roll but I make it with butter instead of mayonnaise. Not particularly lo-cal." He hesitated then added, "However, from my vantage point you could put on a few pounds."

Molly smirked. "I know, depression isn't conducive to eating, at least not for me." She ordered the lobster roll, which came with chips and coleslaw.

Fred punched in her order on the computer screen behind him, then returned. "How about a drink while you're waiting? On the house."

"Thanks. Chardonnay?"

"One chardonnay coming up." Fred placed the glass in front of her, poured a good six ounces, then moseyed to the other end of the bar to wait on other patrons.

Molly sipped the icy golden liquid, her mind racing. What a fucked up day. She felt horrible for Ian locked in the holding cell in the courthouse basement. She could wring that judge's fucking neck. She'd gotten into this line of work to serve justice, furthering her commitment with law school. And yet, in her eight-year career she'd seen plenty of injustice, people who became obsessed with their power, or their knowledge, adept at skirting the law. It could get to you if you let it. She reflected on her recent circumstances, particularly her ninety-day funk. Three months when she could have been out fighting the good fight. Loathe to admit it, she'd become numb. Anesthetized to the world, her daughter and pretty much everyone and everything. Yet she was beginning to feel again. Anger at the man who'd robbed Jonathan Ogburn of his innocence and the choice to declare his sexuality on his own terms, and the judge, who the hell did she think she was?

And then there was Ian. Had he been the one to wake her from her gloomy sleep? Her own Prince Charming? If she was honest with herself, she'd never felt that way about Sam. They were good friends who turned into something more. And she'd always thought that was the best formula for a relationship. But Ian ignited a fire in her that was different, new, something she'd never experienced before. She often wondered about the attraction between men and women. On the job, she'd seen plenty of abuse in relationships, often wondering why someone could be attracted to an obviously deviant or law-breaking individual. Did it come down to biology? Were you at the mercy of your hormones? And the attraction to Ian was something she couldn't deny any longer.

She finished her wine just as the to-go food arrived. The waitress swiped her credit card and she headed back to Ian's car, giving it the once over before getting in. The rims sparkled, the onyx paint gleamed. She wondered if Ian was this fastidious about his living quarters. Most guys she'd known weren't exactly neatniks and an unexpected guest, especially a female, would be unwelcome. She was well trained in assessing humans, but somehow she didn't think Ian fit that stereotype.

The garage opener was attached to the sun visor and she pressed the button and parked the BMW next to a bright red Jeep Renegade with a surfboard strapped to the top. Apparently Ian was a surfer dude. She walked up the two steps to the access door and punched in 7335#. The panel beeped and turned green and she opened the door leading into the kitchen. The aroma of bleach and some sweet fragrance perfumed the air. Hmm, maybe Ian's cleaning personnel had been here, which might be why he wasn't hesitant to allow her overnight privileges.

She placed her food on the gray granite counter along with her purse. Daylight waned, so she flicked on the kitchen lights and strolled into the living/dining area. One large space with lots of windows and glass doors leading to a deck overlooking the bay. She neared the doors, slid them open and stepped out. The briny air filled her nostrils, the cool summer breeze swept her hair into her face and she tucked the wayward strands behind her ear. She thought of her parents' beachside abode. She was looking forward to spending a few days there, sunning and swimming, building sand castles with Justice, imbibing ice-cold gimlets and indulging in her father's masterful cuisine. Cooking together had been a true joy in her family. The three of them, chopping and stirring, tasting to adjust seasonings and eating at a sumptuously adorned table. No paper plates or napkins allowed in the Masterson household.

White wicker furniture filled the space, two chairs with dark green cushions and a small cocktail table. To the left, a table sat four, a matching green umbrella in the center, its ribs collapsed. She pictured sitting here with Ian, feet propped on the small table, sipping a glass of wine. Good God. *Stop it.*

Further exploration yielded a large master bedroom festooned in shades of gray, a king-sized bed the center of attention. The second bedroom had a nautical flair, light blues and taupe, shells and beach scene paintings, the lamp bases filled with multi-colored beach glass shards.

Molly stripped out of her clothes and headed for the shower. The hot spray pummeled her tired bones. The day had taken a turn she hadn't seen coming. She closed her eyes and shampooed her hair, relishing the warm water. She towel-dried her tresses fingering the damp stands into place. Maybe she'd see if she could pilfer a tee shirt from Ian to lounge in for the evening.

Returning to his bedroom, she hesitated. Not a good idea to be rummaging through someone's drawers. What if she found something she didn't want to find? Like... Good God. A blindfold, handcuffs, restraints? Stay away from his night-stand, she decided. That's where most people kept their personal stuff... condoms, lube. Opening the top drawer of his dresser she noted socks and boxer briefs, careful not to touch them. Touching someone's underwear without their knowledge would be kind of pervy.

Next drawer: sweat pants. Next: shorts. Maybe the closet. It had built-in bins on one side, the rail on the other. Talk about a neatnik. Suits and shirts arranged by colors, most likely all fresh from the dry cleaner. Score! Tee and sweat shirts folded neatly in the bins. She selected a gray one with the Under Armor logo. She'd take it home and wash it tomorrow before returning it. She entered the bathroom and washed out her panties, laying them on the tub rim to dry.

Ian had an open bottle of sauvignon blanc in the fridge and she poured some into a wineglass she found dangling from the rack over a side counter, then settled in front of the

TV and munched her food, the lobster roll as scrumptious as promised.

She called to say good night to Justice who rattled on about the visit to the museum, the day at the park, and especially the chocolate ice cream with rainbow sprinkles. "Daddy wants to know when you're coming home, Mommy," Justice said.

Molly swallowed hard. *Don't go there.* "Tomorrow," she said.

"Okay. Night, Mommy."

"Night, sweetie."

Molly discarded the paper wrappers and washed the wineglass, placing it back in the rack, then watched reruns of SVU, Law and Order until her eyes grew heavy.

She reset the house alarm. Returning to the guest room, she pulled her ever-present toothbrush from her bag, brushed her teeth, ready to turn in for the night. She plugged her charger into the wall outlet and connected her phone. She wished she could talk to Ian. See how he was doing. It must be awful in that dismal cell. Hopefully, he wouldn't have to share it with some derelict.

His phone… she should charge it. Pulling it from her bag she entered his room in search of a charger. Probably near his bed. A bedside clock announced 10:07 pm. Molly moved closer. It had a charging station so she sat on the bedside and plugged it in. His lock screen flashed, a list of messages, no names she recognized. His office must be a zoo, people abuzz about this absurd debacle.

Molly ran her fingertips over his pillow, wondering which side of the bed he slept on. Or had he adopted her practice of sleeping in the middle, a way of disenfranchising the concept of another person sleeping beside you. She picked up the pillow and hugged it to her chest, then collapsed backward across the quilted coverlet, eyes fixed on the ceiling.

The pillow smelled like Ian. The scent brought her back to the porch last night. His first kiss sweet, gentle, delicious. But the second? Scorching, demanding, her hands pinned to her sides, rendering her shaky and off-balance, shivering with delight as he pressed against her. She craved him. Needed more. Needed his essence, his warmth. And obviously, he was a man not used to being denied.

The door alarm beeped. Footsteps.

Chapter 18

Molly's service revolver sat on the nightstand next to the bed in the guest room. Should she run for it? But the alarm wasn't blaring to announce an intruder. It had only beeped a few times, like someone putting in the code.

He walked into the bedroom. Molly sat upright and froze.

"Well, well, well, what do we have here?"

She squeezed the pillow tighter, a shield concealing her nearly naked body. "What are you doing here?"

Ian removed his suitcoat and threw it on the bedside chair. "I live here."

"I know that, don't be an ass. How did you get out of jail?"

"Brian sprung me."

"How did you get home? I have your car."

"I was going to Uber but I didn't have my phone. Brian offered to drop me off. I thought of calling, but I don't have your number memorized."

She jumped up from the bed throwing the pillow on the

bed as if on fire, using her folded arms as replacement armor. "Okay, I'm a shitty person. Except, not really. I came in to find a phone charger for your phone and, well, I sat down to plug it in and got... ah... I don't know." Heat flooded her cheeks. She dropped her arms, clasping them behind her back and focused on her bare toes, wishing she wore her usual red polish. At least then her toes would match the color of her face.

Ian pulled his slackened tie from his shirt collar and threw it on the coverlet and began unbuttoning his shirt. "I'm not offended, in fact I'm overjoyed to find you lying across my bed. And you look sexy as hell in my shirt." As if she were in protocol. Eyes down, her hands behind her back, and probably a good chance she wasn't wearing any underwear.

Her gaze met his. She ran her fingers through her tousled locks. "I took a shower and borrowed a tee shirt to sleep in. I hope you don't mind. I'll wash it and give it back to you."

"I don't mind. I'm just glad you didn't shoot me. I should have knocked or announced my arrival but I didn't think about it until I was already in. I thought maybe you were asleep and didn't want to startle you."

Molly chuckled. "Yeah, pretty risky, mister. Good thing my Glock is in the other room."

Ian moved closer. "Can we talk about last night now?"

Molly's big brown eyes would be his undoing. Her flawless skin, her disheveled dark hair, he wanted his hands in that hair. He wanted his hands everywhere, to kiss her, everywhere. Give her pleasure beyond her wildest dreams. To take what he wanted, but to give her more, to have her surrender to him. To *submit*.

"It was just a kiss. It didn't mean anything," Molly said.

"I beg to differ. I think we both want this, and a lot more than a kiss. I want to please you, make you come, hard and often."

He was close enough to feel the heat wafting off her body. Her cheeks flushed, the little blue vein in her neck throbbing.

Molly averted her eyes. "You don't want to have sex with me. You're a Dominant and I could never be submissive. In fact, with Sam, I was the aggressor. The more experienced one. I don't think you and I are compatible."

Ian chucked her chin up with his knuckle and forced her to focus on him. "I heartily disagree." He noticed she held her breath. "Breathe, baby. Don't want you passing out on me." He watched as she inhaled through her nose, her breasts rising, then exhaling slowly through her mouth. Sweet, sweet honey breath.

He stepped back, pulling his shirttail from his pants, unbuckling his belt and adding the items to the clothes pile. He sat on the bed and pulled Molly down beside him. He faced her. "Was your married sex life fulfilling?"

Molly hesitated before answering. "Of course. You know, it… ah… loses some of that initial thrill, but that's true for everyone."

"Did you orgasm every time? And better yet, multiple times?"

Molly's forehead wrinkled. "What? Nobody does."

"What about a vibrator. Do you have one?"

"Not since college."

"Did you enjoy it?"

Well, yah, what woman didn't? "Let's just say it's the express elevator to Nirvana."

"I like imagining you on your back, legs spread, a thick plastic cock plunging in and out of your pussy." He slipped a hand under the back of her t-shirt, his fingers stroking her overheated skin. "No comment?" He studied her plush lips, her teeth biting the bottom one. "Darling, I think you're severely deprived in the passion department."

"Well, don't get your hopes up. I'm not submissive."

"Too late, my hopes are already up. And so is the rest of me. And don't tell me you weren't into it last night. When I restrained your arms so you couldn't move, your pulse galloped."

Molly folded her hands in her lap and her chin dropped. "You just surprised me. I've never really been with someone who made me feel that."

"Like losing control? Having a man take whatever he wants from a willing woman? To let your guard down, be vulnerable?"

Good God. Molly had no response, her mouth as dry as the dessert. She'd never pondered a man using a vibrator on her, never thought a man would enjoy that, yet she had to admit —Hot, incredibly. Ian had her trapped in an oxytocin maelstrom, a tornado so powerful, so sizzling, she wanted to jump him. It would just be sex and nobody would have to know. The idea of someone new, someone who desired her this much? A heady proposition. She wanted him to throw her on the bed and ravish her... a fantasy she rarely sanctioned in her imagination. But now, she wanted, craved, needed.

"I think it's too late for you to say no. I know an aroused woman when I see one and you're showing all the signs. Let me please you."

Molly laughed. "You want to have your way with me, Sir?"

Ian smirked. "Oh, don't tease me, darling. If it's yes, then be prepared to be ravaged."

It's just a game, Molly thought. An adult game. She could role-play. It might be fun. But to what limits? Would he use restraints? Did he have other sex paraphernalia hidden in secret places? And why couldn't *she* shackle *him*?

"Where's that head of yours at, darling?"

"What do you have in mind? Will you tie me up and stuff?"

"That's for me to know and you to find out. You can have a safe word so if you become afraid or uncomfortable I will stop."

The idea of not knowing what he would do had her insides coiled tightly, ready to unfurl in a nanosecond.

"So, what say you, little subbie? Want to play?"

Molly held her breath, her heart pounding, her entire body throbbing.

"You're thinking too much. I need to shut off that brain of yours."

"What? What's wrong with thinking?"

"Not during sex. It's more about feeling."

Huh, kinda made sense. "I guess I'm game."

"Excellent. I'm going to take a quick shower." His hand traveled from her back to her side, inching down her hip to her thigh. "No underwear. Good girl. Now lie down." Molly reclined on the bed's center, head on a pillow. "You are to remain on the bed and wait for me."

Good God. Was she really going through with this?

Chapter 19

F resh from the shower, Ian wiped the fog from the bathroom mirror and studied his reflection. Too impatient to shave, his stubble would have to do, besides, women were a fan these days, confessing it provided welcome stimulation. He towel dried his hair and combed it off his face, an errant strand falling across his forehead. He was psyched to show Molly a great time, cognizant her impressions of what went on at the club might be making her fearful. He'd have to figure out just the right mix, the perfect cocktail of trepidation, kink and safety… trust. If this went well and she didn't run for the hills then he might find his way into her heart. A grieving heart he hoped he could *unsadden*. Would the jagged edges of their broken hearts fit perfectly together as one?

He returned to the bedroom, towel wrapped around his waist. Molly hadn't moved an inch, her hands at her side, eyes fixated on the ceiling. He stopped at the foot of the bed and crossed his arms over his chest. "We still a go?"

An uncertain moment passed and she nodded.

"First, birth control? Condom?"

"I'm still on the pill." Although, Molly wasn't sure why. She'd thought of stopping every month. "Not really a condom fan. I haven't been with anyone else in years so I'm STD free."

"We get tested regularly at the club so I'm good to go. And no condom makes me a happy guy. So, here are the rules. I am in full control. You are not permitted to speak unless I ask you a direct question. You are to address me as Sir or Master. Your safe word is red, so if you get uncomfortable, use it. You can say yellow if you're getting close to red, green if I ask you and it's all good. And remember 'ouch' isn't a safe word."

Ouch? Molly peered at him, her eyes slightly narrowed. "Why would I say ouch?"

"I might be inclined to spank your adorable ass."

"What?"

Ian grinned. "How do you feel about getting tied down?"

"Hot."

This time he outright laughed. "My, my, aren't we embracing the life."

"Don't get carried away. This is a one-time deal, an experiment, living out a depraved fantasy. And I'm not sure how obedient I can be. It's not exactly in my repertoire."

"You will obey, or you'll definitely earn a spanking."

Ian's arms crossed over his chest made his already massive biceps bulge. He dazzled her. His naked chest and solid shoulders sent a delicious shiver through her nether regions. So wet already. She'd never had sex with a guy as stunningly handsome as Ian. His body so much bigger and stronger than hers, the power of his musculature unmistakable. She imagined he could move her around like a rag doll, fuck her like a Barbie, putting her in any position he wanted, *doing* whatever he wanted. Tying her to the bed, she'd be totally at his mercy. Good God. And she wanted this, wanted it bad. She'd play by the rules, follow his orders and find out what it felt like to... did she dare say it? *Submit.*

"Just one more thing," she said. "What about pleasuring you? Don't I get a say?"

"Not tonight you don't. If there's a next time, I'll decide how much freedom I will allow. I don't give up the reins easily or often."

"I've never heard a guy say that before. In fact, most guys want more pleasure than they give."

"Hence, the dearth of orgasms in the female population. Personally, I think it's an epidemic. Especially among the married ones. It's sad, really."

Molly had to admit Ian was probably accurate in his assessment and he likely heard plenty of laments at the club.

"Enough," he said. "You're done talking. You're in protocol. I intend to explore every inch of you and I won't be satisfied until I hear you scream your release. And more than once."

Experienced as Molly was, she'd never been multi-orgasmic and doubted it would happen tonight. And she was *never* noisy. But she wasn't about to stifle his enthusiasm. Bring it, mister.

Ian grabbed her ankles and dragged her to the foot of the bed. "Up you go, darling," he said, pulling her to her feet. "Time to lose the shirt." He pulled it up and over her head in one fell swoop, tossing it over his shoulder. He picked her up by the waist and flipped her back on the bed, then reached underneath to yank down the coverlet, the cool sheets a startled contrast to her overheated flesh. "Don't move."

Ian entered his closet and returned with a black pinstriped necktie, the one discarded earlier on the bed, a deep jade green. He dropped the towel and Molly's eyes widened, his massive erection on full display. Good God. She'd never been pounded by a guy with a dick that size.

Ian crawled onto the bed next to her and straddled her hips, his erection against her belly. "I'm tying your hands to the headboard." Molly gazed over her head at the metal frame, wondering if all Dominants possessed furniture that enabled restraints. Probably. He selected one wrist and looped the tie around twice then secured it to the frame and did the same to her other, several inches separating them. He moved farther down the bed and dragged her down by her legs, extending her arms taut. "You okay?"

"Yes," she said.

"Yes, what?" Molly frowned. "Use my title."

"Oh, uh… yes, yes, Sir."

"Give me a color."

"Green, Sir."

Ian hiked her knees up and spread them wide. His eyes probing her wet folds. She should be embarrassed, most of her lovemaking took place in the dark, or semi-darkness, okay, and sometimes the occasional nooner, yet it usually proved fast and furious. No guy had ever viewed her this intimately. She desperately wanted him to touch her. Wanted his fingers inside her. And his mouth, his tongue… Oh God.

Instead, he lay atop her, his weight pressing her deeper into the mattress. He ran his fingers up her arms, massaging, making little trails up and down, up and down. She shivered and laughed.

"Ticklish, little subbie?"

"Maybe," she said.

He leaned in, pressing his lips against hers, his fingers intertwined with hers on the headboard. He nibbled her bottom lip and her mouth opened, waiting for him to enter. She breathed him in with deep inhalations, his scent filling her lungs, satiating some unknown hunger. Their tongues touched, his mouth crushing hers, their tongues intuitively dancing. He plundered her mouth, consuming her, eating her alive. She struggled against the restraints, her fingers clutching his hands. She desperately wanted to wrap her arms around him, claw his back, hold him close. But she couldn't move, trapped beneath him.

He kissed her senseless then dragged his tongue down her neck and nipped a breast, taking the firm peak into his mouth. He sucked hard and her toes curled, her synapses firing erratically. A low moan left her and she yearned for more.

Molly's scent drove him wild. An intoxicating drug that made him dizzy with lust. Her body lean and hard, yet her breasts plush, a cushion he could sink into, lose himself in. He moved to the other breast, squeezing, manipulating, licking, seizing the nub with his lips. He took it into his mouth, his tongue circling the areola, pulling on the nipple before releasing it. Molly moaned. He glanced at her face, eyes closed, lips tight. He surmised she was used to being quiet during sex, but that was all about to change. He'd make her scream, wrench her out of her sadness, banish it to hell where it belonged. And his along with it.

He kissed her again, then slid down her body and opened her knees wide. She was so wet. He wanted to plunge his cock inside, hard and fast, building the rhythm until they both bellowed their release. Not yet. Not even close. He needed to pace himself. He leaned his shoulder on the soft inside of her thigh and placed a finger on her clit. Molly shuddered and gasped. He circled his finger around the swollen nub, around and around, but not exerting enough pressure to make her come.

"Oh God," she uttered.

"You'll be worshipping me soon enough." Ian smiled. "For now, just call me, Sir."

First one finger, then two, he probed deep, in and out, curling his fingers upward to massage the sensitive spot against her pubic bone.

"Oh my God, Ian, I think I'm going to come."

"Not yet, sweetheart. Too soon."

"What?"

He pulled his fingers out and gazed up at Molly, her head off the pillow, her eyes peering into him. "You do not have permission to come."

"That's ridiculous, isn't that the point?"

"We'll talk about this later. Be quiet. You won't come until I say so."

Molly couldn't believe her ears. She couldn't hold it back and she shouldn't, should she? But she'd agreed to obey and she must follow through. And, well, now that he quit his ministrations, the wave lessened, which kind of disappointed her.

"Let's change it up," he said. He flipped her over gingerly, her hands still tied to the headboard yet now her arms were crossed at the wrists. "Have you done much anal play?"

Oh God. She never even thought about this happening. In her deepest darkest fantasies she'd imagined it but never did she think it would creep into reality. And she wasn't sure she wanted it to.

"No, I'm not sure…"

"We'll go slow. See how it feels."

He reached for something in the nightstand, then spread her cheeks with one hand, a cool liquid trickling onto her flesh, traveling downward between her legs. A finger circled her anus. She tightened her butt cheeks and held her breath.

Chapter 20

"Breathe, darling. You need to relax or this will be uncomfortable." Damn, he could read minds, too. He switched to massaging her buttocks, venturing in between, caressing gently. "Breathe in and let it out slowly," he urged. "Keep doing that."

Molly obeyed and on the third breath he breached her entrance, his finger pushing in, deep, deeper. He built a rhythm, faster and further. All her nerves tightened, tension escalating, the need to come nearing the crest again. His lips nipped a buttock, his tongue laving her overheated skin, the sensation driving her mad, her body squirming as she tugged at the restraints. His fingers retreated and he rose, kneeling between her spread legs. He pulled her up onto her knees, all her privates exposed. A hand landed on her buttock and she yelped. Again, he did it again, and then a third time. Her skin flamed, and not just her bottom, every inch of her. He shoved a finger into her ass again, while the other hand pressed against her vagina. Too much, too much. Her panting breaths signaling she was at her limit. What would he do if she came without permission? Spank her some more? Oh God, no… *yes.*

"Come, darling. Let go."

He pinched her clit and the wave crested, breaching the wall, sending her skyward into the carnal cosmos. She pressed her forehead into the pillow, her body rising to meet his. She grasped the ties binding her to the bed, holding on for dear life for fear she'd wind up on the ceiling. A feral scream filled the room, her body in spasms, convulsing, every nerve firing in synchronicity. "Oh my God. Jesus. What the hell?" Unable to catch her breath, she reverted to Ian's prior instruction, breathing in and letting it out slowly until her heartbeat began to slow.

Ian laughed and turned her over, her back against the warm sheets again. He straddled her hips, his erection standing proud and strong. And talk about control, he must have amazing fortitude to have not come himself. Sam never lasted very long. "That, my dear, was one outstanding orgasm."

Molly licked her lips, dry from all the panting, her breaths still too rapid. She opened her eyes and feasted on Ian's handsome face. "I-I didn't know. In the past it's been more of a… I don't know… kind of a tingle. Nothing like that."

Ian's weight pressed down on her thighs, his arms crossed over his chest. Those bulging biceps again. "And we're not done yet, little subbie."

"What? No way. I can't do that again."

"You can and you will." He rose from the bed and went to the bathroom. Molly heard the rush of water in the sink and then he was standing at the bedside again. "Now for the really good stuff." His erection in hand, he pulled on it several times. "I'm going to fuck you hard. I want another scream and a mind-blowing climax for us both."

Shocked at Molly's responsiveness, Ian wanted this night to go on forever. He'd had plenty of sex, and screwing Rebecca was great, although she never embraced the level of kinkiness he thought Molly might. The idea sent his libido into the stratosphere. So much more he wanted to do to her, to show her, to challenge limits. His level of excitement kept skyrocketing, however, he couldn't control his orgasm much longer.

Ian crawled onto the bed and lay alongside Molly's warmth, his head propped up with his hand. He ran his fingertips down her belly, dipping them between her legs. "You're very responsive, and very wet. I like that very much." He kissed her hard and kept kissing her, his intrepid hands roaming her body.

"Spread your legs," he ordered.

Molly opened her knees slightly, he immediately took charge, pulling one thigh back, then the other, opening her to his touch. He probed her wetness with two fingers, adding a third. She wiggled and writhed, pushing her pelvis upward, pressing her pussy into his palm.

His tongue nibbled a breast, then traveled down her belly. He kissed her wet folds, licking and sucking on her clit. "Oh God" she said. "You're killing me."

He chuckled, his lips against her wet flesh. "It will be a sweet death then."

Molly couldn't fathom she was riding the crest again. Her breath came hard and fast and she feared the rest of her would too. Would he allow her orgasm? She listened to her own rapid breathing. Her belly tightened, her mind thinking about the moment his enormous dick would enter her.

He knelt between her spread legs. His hands rested on her knees then slowly traveled up her thighs. The rushing sensation sent her mind into overdrive wondering what he'd do next. His hands stopped and squeezed her thighs, then resumed their advance up the length of her legs. His thumbs pressed against the insides of her thighs. Each beat of her heart a drum calling him closer… closer… inside. His hands slipped a little farther and she stopped breathing. He gripped her buttocks and pulled her forward, his warm lips against the skin of her inner thigh. He covered her clit with his mouth. Wracked with overwhelming desire, her circuits blown, she cried, "Oh my God, Ian, you have to let me come."

"Soon," he mumbled against her moistness, the vibrations inching higher. With one jerk, he angled her up to him. His tongue came slow and strong, coaxing, laving tender spheres around the border of her clit.

Her fingernails dug into her palms. She wanted to grip the hair on his head and pull him to her. The rumblings of an orgasm barreled toward her, a speeding train with a madman at the controls. She didn't know whether to fight or flee… she didn't have permission to come. She couldn't lose control.

"Come for me, baby," he whispered. He tore it out of her, relentless, sucking on her clit until she came. Eyes shut tight, she hollered something unintelligible. Again. After several seconds he rose up and lay atop her, his weight grounding her like one of those weighted blankets that put you on the express train to dreamland. She opened her eyes, and they were nose-to-nose, eyes alight.

"Well done, little subbie. You're fucking adorable."

He deftly untied the restraints, and she circled her arms

around his neck. Molly didn't know what to say. Yes, it was fucking incredible and they hadn't actually even fucked. He moistened her dry lips with a gentle kiss, biting her bottom lip, then retreating. "And now for the *piece de resistance*," he said.

Molly chuckled. "Talking dirty to me in French?"

"*Oui*, madam. I'm going to fuck your brains out."

"In case you haven't noticed, my brains are already all over the pillow."

"Yuck, terrible image. Let's move on."

Ian pressed a leg between hers, spreading them, his cheek against hers. She needed him inside her. Could he tell how much she wanted him, how badly she needed it? He took his time, moving slowly, purposefully, torturously. Her legs trembled and she arched her back, pressing her chest into him. Her pulse roared in her ears. Completely vulnerable. At his mercy. The head of his cock touched her outer lips, and it pushed in slowly, relentlessly, so she felt each thick inch, the deliberate motion of each thrust giving her time to wonder how he'd fit. She moaned as he slowly impaled her, dropping her hands to the small of his back, she clutched him to her. She felt stretched, full, on fire. He fucked her, his fingers digging into her hips as he drove in and out in long, strong, punishing thrusts. Her body opening and closing, drawing him in, contracting around him, and finally bursting in great shuddering waves.

She rode the feeling home. Or was it into oblivion? A jolt rocked her body and she screamed something. Not words. He drove into her with one final thrust and she felt him come hot and hard, felt him shudder, then he fell onto her, leaving them both motionless. A tear trickled into her ear. Not a tear of sadness this time. A tear of joy. She ran her fingertips up and down his back, stroking, caressing, then wrapped him tightly in a forever hug. Her mind whirled. Who was this man, this magician? This *Dominant.*

Forehead to forehead, her breathing calmed in synchronicity with his, and she inhaled the warm puffs of air as he exhaled. Never had she felt so close to a man, so intimate, vulnerable, willing to give herself openly and freely to do with as he wished. She felt peaceful for the first time in months. It had unbound her, and shockingly she admitted to herself that submitting was *freedom.*

Ian rolled off her and the loss of his weight left her feeling bereft. He slid an arm under her neck and she turned toward him. She stroked his cheek and kissed him gently. "Thank you."

Ian smiled, his hand caressing her arm. "I'm not sure for what, but you exceeded my expectations. You were amazing. And definitely submissive."

"I don't know what to say to that. Never in a million years did I think I'd ever experience something like this. I finally understand why the French call it *la petite mort.*"

"What does that mean?"

"The literal translation is *little death.* It means the brief loss or weakening of consciousness, the sensation of post orgasm is likened to death."

"Hmm, I think in the BDSM world we call it subspace."

"Subspace?"

"It's a trance-like euphoria generated by overtly intense feelings and emotions. You get the sensation of flying or floating, like being drunk or high. Subs feel immense joy and often are incoherent and dizzy for a period of time. Dominants watch closely until their sub recovers."

"Well, I think I was damn close."

"You were. And there's so much more to explore."

"Well, whatever we call it, I liked it. I liked it a lot."

"So, this isn't a one-time deal?"

Molly laughed. "No way, mister. I will demand a repeat performance."

———

The thrill of Molly submitting sent Ian into whatever the opposite of a tailspin was, up and up, a supernova erupting on the fiery surface of the sun.

Chapter 21

They lay tangled in each other arms, Ian's leg slung across her pelvis, his warm breath sending little shivers down her spine. If someone had told her the best sex of her life was right around the corner, she would have laughed and called them a liar. But now? She fucking loved every minute.

"Tonight meant a lot to me," Ian whispered. "I've been in a bad place for a long time."

"Same here, but I wouldn't have guessed, you seemed upbeat and professional when we met." Molly kissed his cheek. "How did you cope after Rebecca's death?"

"I didn't. I was pretty much a slut after Rebecca died. Lots of angry sex. I screwed anyone I could find. But I never gave out my number, never brought anyone home and if I went to some chick's place I left as soon as she fell asleep. Didn't even leave a note. No repeat encounters."

Molly didn't respond and he was relieved. Seriously, what could someone say about his sordid confession? "You know how there are those different stages of grief? I just couldn't seem to move out of the anger phase. I'm not proud of who I was in those months."

Molly laid a hand on his chest. "What happened to help you move on?"

"My mother."

Molly lifted her head off the pillow. "Do tell?"

"She's always had kind of a sixth sense. As a kid she always seemed to know when I fucked up before I confessed. So, she came to my house one morning and let herself in."

"Your mother had the key to your place?"

"They own the townhouse as a rental property. I lived there for free when I was in law school. When I got my first job I started paying rent. Rebecca moved in and after the wedding we were going to get our own place. Anyway, I was dead to the world, having drunk and screwed to excess the night before. She dumped a glass of ice water on me. She's lucky I didn't punch her."

Molly laughed. "That's one tough cookie."

"Yeah, she is a force to be reckoned with. She said, 'Ian Thomas Turner, get your ass out of bed. I'll make coffee and I want you at the kitchen table in five.' She marched out of there and I heard her slamming things in the kitchen."

Ian stroked her arm, squeezing her shoulder, landing a kiss on her cheek. "She really reamed me out for sleeping around and ditching my family. I still don't know how she knew, but then again she does know *everybody*. She reminded me when people are at their worst, they need their family. But I argued that it just made me feel worse. Rebecca had been by my side at all our family gatherings and I couldn't bear it, it just reminded me she was gone. I even blew them off for Christmas and went skiing by myself."

Molly circled his nipple with her fingertip. "I guess I was just the opposite. I think I skipped the anger stage. After Sam died I just became numb. I couldn't feel anything and I never thought I would again. I thought Sam was my soulmate and figured you only got one of those in a lifetime."

Ian rolled onto his side, their eyes met. "It's easy to think that when you find what you think is the love of your life."

Ian wanted to confess his instant attraction to her, even though he wasn't much of a believer in love at first sight. Attraction, yes, love, not so much. He and Rebecca met in law school and she was dating a friend of his. He considered her a friend, a study buddy until she broke off her relationship and they admitted a mutual attraction. But it was one that had grown over time.

Nervous about pushing Molly too hard, he resolved to go slow with the L-word. Usually guys were the ones who freaked at that word, but Molly wasn't ready. He must be patient and hoped she might feel differently in the not-too-distance future.

"Do you want me to move to the other bed?" Molly said.

"What? No, of course not."

"I know a lot of guys are down for the wham-bam but not so much for cuddling. I won't be offended."

"I would be offended. Stay put."

Molly wasn't sure sleeping together would result in productive sleep, but having a warm body next to her was a welcome relief. She turned on her side and Ian pressed his chest against her back and slung an arm over her waist. Molly prayed for sleep.

She woke, Ian on his back and her arm over his chest. She

studied his square jawline, his beautiful face, peaceful in slum-ber-land. She peeked at the bedside clock: 7:04 a.m. They'd have to hustle to get to Ian's office by eight. Exiting the warm cocoon, she tiptoed toward the guest bath to shower. A premium eucalyptus-lavender bodywash – were all Doms so hopelessly metrosexual? – followed by a steamy rain-shower rinse— breathe, that's it, breathe, inhaling and exhaling oh-so-slowly— became a too-brief respite from the unvarnished world, the concrete jungle that awaited. Molly towel-dried, listening to the running water in Ian's master bath. Probably a good thing they didn't bathe together, they'd just get dirty all over again.

Dressed in her clothing from the prior day—luckily her outfits were more forgettable uniform than look-at-me couture, so no one would probably notice—she stood before the vanity mirror and applied her makeup. His reflection appeared behind her. He tied a royal blue tie, his white starched collar up, no suit jacket and his IT cufflinks sparkled in the bathroom lights.

"I thought maybe you were running off," he said.

"I don't have a car."

He pulled one end of the tie through the loop and pulled it tight, straightening the knot. Molly held her breath as the image of him tying her to the bed surfaced.

"You could have stolen mine, but then I'd have to arrest you, handcuff you, and probably spank you."

Molly paused, eyeliner pencil in the air. And now she was wet. "You're the jailbird, baby, not me. Here's a tip. Please don't bend over to pick up the lavender soap."

Ian chuckled. "Touché."

Molly finished applying her makeup and zipped every-thing into her bag. She faced him, his appearance profes-sional and damn fine. She still couldn't believe she'd had the night of her life with him. She shook her head. "Let's get a move on, can't be late." She brushed past him but he grabbed her arm and pulled her into his chest.

"I promise I won't pressure you but I want to spend more time with you. Any way you want. Just tell me what you want. I'm pretty sure I'm falling in love with you."

"That's ridiculous. You barely know me."

"I know enough. Besides, you interrogate people for a living. Tell me I'm lying."

She gazed into his ice blue eyes and her heart slowed, expanded. Yeah, telling the truth, but… what did *she* want?

Chapter 22

No traffic, they arrived at Ian's office before eight, Sylvia and ADA Alicia Lopez waiting in his office. Their conversation en-route encompassed strategies for investigating Judge Smoot and what actions they should take, and Molly was thankful they avoided the *personal stuff*.

They neared his office and Ian said, "Ready to kick some judge butt? I feel like Batman and Robin."

Molly frowned. "Oh yeah? Make that Batwoman and her trusty sidekick."

He hesitated before answering. "Can I at least be Nightwing?"

"I'll consider it." She held the door for him.

Sylvia had made a pot of coffee and Ian raised an eyebrow in her direction. "Thought we needed to move fast… don't get used to it," she said.

Ian smiled and poured himself a cup then offered the pot to Molly. They sipped coffee, sitting around the conference table. "Molly and I will head down to the Clerk's Office to obtain Judge Smoot's conviction and sentencing records. We'll meet you back here and review them for anything suspect." He turned to Alicia. "How's your schedule for today?"

"Don't have to be in court until two, so I'm yours till then."

He nodded. "Sylvia…"

She stopped him. "Already cleared your schedule and the DA said to bring him into the loop as soon as you know something."

"Okay, then, let's go," he said to Molly.

The Clerk's Office looked like something out of the 1950s and Molly wrinkled her nose. "Haven't they heard of computers?" she asked Ian.

"We're working on it but there's a lot of paper to transpose. You should see the evidence locker. It's worse."

Molly put her hands up. "No thanks."

"I reckon the FBI is a little more up to date?"

"Ya think?"

Molly approached the man standing at the Formica counter. She flashed her credentials. "Special Agent Molly Masterson. I'd like access to Judge Smoot's records. Convictions and sentencing."

"Yes, ma'am," the clerk said.

A taller bald man appeared behind him. "I'm the senior clerk. You'll have to fill out the forms and we'll get back to you."

"How long will that take?" Molly asked. "Wait, don't tell me. Several months?"

"At the least," he said.

Ian laid his forearms on the shabby counter. "I would like that expedited."

"No can do, not even for you." The clerk slid the forms across the countertop toward Molly. "Leave them with me when you're done." He walked away.

Ian and Molly stared at each other. "Can't you override the clerk?" she said.

"No. Maybe Brian can help."

"What's your boss's name?" Molly asked the assistant clerk.

"Nathan Bates."

Molly texted Lily. *"Run the name Nathan Bates ASAP. I want everything you can find on him. And while you're at it run Judge Vera Smoot's financials. See if anything wonky shows up."*

Lily answered in the affirmative.

They walked up the stairs, but before they could reach Ian's office they were intercepted by a court officer. "Judge Smoot wants to see you both in her office."

"Now?" Ian said.

"Yes, sir."

"That didn't take long," Molly said. "I'm guessing the clerk tipped off the judge. But why? Makes me think he's in this up to his ears."

"Right this way," the officer said, extending his hand.

They entered the judge's chambers where she sat behind her desk, leaning against the chair back, clad in a dark red suit and white satin blouse, her fingers steepled under her chin. "Sit," she commanded.

Molly and Ian settled into the two russet leather chairs facing her.

"Why is the FBI interested in my records?"

"Why don't you want us looking at your stats?" Molly said.

The judge smiled and sat upright, her hands folded atop the desk. "We're off the record. All friends here. I just want to know why you are interested in me?"

"You don't have to answer that," Ian said to Molly.

Molly ignored him. "We don't understand why you're

sending this kid out of state, away from his parents. It's an unnecessary hardship."

"There are never any available beds in-state. I've stopped trying."

"Besides," Molly said, "you're sending him to a facility for sex offenders and he's not a sex offender."

The judge sighed. "I heartily disagree. I'm so tired of kids getting away with these sordid behaviors. Too many teens are sexting, it's an epidemic that affects college admissions, future employment, and contributes to society's overall lack of morals. Somebody has to do something and I'm up to the task."

"I think you just get off on the power," Molly said.

Ian cleared his throat. "I think what Agent Masterson is saying is you're levying convictions and issuing sentences way outside the guidelines."

Molly glared at Ian. "I can speak for myself, Chief ADA." She turned toward the judge. "Something is off about this whole thing and I intend to find out what."

The judge stood, her face flushed. "The FBI doesn't have the authority to sanction me."

"Oh no? Watch me," Molly said.

"I'm holding you in contempt, Agent Masterson. Officer?" she yelled. He immediately entered. "Take Agent Masterson down to lockup for contempt."

Molly smirked, her arms crossed over her chest. "I thought we were off the record... all friends?"

"Not any longer."

"Take her now," she instructed the officer.

The clerk came close and grabbed Molly's upper arm. "Don't," she said, pulling free.

"Judge Smoot," Ian said, "with all due respect you're making things worse for yourself."

"Enough, counselor or you'll follow her and earn yourself another fine."

Ian put his hands up. "Fine, but this isn't over."

The court officer attempted to take Molly's phone when Ian intervened and secured it in his pocket. Molly faced Ian through the bars in the holding cell.

"Hey jailbird," he said, contorting his features into what he hoped was pure sympathy.

"Birds of a feather."

"This is absurd."

"This damn judge is over the edge, big time. Something's not right." Her phone rang and Ian handed it to her. "Lily," she said. "What did you find?" She put it on speaker phone.

"Mr. Bates makes $56K a year but drives a brand-new Mercedes, owns a million-dollar property in the Bahamas and a $500K home on the water in Sayville. Doesn't add up. But he makes the judge's docket so he funnels cases to her that fit the profile. The judge has an offshore account that shows regular payments from a place called Bay Pointe Juvenile Detention Center in Massachusetts. And, get this… the Judge's cousin runs the detention center and gets a commission on each new inmate. I was also able to access the judge's conviction record. She sends kids there for pretty minor stuff, like public urination."

"Thanks, Lily. That's a huge help. How's everything going there?"

"We've apprehended seven new suspects. Our tech team is cracker jack. Rob's impressed."

"Good work. I should be back in the office tomorrow. I'm currently… uh… tied up."

The call ended and Ian said, "I'm going down to get the

clerk and squeeze him. He can either be a cooperating witness or a co-conspirator. I think he'll make the right choice."

"Good. Then get me out of here."

Ian came close and whispered. "I'd like to have you under lock and key, but not here."

Molly gasped. "Shuuut up…"

He smiled and disappeared up the stairs.

Ian returned thirty minutes later with another court officer who unlocked the cell door. "Brian intervened, the clerk turned state's witness, and Judge Smoot has been arrested."

Molly exited and accompanied Ian up the stairs. "We've dropped the charges against the Ogburn kid, vacated the sentence and expunged the record."

They entered his office and Molly slumped into a chair. "What a fucking day." Only to be outdone by the *fucking* night she'd had. She ran her fingers through her hair wondering if she looked like something the cat dragged in. In yesterday's clothes and drip-dry hair. Good God. Time to go home.

Chapter 23

Molly spent the next few days reviewing cases with Matt and Lily, reporting stats to Rob—who invited the Assistant Director in via conference call so he could hear Molly's assessment firsthand. They kept making excellent progress.

She sat at her desk evaluating new leads from the tech crew and munched on a sandwich Colleen had prepared. Ian remained in her thoughts almost constantly. With the Ogburn case closed, she had no excuse to see or talk to him and it left her feeling forlorn. Should she call him? She wanted to see him again, but would she? Maybe enjoy an encore from the other night? They could keep it casual. Although that level of sexual intensity didn't seem casual at all, it was both larger than life *and…* intimate.

No matter how many times she rationalized it, she still couldn't see her way into a relationship with him. Yet her mood had shifted from interminable sadness to something more positive, upbeat even. Matt had sensed it upon her return, interrogating her, calling her *jubilant,* an adjective no one had ever thrown her way before. She couldn't deny her feelings but was reticent to name them: overjoyed, exuberant, exultant? Or just plain happy.

In some ways it felt like a malignant mass had been surgically removed from her chest. A new freedom, the need to reach out, to touch someone, which sounded like a bad commercial or at the very least an overused cliché. Ian confessed he wanted more than sex. Was she crazy? A hot guy, expert between the sheets, who wanted a relationship? With her? Most women would jump. Why shouldn't she? She shook her head and sighed, stowing her wrappings in the bag and tossing them in the wastebasket. Her phone rang. Ian. Overjoyed, she tried to steady her voice.

"Morning, counselor."

"Hey, how are you?" he said.

"Great, how about you? Any fallout out from the Ogburn case?"

"It's eerily quiet actually. The bench is keeping a low profile now that one of their own has been jailed. How's it going with the task force?"

"All good. We've cracked nearly a dozen cases. Everything is running smoothly and Lily and Matt are amazing. The Assistant Director even added his praise."

"Awesome. You'll be in line for another promotion before you know it."

"I've got plenty to keep me busy right now, thank you very much."

"Listen, I called because I wanted to know if you have plans for The Fourth?"

Molly bit a fingernail. Her stomach did a somersault. "I'm taking Justice out to visit my parents in Montauk and plan to leave her there for two weeks. Still trying to decide what to do with her for the rest of the summer. I'm researching day programs at the museums and such. Art or music classes maybe. My nanny can work the summer but she's taking a class these next two weeks. And I can't take too much time off since I've just returned from leave."

"I'll be out east for the weekend and I'd love to see you."

"That would be nice." He'd be at the club. Having sex with other women. Okay, so she went from not wanting a relationship to being jealous in less than a nanosecond? Good God.

After a pause, Ian said, "Please tell me if this is over the line, but you said your parents live in Montauk and since I'll be in that general vicinity, I'd love to meet your mother, and your dad too."

Bringing Ian home to meet her parents? That sounded wrong. They'd think she was moving on... Was she? Had she? Maybe... "Speaking of over the line, what about you? Don't you work at the club on the weekends?"

"The club is shutting down for renovations and it will be closed for a few months, so I'm free Saturday and Sunday. And honestly, I'm rethinking my involvement there."

What did that mean? She didn't dare ask.

"Well, I'll see if my parents have plans."

"Okay," he said, his apparent disappointment pinging her stomach. Like that puppy she'd recently kicked. Her chest tightened. Ian had no family nearby and it was a holiday, and he was a friend. She did a one-eighty. "You know what? Stop by. Even if they're busy we can hang out at the beach. And my mom loves an adoring fan."

"Great. Saturday then?"

"Yes, tentatively. I'm heading east Thursday afternoon."

"I'm leaving Thursday afternoon too, hopefully to avoid the onslaught of cidiots."

"Hey, watch it buddy, technically I'm a cidiot."

"Present company excluded. You may be from the city but I'm sure you don't act like the rest of the city idiots."

Molly chuckled. "I'll text you Saturday and we'll make a

plan." She wondered where he was staying. Did she want to know?

"Sounds good." He paused again. "Listen, Molly, we have to talk."

She closed her eyes and pinched the bridge of her nose. "I know. I still need to sort some things out but I promise to find some time this weekend."

"I'm holding you to that. Don't make me tie you down."

Molly gulped, summoning the memory of their recent encounter. She enjoyed the bondage aspect, and well, everything else. "Tempting, but not necessary."

She'd barely put her phone down when Alyx called. "Hey, there's going to be a party at the St. Andrew's Club on Sunday. Jack, the owner is starting a major renovation on Monday and there will be limited access so he's hosting a big barbecue for all the present and past members as a sendoff before it closes. I thought maybe you'd want to come as our guest. Ian will be there."

Huh, Ian hadn't mentioned anything. Maybe he didn't want her there. Did. She. Dare? Go to the club? And did she dare tell Alyx she'd slept with Ian? "I don't know if the club is something I want to experience."

"It's just a barbecue, any kinky encounters will be in the private rooms. The rest of the equipment will be gone by Sunday."

"I'm not sure Ian would want me there."

"Unless my ability to read people is seriously compromised, and I'm sure it is not, I'd say he's really into you."

"Come on, Alyx, he has sex at that place. Probably with a lot of women. Maybe men too, for all I know. I doubt he'd want me invading his territory."

"Whoa, take it down a notch. It's just a party. There will be no club activities. And you need to get out. Maybe you'll meet someone else there."

Good God. Never in a million years did she ever think she'd venture into the BDSM lifestyle community. And she wasn't sure she would now. "I'll think about it. Ian is stopping by my parents' house this weekend. I'll mention it."

"Wait a minute. Ian's meeting your parents?"

"It's not the way it sounds." The lump in Molly's throat strangled her voice. Just thinking about Ian set her pulse throbbing. "I'll agree we enjoy each other's company but it turns out he's totally into my mom's work. He wants to meet her and you know she always appreciates an adoring fan."

"Did you sleep with him?"

"What? Why would you think that?"

"Because you sound like you can't catch your breath just at the thought of him. Either that, or you're having a heart attack."

"*Alyx.*"

"Yes, Moll*y*."

Molly sighed, her forehead in her hand. "Guilty as charged. But it was an accident. I didn't plan on it. And only one time. I'm not interested in a relationship. I was very clear about that."

"You slept with a Dominant, which isn't an everyday experience, so spill the damn tea, and there better be some Long Island in it."

Molly's heart pounded. Fessing up, saying it out loud made it all too real. "Fucking Long, *Long* Island with a splash of Sodom and Gomorrah mixed in."

"Ha! I knew it. I tried to walk away but I couldn't. The pull was too great. It would have been the biggest mistake of my life."

"God, Alyx. I don't know what to do. I like him, he's a great guy, not to mention incredibly handsome and his talents between the sheets, undeniably mind-blowing. But Sam has only been gone three months."

"Look Molly, I have no idea what it's like to lose a spouse and the thought of it terrifies me. But I also believe there is more than one person out there for all of us. And you can't choose the timing. Yeah, maybe it's too soon by some people's standards but what if the opposite was true? You walk away and nobody else ever arrives?"

Molly considered Alyx's words. Made perfect sense. What if she turned Ian down and was alone for the rest of her life? In some ways she'd felt that should be her punishment, a life sentence of loneliness. But why? None of it was her fault. She'd been through the what ifs... what if they'd not gone to the party that night, what if she'd been driving, what if they'd left a few minutes earlier or later... what if, what if, what if.

"I don't know. I don't know what to do."

"Well, I say, don't overthink it. If being with Ian feels good, then let yourself feel good. There's nothing wrong with it. And if a relationship is right, you'll know. Give yourself some breathing room."

"Good advice. I'll speak with Ian and see if he thinks coming to the party is a good idea. Justice will be at my parents' so I could get away."

"Great. Hope to see you there. Love you."

"You're the best."

Lily walked through the open door to Molly's office. "We've got eleven new cases."

Chapter 24

I an had difficulty concentrating on work Thursday morning. Sylvia reviewed his agenda for the day, but his mind was undressing Molly, overly anxious to see her again this weekend. "Ian?" Sylvia's voice brought him to attention. "Where's your head? It's certainly not here."

"Sorry, Sylvia. What?"

"You have lunch at the Rotary Club at noon. You're receiving their service award."

"Right. I'll drive myself and then I'm done for the weekend. What about you, are you doing anything for the holiday?"

"My son is having a get-together over at Davis Park. They've rented a house for the month. Get to play with my granddaughters. I build an outstanding sand castle and I make a mean margarita."

"Nice. Have a great time and I'll see you back Monday morning."

He returned home from the Rotary Club luncheon to pack. He hadn't made his bed since Molly slept over, and he always kept things tidy. The day didn't feel like it was off to a good start if he didn't. Although that particular day had begun beautifully.

He stood at the foot of the bed and stared at the rumpled bedding, an erection imminent, as the memories of their incredible night surfaced. For a first-timer experiencing kink, Molly had proven willing, compliant, nubile, intoxicating. A lifetime with Molly wouldn't be enough. He loosened his tie and pulled it from underneath his collar. The two he'd used to bind Molly still lay on the floor near his feet. Plucking them from the carpet, he wrapped the green one around his hand, pulling it tight. He imagined it to be Molly's wrist, then an ankle. His dick stood at attention. He closed his eyes and inhaled the lingering wafts of Molly's scent, exhaling slowly. A smile stretched his lips wide.

Naked, he entered the shower, working his erection for release. Dressed in jeans and a navy tee-shirt, he packed his brown leather duffle. He wanted to put the top down on the Jeep but the day had turned drizzly and nixed that. He double-checked to make sure his surfboard was securely fastened to the Jeep's roof, then headed out, praying traffic wouldn't be a bitch.

Justice sat on the floor of her room, making Sparkle dance in a circle as she sang *Ring Around the Rosie*. "Justice, stop dilly-dallying and put your shoes on," Molly ordered. She packed the last of Justice's things for the two-week stay with her grandparents and zipped the pink and black polka dot bag.

"Okay, Mommy." Justice donned her pink Nikes, the ones Sam's brother had given her. Sneakers were his thing. He had a massive collection, many still pristine in the boxes they arrived in. He bought Justice sneakers for every occasion where a present was required. And they were darned cute.

"Grand-mère has plenty of books, paints and crayons, and beach toys. And your bike is there. Is there anything else you want to bring?"

"Just Sparkle." She hugged the furry white unicorn to her chest and kissed its head.

Molly's phone pinged. Lily. "What's up?"

"We sent agents from the Massachusetts office to bring in the judge's cousin for questioning. He's in the wind. They checked his residence also and his bank accounts have been emptied. We put out a BOLO."

"Okay, keep me posted. I'll tell Ian, maybe we can squeeze the judge."

"No problem."

"How's progress on the new cases?"

"Tricky, we get video but it's usually routed through a proxy server. One went to a server in Cypress."

"Yeah, these guys are good. VPNs are tough to trace."

"Exactly. We've got guys working the weekend, hopefully we'll track a few more down."

"Good work. Are you at least taking some time off for the holiday?"

"Nah, working, I don't have much of a life these days. It's all about work."

Molly wondered if Lily was simply committed to the job like any good intern would be. Trying to impress the boss, learn everything she could, gain experience. She'd keep an eye because she knew all work and no play was unhealthy.

Unexpectedly, the traffic had been light and Molly attributed it to the rainy weather. If it had been a beautiful beach day many of the *cidiots* would have left a day early like her.

Pulling the black Escalade into her parents' driveway she threw it in park and killed the engine, then freed Justice from the car seat. The door opened and her parents waved, then opened their arms and scooped Justice into a three-person hug.

Molly hauled the bags out of the back and headed for the door, inhaling the briny ocean air. It had poured for most of the trip, even a few cracks of thunder, but the rain had finally tapered off. The sky still overcast, the scent portended sun and fun for the weekend, which, if you believed the weather report, promised to be as flawless as those paintings by Henri Matisse.

"*Ma jolie fille, bienvenu,*" Alyene Bouchard exclaimed, pulling Molly into her arms and kissing her cheek. "I'm so happy you could spend time with us this weekend."

Justice clutched her grandfather's neck, his arms securing her on his hip. "Sweetheart, how are you?" he said to Molly.

Molly surrounded his shoulder with an arm and pecked his cheek. "Doing well, Dad, *merci.*"

"Come, come," her mother urged. Howard Masterson returned his granddaughter to the ground and picked up Molly's bags. Her mother held the door and the family parade marched inside.

The house smelled aromatic, sweet and savory, intimating her mother had baked—her specialty—and her father had cooked up something scrumptious in his commercial-grade kitchen.

"Hungry?" her father asked.

"Famished," Molly said.

"Me too," Justice said. "Grand-mère, did you make cookies?"

Alyene Bouchard put her hands to her lips, her eyes big as balloons. "*Ma chérie,* how did you know?"

Justice smiled, pumping up and down on her pink-sneak-ered toes. "Because you're the yummiest grand-mère in the world!"

"Come, they're peanut butter blossoms, your favorite." She tugged Justice by the hand toward the kitchen.

"They're still Daddy's favorite too," Justice said.

Her mother came to a short stop and gazed over her shoulder.

"It's okay," Molly said, "she talks about him a lot, sometimes like he's still here. I'm just trying to go with it for now."

"Of course," her mother said, rubbing the top of her granddaughter's head. "Daddy watches over you from heaven."

"Not in heaven. Daddy is staying right here with us. For as long as we need him."

Everyone exchanged slightly nervous glances and faux smiles.

Justice and her grandmother disappeared into the kitchen. "How are you doing?" Molly's father said.

"Better now that I'm back at work. It's good to have a purpose again. Something to occupy my time."

Her father rubbed her back. "I agree. I was worried, you were wallowing in sadness for so long. And yet, *my heart* was broken, I could only imagine how horrible it was for you."

They had her father's famous Béchamel lasagna with sun-dried tomatoes and sautéed mushrooms for dinner, accompanied by a crisp chardonnay, and her favorite salad, Caesar with homemade croutons, freshly-shaved shards of parmesan, and real anchovies in a garlic-lemon-olive oil dressing.

Molly had been blessed with a toddler who ate everything. She'd often witnessed others who only consumed yogurt, fruit, and boxed macaroni and cheese. Right from the get-go Justice embraced everything offered, even her grandfather's exotic concoctions. Much to everyone's astonishment, she slurped down raw clams at the age of two, followed by things like paté, marinated artichoke hearts and Spanakopita.

"*Bien joué,*" Alyene said to Justice, spying her clean plate. "How about a cookie?"

"Yes, please," Justice said, clapping her hands together. "I finished all my dinner."

"*Oui,* you're such a good girl," Alyene said.

Molly helped her father clear the table and tidy the kitchen while her mother chatted up Justice with plans to build a massive sandcastle tomorrow morning and have a picnic on the beach.

"Grand-mère, guess what?"

"What, *Ma chérie.*"

"I'm going to the 'lympics," Justice said through a mouthful of cookie.

"The Olympics?"

"Mommy said I could and she even got me a coach."

Alyene Bouchard studied Molly's face, who'd stopped midway through drying the lasagna pan. "Do tell," she said.

Molly smiled, recalling Justice's proposition to Ian and his diplomatic acquiescence. "She saw something on television about the summer Olympics and asked Colleen about it. She decided she was a really good swimmer and wants to get a gold medal. Then, she found out Jamie won a gold medal for skiing and that sealed the deal. The glitch was Jamie said her father had coached her, he is a ski instructor. But then we got into the whole 'I don't have a Daddy to coach me' thing and Jamie explained not everyone has a daddy and we could get a coach instead."

"Ian is going to be my coach," Justice said, her eyes alight, her smile stretched impossibly wide.

"Oh," her grandmother said. "Ian?"

Here we go. Molly had planned on bringing up Ian,

except not quite yet. "A friend," she said, stowing the lasagna pan in the drawer under the stove.

Her mother's eyes flickered. "A new friend?"

"Yes, we worked a case together recently and…" Molly sighed, resting her backside against the counter, her hands grasping the gray speckled granite.

"Go on," her father said.

"Yes, details please," her mother added. "Does he work for the FBI?"

"He's the Chief ADA for Suffolk County and we had a case out there."

"Is he single?" her mother asked.

"Yes."

"Cute?"

"Gorgeous."

"How old?"

Good God. The inquisition had begun and there would be no escape.

"Daddy says he likes him," Justice said.

Molly gasped.

Chapter 25

Ian checked into Daunts Albatross Motel in Montauk, not his usual haunt, but more proximate to Molly's location. He ate at the nearby clam bar—fried clams, French fries and their famous apple cider vinegar coleslaw—and sucked on a brew. The rain had abated and the sky began to clear so he finished his beer on the deck. The red sunset portended a picturesque day tomorrow. He thought of that old adage fishermen quoted about red skies in the morning and at sunset, but could never remember which was bad and which was good. The sing-song of the phrase rhymed morning with warning so he figured that was probably the bad one. Tomorrow would be exceptional, he told himself.

The evening still young, he stopped at the club for a drink before returning to his lonely room. It was the last night of regular festivities, the rest of the weekend reserved for long-time members and unattached submissives as a good deal of the equipment had already been moved out. He wasn't on the schedule tonight and could play if he cared to, but he didn't want that. Something had changed in the last

Unsaddened

few days. He only wanted to play with Molly. But he didn't want it to just be play. He wanted more. Something real. His phone rang. "Hi, Mom."

"Hi sweetie, how are you?"

"No complaints. Spending the weekend out east, surfing, catching some rays, and having dinner with a friend."

"Wonderful. Of course I keep hoping you'll venture back home one of these holiday weekends. Everyone misses you."

"I promise to get home soon. What are you guys up to?"

"Going to Uncle Billy's lake house. Your sisters and all your cousins will be there. They'll be asking for you."

"Tell everyone hi, and I'll see them soon."

"Your dad says, hi."

Ian's father barked into the phone. "Get your ass home for a visit before I disinherit you."

Ian laughed. "Okay, Dad. Although I doubt there's much money left because you two spend it all on the less fortunate. Not that there's anything wrong with that." His father's deep laughter rumbled.

"Anything new?" his mother said.

Ian wanted to tell her he met the most amazing woman, someone he might be able to bring home. But he didn't want to get his parents' hopes up. Damn, he shouldn't get *his* hopes up, but alas, too late. He was in— hook, line and sinker. He just hoped he didn't wind up at the bottom of the emotional ocean. He'd been there once and nearly drowned. "Maybe, I made a new friend." Jesus, sounded like the first day home from kindergarten.

"Oh? Someone of the female persuasion?"

"Yes, her name's Molly, she's a special agent for the FBI. We worked a case together and grabbed a drink one night. But her husband died several months ago, a car accident, and I'm not sure she's ready to move on." Okay, that was way too much information. His mother always got him

163

to spill stuff he vowed to keep in the vault. Her super-power.

"Sounds like you two have much in common. It might be good for you both."

And... she was reading his mind. Again.

"Well, we'll see, I'll keep you posted. I'm hoping to see her this weekend."

"Fingers crossed. I hope it works out for both of you."

They bid goodbye and Ian tucked his phone in his back pocket and wondered what Molly was doing at this exact moment.

Molly sat in the oversized brown wicker chair on the back deck and nursed her second chardonnay. The crimson sun kissed the horizon and the waves broke gently on the sand, a quiet surf, not the raging white-capped breakers of an impending storm. She'd tucked Justice into bed, having put off further explanations of Justice's recent tendency to blurt out statements from dead Sam. Her parents sat on the matching loveseat, holding hands, wine glasses perched on the side tables. "How long has she been talking about her father like that?" her mother said.

Molly detailed the incidents, the one regarding the exploding light bulb garnering shock from both the Master-sons. "I don't know if I should do anything or just wait it out. Brush it off as the musings of an imaginative child."

"Like what? Take her to a therapist or... a psychic?" her mother said.

"The thought of both did occur to me."

"Don't jump the gun," her father said. "I'd give it time. She doesn't seem distressed and maybe it's just her way of coping. Death must be difficult for a child to understand. Look at how hard it is for the rest of us."

Molly twirled the wineglass on her lap, then sipped. "That's pretty much where my head is at. Until it becomes a problem, I'll just play along."

"Now, let's talk about this young man. What's his name, Ian?" her mother said.

Molly smiled. "Ian Turner, he's from Detroit. Actually, he's a big fan of yours."

Alyene arched her eyebrows. "Pray tell, darling? How so?"

"He attended your show in New York City that year, when I was in college. It was extra credit for his art history class. He says he fell in love with your work."

"I'm liking this guy already," Alyene said. She smiled at her husband.

"He'd like to meet you both. I told him maybe he could come for dinner. Perhaps Saturday night?"

"We'd love to have him," her mother said.

"Is he a meat guy? I could do steaks or ribs," her father said.

"Dad, I hardly know him. He likes seafood, there's a place near his condo that serves amazing shellfish but I don't get the feeling he's a picky eater."

Her father clapped his hands together. "Excellent. I'll plan the menu and run it by you."

Alyene picked up her wine glass and emptied the last inch. "You said that restaurant was near his condo. Have you been to his place?"

Good God. Her mother was like a dog with a bone. She wouldn't let this go until she extracted every tasty morsel. "Not really any of your business." Molly poured another half glass of wine.

"Since when? You're always my business."

Her father frowned, but she wasn't sure if he was disappointed in her comment or her mother's. "Sorry, that was rude. I'm just not sure I want to talk about this yet."

"Molly, I'm only concerned for your happiness. And for Justice."

Molly put her wineglass on the side table. "It's only been three months since Sam died. I shouldn't be even considering seeing another man."

Her mother guffawed. "Really? Who made that rule?"

"Mom, seriously. It's inappropriate." She crossed her arms over her chest.

"Not to me it isn't."

"Me either," her father said. "Speaking of nobody's business, I wouldn't give a shit what anybody else thinks. If you want to spend time with him, do it."

Molly's head pounded, maybe the chardonnay. "Well, for now, he's a friend. I'm trying not to overthink it, which seems to be a problem for me these days." She'd kept her mother at bay, at least for now, having no intention of revealing her overnight escapade at Ian's place.

Ian downed the last of his scotch. He surveyed the crowd, an array of fetish wear, riding crops, handcuffs... masks and ball gags on display. Women and men shrieking their release, moans and yelps as whips made contact with flesh or a hand struck reddened buttocks. The music blared, the beat pounding his eardrums in a frenzied rhythm. He'd only had one beer and a small scotch so it couldn't be the alcohol, but suddenly he had a throbbing headache. Perhaps the week was taking its toll. The Ogburn case had been stressful, getting locked up and fined... but then vastly diminished by spending an amazing night with Molly. Something about her calmed him. He'd never relied on a woman much before. Rebecca was an independent, brilliant woman, and in many ways she shared Molly's characteristics. But Molly made him feel like she was an equal partner, able to carry any burden, to stand beside him and even take charge if he needed it, something he never imagined. Dare he say it? He felt *protected*.

A finger tapped his shoulder. "Master, how are you tonight?"

He turned on the barstool. She wore a leather bustier and a minuscule patent leather skirt. "Fine, thank you, Kelly. How are you tonight?"

"Well, thank you, Sir. Do you have time for me tonight?"

Ian tightened his lips. He wasn't on the schedule until tomorrow night, but he was allowed to play, and normally, he would. Sunday night the club would shut its doors to the general clientele for an extended period. "I'm not working," he said. "How about tomorrow night?"

Kelly curled her bottom lip. "Boo-hoo. I was hoping to play with you tonight."

"I'm on my way out. Tomorrow. Promise." However, his heart wasn't into it. Shockingly, neither was his dick.

Chapter 26

Breakfast consisted of homemade blueberry pancakes with her Dad's crème fraiche, crispy bacon, and freshly squeezed orange juice.

"Can I have another pancake, Grand-père?" Justice asked, holding up her plate.

"You've already had two," Molly said. She'd barely finished two herself.

"Of course, sweetie," Howard Masterson said. "I wish your mother had your appetite." He narrowed his eyes at Molly. "You could afford to put on a few pounds."

"Fine, hit me up," Molly said, offering her plate alongside Justice's in a Dickensian pose.

Justice smiled. "Daddy says, 'good girl,' Mommy."

Her mother, who'd been pouring coffee, stopped and turned, cup in hand. She sipped, her eyes peering over the rim at Molly. Howard delivered pancakes as requested and both returned their plates to the table. Nobody said anything. Molly downed the remainder of her orange juice and slowly replaced the glass. What she said next was important.

"Is Daddy here?" she asked Justice.

Nobody moved.

"Of course not, silly," Justice said.

Molly reached over and slathered crème fraiche on Justice's pancake, cutting it into four-year-old mouth-sized morsels.

"Do you see him?"

"Mommy…" Justice's shoulders deflated in a dramatic pose. "I told you already. I don't see him I just hear him. He died, remember?"

Molly feared she'd never get a mouthful of pancake past the lump in her throat, but she cut it up anyway and poured herself more orange juice. "Of course," she said, "I remember. Does Daddy have anything else to say?"

Justice shrugged. "Nope."

"Okaaay, then…." The three adults made eye contact, sideways glances and raised eyebrows darted around the room like ping-pong balls in a windstorm. Molly ate silently, finishing her breakfast, then cleared her place. Her parents sat at the table, drinking coffee.

"Can I go play?" Justice said.

"Of course. Why don't you draw some pictures for Grand-mère and Grand-père so they can put them on the refrigerator. Then we'll get ready for the beach. But first clear your place."

Justice slithered off the chair, took her plate and silverware and deposited everything on the counter. "Can we build a sand castle?"

"Absolutely. The biggest, best one on the beach."

"Yay." Justice clapped her hands then ran from the kitchen.

Molly rose and poured a cup of coffee and sat beside her mother. "Freaky, right?"

Her mother clasped her hand and squeezed. "I'll admit it takes you aback for a second, but I think not overreacting is the best way to handle it. It seems perfectly natural to her."

"I agree," her father said. "But it does make me wonder if it's really him talking to her."

"What?" Molly said, her mouth agape, coffee cup halted mid-sip. "You believe in ghosts?"

Her father hesitated, gulping coffee then. "I don't know what I believe, but I can't say for sure they don't exist."

Molly hung her head in her hands. "I guess I don't know what I believe either." She gazed up. "But seriously, if it's true, is he going to hang around forever? The idea of him watching us is creepy." She thought of her night with Ian. Could Sam have been watching? Good God. A horrible thought. Maybe he was tied to Justice, or the house, yet apparently he'd followed them here… were their rules for ghosts? Perhaps she should study up. Okay, that was totally absurd. There would be no facts, only lore, ghost tales, and that would be as reliable as… well… absolutely nothing.

"Let's put it away for now," her mother said, bringing Molly back to the here and now.

"Agreed," Howard said. "Let's pack up for the beach. I've made potato salad and ham sandwiches. I'm grilling sea bass for dinner."

"Delish," Molly said.

———

Ian rose at dawn, grabbed coffee and a bagel at a nearby café and headed for the ocean. Surfers dotted the water, the beach empty save for a few early morning joggers. He settled on the sand in his shortie wet suit, munching his bagel, drinking coffee and savoring the solitude and serenity before the masses inundated the beach. The inclement weather yesterday gave the waves a little pep and he paddled out into the deep. After several hours riding monster waves, with only one epic wipeout, he collapsed on the warm sand, an immense sense of satisfaction swelling his chest. Nothing could compare with a perfect morning surfing. Well, maybe a night with Molly might compare, no… exceed. By about a light-year.

Molly watched as Justice frolicked at the water's edge with her grandfather. He had her by both hands and lifted her up each time a wave crashed onto the shore, saving her from a salt water deluge. Justice giggled with unadulterated glee.

Molly lowered the back on her beach chair and let the sun's rays bake her, hopefully to a golden brown. She tanned easily and rarely used sunscreen and a tan always made her feel healthy, although the reality was probably the complete opposite. Molly felt more content, happy even, than she'd felt since Sam's death. For the first time she felt inspired, like there was more life to live. More happiness, and maybe more *love*. The recent encounter with Ian weighed heavily on her mind. She still couldn't understand his claim that he'd fallen for her at first sight. Perhaps he was still too desperate to replace his lost love, a woman to have and to hold for eternity?

Her mother had gone back to the house to refill the iced tea jug after lunch and Molly considered taking a nap, Justice remained in play mode with her grandfather. She removed her sunglasses when she heard her mother exclaim, "Look who's here."

Molly peered over her shoulder, squinting, her hand shielding the sun. Two well-built men, dressed in board shorts and tank tops stood above her. She waited for her mother to identify the strangers.

"Hey, Molls, good to see you."

Molls? Only one person had ever called her that. John T. Shadow. Good God. She sat up, donning her aviator shades. Damn. Had her mother set her up?

He crouched down beside her chair. "How ya been?"

"Good, you?" Handsome as ever with his cropped dark hair and chiseled jaw, tanned rock-hard shoulders on full display, his chest barely contained under a black tank top. A plethora of tattoos. A silver chain around his neck glinted in the brilliant sunshine. Behind those Ray Bans were stunning blue eyes that could melt you at fifty feet. All the girls had an eye for John Shadow, who often just went by the moniker Shadow. The name itself projected a dark and mysterious image, unsettling, intimidating, and forbidden as two porn stars sneaking into heaven.

"Great. Been surfing all morning. I gotta say you look amazing. The years have been good to you, Molls."

Yeah, that's because the last time he saw her she was a total dork. A knot tightened her stomach. They had been classmates in high school… when she was a nerd and a prude. He'd tried to kiss her once and she wouldn't let his tongue into her mouth. He never embarrassed her over it, but she'd been mortified, even to this day.

"This is my surfing buddy, Jax. Jax, this is Molly Masterson, we knew each other in high school."

"Any friend of Shadow's," Jax said with a chin-nod.

"Do you still go by Masterson? I know you married."

"Masterson is fine. And I'm not married anymore."

"I heard about the accident. So sorry."

"Thanks. So I lost track of you. Are you just out here surfing?"

"I live here," Shadow said. "I work for the FDNY, I'm a firefighter. Work three-day shifts and stay in the city. The rest of the time I hang out here. Sweet life." Shadow settled cross-legged on the sand, elbows resting on tan muscular thighs, hands clasped between them. Looked like he planned to stay a while. His buddy sat beside him in the identical pose.

"Iced tea?" her mother offered.

"No thanks, we're on our way to Buster's. A few brews before we head over to the club tonight."

What club? Maybe The Stephen Talkhouse in Amagansett? They had great bands, often really famous groups looking for an intimate acoustic setting. She'd seen Coldplay there once.

"So, what are you up to these days?" Shadow said.

"I'm a special agent for the FBI. I work sex crimes. I live in SOHO." Justice bounded onto the blanket, Howard not far behind, and plopped down on Molly's lap. "And this is my daughter, Justice." She turned to her daughter. "This is my friend John and his friend Jax. Say hello."

"Hi," Justice said, adding a pert wave.

Shadow smiled. "Hello there, darling. Nice to meet you."

Justice stared up at Molly. "Daddy doesn't like him."

Chapter 27

The awkward moment lingered and Molly, tired of explaining Justice's obsession with Sam's supposed messages from the *other side*, sloughed it off in the usual manner. John appeared unfazed and extricated himself graciously with... 'gotta cut a kid some slack'.

John and Jax left, John promising to stay in touch. Molly's mother saw them out and didn't return to the beach. Molly and Justice built the promised sand castle and she even allowed Justice to bury her in the sand. Her dad reclined in his beach chair reading the new Tom Clancy book.

Escaping her sand coffin, Molly battled through the breakers, enjoying a leisurely swim. As much as she tried to dismiss it, her ire simmered at the thought her mother had invited John Shadow over with the intention of Molly going on a date with him. How had she managed that anyway? Some strange coincidence like bumping into him at the grocery store? She didn't think her mother even knew John Shadow. It wasn't like Molly ever brought him around the house. Okay, he was popular, held the touchdown record for her high school football team, but she didn't remember her mother ever attending anything sports related.

The afternoon waned, the sun drifting toward the horizon. "Time to get cleaned up, sweetie," Molly said.

Her father closed his book. "How about an outdoor shower?"

Everyone knew Justice's affection for the outdoor shower. Justice jumped up and started removing her swimsuit. "Whoa," her grandfather said. "Let's wait till we get in the shower." He rose, grabbed a towel and walked Justice toward the wooden cubicle at the far right of the deck.

Molly packed up the beach toys and chairs, stowing them in the shed, then collected the remaining towels and blanket. She headed for the kitchen where her mother emptied the dishwasher. She couldn't shed her irritation at her mother's obvious intervention. She tried to talk herself into keeping her mouth shut, yet couldn't. Arms crossed over her chest she leaned a hip against the kitchen counter. "I can't believe you tried to set me up with John Shadow."

Her mother retrieved a glass from the dishwasher and placed it in the overhead cupboard. "I wasn't really thinking that way. I just thought it might be nice to see an old friend."

"How do you even know him. It's not like we hung out."

"I always knew you had a crush on him."

"Mom!"

"Oh stop, it's not like I invited him to dinner. I often see his mother in town and the other day I ran into her at the farmer's market. We started chatting and I mentioned you were coming out for the weekend. She told me her son lived on Beech Tree Lane, right around the corner. I said she should tell him to stop by."

"Sam's only been dead three months. I'm not ready to move on. I don't think I ever will."

"Well, you've invited Ian to dinner. Seems like maybe thou doth protest too much."

Molly smacked her forehead. Ian had said the exact same words to her, only he was referring to something a bit different. "I told you, he's just an acquaintance. Barely even a friend. I've known him like a week."

"Well, your father and I knew we were meant for each other the moment we met."

"That's bullshit. Nobody could know something like that."

Her mother slammed the dishwasher door shut and faced Molly. "Don't tell me what I know and what I felt."

Justice bounded into the room wrapped in a blue and white striped beach towel, her hair a wet tousle, Howard at her side. She frowned at Molly. "Daddy says…"

"Don't Justice," she pointed a finger at her, "don't you dare tell me what Daddy is saying. I never want to hear you say that again." Her parents' jaws dropped. "You know," she said, glancing first at her mother, then her father, "I need to go for a walk. I'll be back in a while." And she flew out the back door. She broke into a run, her feet pounding the sand until the crowd had thinned and she was alone. Her pace slowed and she tried to catch her breath. She bent over, hands on her knees and screamed, "F*uuuuck*!" She exhaled slowly, striving for calm. But the dam broke and the tears flowed. Dropping to her knees, she collapsed on her back and covered her streaming eyes with her forearm. The sobs came in an endless rhythm, like the ocean waves pounding the beach. If only she could turn back the clock so this never happened. Why Sam? He was a good person, a good husband, a good father. He was globally conscious, recycled, gave to charity, even volunteered at pre-school when he could. Okay, now she was waxing pathetic. Bad shit just happened, bad luck, and it had nothing to do with what you projected into the universe, no such thing as karma. Probably.

She must have dozed off because when she opened her eyes the sun had sunk low into the sea. Rising, as sluggishly as a ninety-year-old getting out of bed, she trod homeward. Her parents sat on the deck chairs, smoke coming from the grill, Justice clad in her Minnie Mouse pajamas. Climbing the three steps slowly and deliberately, she faced them. "Sorry, I don't know what came over me. I just…"

"No need," her mother said, rising from the wicker chair. "It's been a difficult time. I can't imagine how you're dealing with all this." She embraced Molly, holding her for an extended minute. Molly approached Justice and knelt. "Sorry, sweetie. Mommy was in a bad mood. I didn't mean to yell at you."

"It's okay, Mommy. I still love you." Justice strangled her neck with her tiny arms and kissed Molly's cheek. Molly hugged her back, holding her breath. *Please God, please don't let her give me another message from Sam.*

Ian arrived at the club a little after seven. Zach gave his usual 'bro' greeting while signing in members for the night's festivities. The crowd mumbled and grumbled over the unexpected hiatus while the club shut down for renovations. A few took the positive bent, reminding others how amazing it would be when they returned. Something new and exciting to look forward to.

Ian entered the Master's lounge and locked his personal belongings in his locker, but kept his phone in his pocket in case a break in the case came. He lingered at the sink, studying his reflection. Should have applied sunscreen, his face a touch too red. The door opened and Shadow entered, accompanied by a tall, sandy-haired man.

"Hey, Ian."

"JT, good to see you, man."

"A little too much sun today?"

"Seems so. Great day on the ocean though."

"Where'd you surf?"

"Ditch Plains, you?"

"Kirk Park. This is my buddy, Jax. I'm showing him the ropes, literally." JT smiled. "He has some experience, down in Tampa. An old club where Jack cut his teeth back in the day."

"Welcome," Ian said. They shook hands.

"Thanks," Jax said, "from what I've seen so far, this club is the top of the heap."

Shadow added, "Jack is hiring him as a Master."

Ian washed his hands and ran his fingers through his hair. "Great, we can use the help."

"Take any locker you want," Shadow said to Jax.

Jax pulled a Glock from under his shirt and stowed it in the metal cubicle, then spun the lock.

"He works for the ATF. We met on an arson case," Shadow told Ian.

Masters William, Mark and Jensen entered, laughing, Jensen slapping Mark on the back. "In your dreams," he said.

"Stay out of my fucking dreams," Mark said.

The threesome offered greetings, Shadow introducing Jax to the other Masters.

"You gonna let him work the subbies?" Jensen asked.

"Jack says he's good to go, just keep on eye on him."

Jax narrowed one eye. "I'll be fine. I got some skills the ladies will love."

"We'll be the judge of that," William said. "Plenty of

competition so we'll see how you fare. Although, Ian is the man of the hour these days. The ladies beg to get some quality time with him."

"Begging works for me," Jax said.

"That's bull," Ian said. "You guys are just as busy as I am."

William placed a hand on Ian's shoulder. "Well, that Kelly chick definitely has the hots for you. I think she pouted all last night. I had to spank her out of it."

Ian feared William might be right. He'd promised to work with her tonight and he had to deliver. Mind over matter, he told himself, she deserved his best.

He skipped the drink and strolled the floor, keeping an eye out for Kelly, then venturing into the dungeon to assess the activity. The room was warm, even with the air conditioning set to sixty-eight degrees. He observed a woman in a corset using a small tool to send electric shocks through another woman who wore lacy black lingerie. Across the room another woman handcuffed to a large cross was being spanked with a leather paddle. Toward the back, Master Sam was giving a rope-tying demonstration and on the left wall Mistress Olivia whipped a moaning male submissive wearing nothing but a tiny black leather thong.

He moved closer to a woman suspended from the ceiling. "Evening," he said to Master Grayson. "All good?"

"Master Ian, enjoying ourselves very much."

Ian reached up and slipped a finger through the ropes binding the woman to the ceiling making sure the tether wasn't too tight. He glanced downward, her toes touching the ground to give sufficient support. "Excellent. Have a good night."

Confident everyone was in compliance, he moved toward the exit when he spied Kelly in a dark corner.

He approached. "What are you doing in here alone?"

"I just wanted to watch. I'm still not sure what I like and don't like. I want to experiment more."

Ian glanced at her wrists, crimson manacles in place, but another charm had been added: red for pain.

He placed a hand on the wall and leaned in. "It's risky being in here alone. Masters will assume you're interested in participating and these behaviors are some of the most intense."

"It is intimidating."

"I think you're in over your head. Remember the mantra is safe, sane, and consensual. We take that very seriously and I'm not sure you are in a safe space yet." He shoved a finger into her handcuff and pulled her toward the exit. "I want you out of here."

Her giant eyes found his. "Can you work with me? You said you'd have time tonight."

"Of course, my word is my bond."

Chapter 28

After dinner, Justice tucked in for the night, the Mastersons sipped Macallan on the rocks, relishing the warm night air. Molly loved the back porch of her parents' seaside retreat. The homestead boasted four thousand square feet and the back porch ran the entire rear of the house. A fully appointed outdoor kitchen sat to the left, plus an old barn her mother had turned into a studio, a sacred place, no one entered without permission. If her mother took you inside, you inhaled rare air, indeed.

Molly read her father's scribbles, detailing his menu for Saturday night. Basic fare, yet he always put his personal spin on anything he made. The tastes often subtle, diners at his restaurant remarking at spectacular flavors they couldn't identify. The menu consisted of rib eye steaks with Elote seasoning, a blue cheese compote, marsala mushrooms and hasselback potatoes. Her mom was baking a blueberry pie with fresh whipped cream. Appetizers included cold lobster cocktail and pâté with sesame crisps. "Looks great," Molly said. "I'm happy to act as sous chef."

"Hired," her father said.

"What time for dinner tomorrow? I have to text Ian."

"Let's do cocktails at five."

The warm ocean breeze ruffled her hair and she pushed her bangs off her face with her fingers. She texted Ian. *See you tomorrow? 24 Ocean Breeze Lane. Cocktails at 5.*" She stared at the screen but no gray dots appeared.

The day had taken an emotional toll on her and exhaustion weighed her down. "I think I'm going to turn in early, I'm beat."

"Of course," her mother said.

She lingered a while longer as her parents discussed an upcoming event in New York City. Her mother had an impending exhibition showcasing new work at the Met. Finishing her scotch, the ice cubes tinkled their disdain at the empty glass and she lumbered up from her seat. "Night. See you in the morning."

"Night," they both said.

Having rescued Kelly from the dungeon, Ian wondered what she might be interested in trying tonight. Or, more aptly, what he'd be able to manage. His enthusiasm wasn't at its usual level, and he had to admit surfing had tapped his energy. He probably should have taken a nap. When had he turned into such a wuss?

"Who have you played with in my absence?"

"Masters William and Jensen, Sir."

"What new things have you tried?"

"Nothing, nobody will try anything new without your permission. They said you're in charge of me. No one will fuck me, they said I need your approval."

Ian pinched the bridge of his nose. Of course, he'd made it very clear Kelly was under his control for the duration of her training. And based on her abusive history, no Master would cross that line without his okay. He had allowed Master Edward to work with her one evening but Edward wouldn't introduce new behaviors without his okay. And honestly, he hadn't anticipated her being here *every* night. Her enthusiasm surprised him. "I see you've added a new charm. Who gave it to you?"

"I just asked for it at the bar."

He'd have to find out who that was. "Which bartender?"

"I forget, it was a woman."

That could be any one of about ten people. And he had the distinct feeling Kelly didn't want to get anyone in trouble. "Only I can give you new charms. I'm not sure you're ready for that level of pain."

"Yes, Sir."

He reached down and removed the offending trinket and tucked it in his jean's pocket.

"So you're ready for me to fuck you?"

"Yes, please, Sir."

He needed to get his game face on. His game dick? Autopilot kicked in.

He led Kelly to a leather loveseat and pulled her down beside him. "We will talk first. I want to make sure your head is in the right subspace."

Kelly folded her hands in her lap but her gaze focused on him. "Yes, Sir."

"I'm worried you're moving too fast, however I'm willing to test your limits. If you pass, I'll set you free to work with any of the Masters. So tonight, no limits. If you reach one, use your safe word. Understand?"

"Yes, Sir."

He studied her face for signs of distress. "I'm beginning to think you're not as vanilla as you look."

Kelly smiled. "Perhaps not, Sir."

"Good." Ian leaned against the couch's back and folded his arms over his chest. "Stand."

Kelly immediately complied.

She wore the same outfit as last night. "Lose the clothes."

Kelly unlaced the leather bustier slowly, dropping it behind her. Next, the skirt skimmed down her slender legs and she stepped out. Ian picked up the clothing and placed it on the floor next to the couch. "On your knees, slave position."

Kelly obeyed, sitting on her heels, palms facing up on her thighs, eyes down.

"Excellent, little one." He leaned forward. "Eyes on me." Kelly gazed up. "Follow me." He retrieved her clothing and approached the stairs, his naked subbie following obediently behind.

He secured the key to room #8 and led Kelly inside, tossing the key on the night stand beside the king-sized bed. Stripping down the covers, the black sheets bared, he loosened the restraints from the headboard, opening the buckles. He coaxed the black polo shirt over his head and threw it on the bedside chair. Kelly's eyes lingered on his chest, lips taut.

"I'm going to finger fuck you first and then I'm going to take you hard." Kelly remained silent. Good. "Lie down, on your back. I will restrain you first."

Her frail form stretched out on the sheets, the sight of her scars unnerved him and he tried to shut out thoughts of what she'd been through. *Focus, man.* He removed the rest of his clothing, freeing his erection, and sat on the bed, securing one wrist in the manacle and yanking the tether taut. He tied the knot, then walked to the other side and did the same.

He grabbed a condom from the side table and tore the wrapper open with his teeth, then rolled it on. Crawling on the bed, he spread her legs wide and pushed up her knees.

Her folds glistened. Gratitude streamed through him, around him. Everywhere. She was into it.

He touched her clit, so tight and swollen, it throbbed under his thumb. She whimpered. "Easy, darling, we're just getting started."

She lifted her head to look at him, yet remained quiet.

"You're so wet. I like that very much." He sat between her legs, one hand gripping her thigh while his finger circled her opening. He plunged two fingers in, fast and hard. Kelly moaned and her hips lifted off the mattress. He set his mouth on her, licking, probing with his tongue, then thrust a finger in and out of her vagina again, then two, and then a third. Her body trembled, she squirmed in response to his relentless twisting… twirling his fingers around and around. "Not yet, darling. You do not have permission to bust."

"Please," she begged.

"Shush, no talking. You will obey."

He pressed his thumb on her clit and she shrieked, then he used his tongue, circling the tiny nub as it swelled under his ministrations. He felt her body tense, every muscle rigid, then plunged two fingers into her wetness. Thrusting in and out, in and out, he quickened the rhythm.

"Now, Kelly, come for me." The wave hit, her tissues in spasms, clenching around his fingers. She bore down, the vice of her legs around his hand. "Oh God," she said. "Oh God." He massaged her clit with his thumb, drawing out the final shudders. "Well done, little subbie." Her pants came quick and she gasped for breath. He waited until her breathing calmed.

He straddled her thighs, resting his weight on them, erection in hand. "You ready for the big finale?"

"Yes, Sir."

"I'm going to fuck you hard." She clutched the restraints, bracing herself for the onslaught. "Keep your eyes on me."

Her laser focus affirmed compliance to his order. "I want you to remember who you are with. Say my name."

"Master Ian, Sir."

His cock pressed against her core, then slid into her wetness. He circled the head around her clit then pushed in slowly, not sure she could take all of him. He eased out then pushed in deeper. Kelly gasped.

"Green?" he said.

Kelly moaned. "Yes, Sir. The greenest pastures of all."

He increased his speed, leaning over her, hands on either side of her head, he suckled a breast. With each thrust of his cock, she pushed her pelvis against him as if wanting more, needing his girth, thrashing against him in tandem. He grasped her hips and hammered into her, hard and fast. A low growl escaped as he pressed in deep and far. "Come for me, Kelly." Her vagina squeezed his cock, throbbing, sucking him. He shuddered and jerked his release, pleasure exploding outward like a flash-fire. Kelly screamed again, "Oh God, oh God, oh God."

He smiled, glad to provide an experience she'd never forget.

With a quiet sigh, he pulled out, and clambered up to release the restraints. He lay beside her and rested a hand on her belly. "I'm amazed you've come this far in such a short time. I will alert the other Masters that I have released you to the submissive pool. But if you ever need help, just ask."

Kelly placed a hand on his chest and he squeezed it, then released. "Did you receive pleasure, Master?"

"Yes, Kelly. Thank you for your trust in me. I wish for you beauty and bliss." But in truth, he hadn't been fucking Kelly, he'd been fucking Molly.

Chapter 29

Ian slept until eight, then hit the beach, surfing until noon. This time he took a nap so he'd be in good form when meeting Molly's parents. His phone rang. Alicia Lopez. He frowned, she wouldn't be calling him unless there was a problem. "Alicia, what's up?"

"I just wanted you to know Judge Smoot was sent to Rikers to await trial. Last night she got beat up pretty bad. She's in Bellevue."

Ian rubbed his forehead. "What the hell is she doing at Rikers?"

"Apparently, there wasn't space at our usual facilities."

"Well, that's poetic. It's the same argument she used for sending the Ogburn kid out of state."

"Only this happened to be true," Alicia said.

"Still, I ordered protective custody."

"I know, but someone dropped the ball."

"She's no match for the inmates at Rikers. I'm all for her paying for her crimes but I didn't want her to get the crap beaten out of her. How bad?"

"Face is pretty messed up, two broken ribs and collar bone."

Ian squeezed the back of his neck. "Damn. Does Brian know?"

"I sent him a message. Nobody's in the office for the holiday. Just a few of us on call."

"Of course. Well, thanks for the update. You at the office?"

"No, I'm at a party at my sister's house. Is there anything you need me to do?"

"Just keep me posted if you get any updates. Enjoy your party and I'll see you Monday. And if she gets released make sure she's put in protective custody this time."

"Will do. See you Monday."

Ian slumped onto the motel bed and sighed. Judge Vera Smoot would be easy prey for the inmate population. Anyone in law enforcement had a target on their back. He felt a little bad for her, even though she needed to do penance for her sins. Nobody deserved violence.

Molly sliced her way through a dozen peeled potatoes, taking care not to cut her fingers. Chefs owned incredibly sharp knives, which made work a breeze but you could lose a piece of your finger and not know it until the blood splattered the cutting board. She'd peeled them, halved them and the trick was to slice each thinly, not cutting through to the bottom. Once dressed, you baked them and they fanned out like pages in a book. Not only did they look amazing, they tasted fabulous. Crisp on the outside, soft on the inside. She arranged them in a baking pan lined with parchment paper, drizzled them with her father's special melted herb butter, and covered them with plastic wrap. "Done," she announced.

Her mother placed her latticed blueberry pie in the oven and faced her, a smug smile revealing her satisfaction at a job well done.

"Molly, wash the romaine, use the spinner. I've already made the croutons and the dressing," her dad said.

"Yes, sir." The phrase immediately took her back to Ian's bedroom. Tied to his bed. Following his orders. *Submitting.* And three amazing orgasms. An unexpected phantom-pleasure shivered through her.

Her mother nudged her shoulder. "You cold?"

Molly peeled leaves from the head, tore them into bite-sized pieces and tossed them in the spinner. "What? No, I'm fine."

Her mother placed a hand on her forehead.

She sighed, ripping leaves with a vengeance. "Mom, seriously, I don't have a fever."

"Just checking." Her mother studied her face for a too-long moment. "Hmm," she said, one eye slitted. "Something's up."

———

Dressed in a blue-and-white striped button-down shirt, navy shorts and Teva sandals, Ian stopped at the farmer's market and purchased flowers for Molly—wild flowers, daisies for her mother. The bakery and liquor store stood side-by-side. He bought a 'bouquet' of cake lollipops for Justice and a bottle of Courtney Benham Cabernet Sauvignon Napa for her father, *his* father's favorite red.

He bundled everything into the convertible Jeep, having left the surfboard at the motel, and drove the longest ten miles of his life to Molly's parents' house. His body tense, uneasiness about making a good impression niggled him. Seriously? He was a fully grown man. A *Dominant.* Experienced beyond measure. Yet suddenly he was back in high school again, on a first date. Ridiculous.

———

Molly studied her reflection in the mirror. She ran her fingers through her freshly washed hair, finessing a few wayward strands down on her forehead. She applied her favorite shade of MAC lip gloss, Nymphette, smiling as she mused over the name. She pictured a lithe nymph frolicking in the forest... beautiful, young, graceful... adjectives she'd never use to describe herself. But for some reason she felt that way today. Her peach sundress complimented her newly acquired bronzed skin, she'd even painted her fingers and toenails a pastel pink. This time she laughed out loud. The polish was called *bridezilla.* Had she fallen into an alt universe?

She turned left, right, then peered over her shoulder for a rear view in the full-length mirror. The dress had a cutout revealing most of her back. She felt pretty for the first time in a long time, fulfilling her fantasy from the night she had drinks with Ian, when she'd wished she wore something other than her boring black suit.

Justice ran into her room. The child *raced* everywhere, she'd skipped learning to walk and sprinted as a baby instead.

She hugged Molly's knees and gazed up. "You look pretty, Mommy."

"Thank you, sweetheart. So do you. Let me see?"

Justice stepped back and did a ballerina twirl. "Grand-mère got me a new dress."

Molly smiled, her eyes scanning the white dress with tiny pink rosebuds. A pink ribbon surrounded Justice's tiny waist, tied at the back in a big bow. Pink barrettes held her hair off the left side of her face and she had matching pink sandals on her tiny feet. "You're the prettiest girl in the world!"

Justice beamed.

Molly checked the time: 4:45. Her stomach did a little flip. Ian was probably on his way. She entered the kitchen with Justice in hand. "My, my, look at you two," her father said. "My two Miss Americas." He came over and pecked Molly's cheek, then picked up Justice and did the same.

Her mother entered the kitchen dressed in a silky black shift, bedecked in her best silver jewelry, her shimmering white locks tied in a knot high on her head. "And here comes my queen," her father said. "How lucky am I, surrounded by the three most gorgeous girls to ever exist."

Her mother flicked her hand. "Oh, Howard, you always wax so poetic. I'm the lucky one. You look quite dashing yourself." Molly had to admit her father was a handsome man, his thick white hair and tanned skin, dressed in a black polo shirt and khaki shorts. Her parents made a striking couple.

Howard returned Justice to the ground and opened the freezer, filling an ice bucket and walking it out to the outdoor kitchen. Alyene gave Molly the once over. "*Ma chérie*, you look lovely in that dress."

"Thank you, Mother. And thank you for the dress you bought for Justice."

"My pleasure. You know how much I love shopping for her."

Molly picked up the tray of appetizers and carried them out to the back porch. The table had been set with the outdoor china, not the good china, and of course, cloth napkins in a floral print. Red peonies sat in a lavender vase in the table's center, and the tiny white lights decorating the porch lattice twinkled in the late afternoon sunshine.

The doorbell rang and Molly's stomach did another somersault.

Ian stood at the glass door gazing into a spacious foyer with gray beechwood floors and a mirror on the far wall above a half-moon antique table topped with a model of an old fishing schooner. He would have straightened his tie if he was wearing one. A striking gray-haired woman approached, her brown eyes bright, her smile wide. She pushed the door open and he entered. "You must be Ian. So nice to meet you." She extended her hand and he shifted his gifts into one arm and grasped her warm, petite fingers. A hand that'd crafted the most magnificent images he'd ever seen.

"Pleasure, Ms. Bouchard. I'm a huge fan."

"So I've heard. Come in."

Molly appeared behind her, Justice at her side. "Hi," Justice said.

"Well, hello," Ian said. He handed the bunch of wild flowers to Molly and the daisies to her mother.

"Thank you," they both said.

He kissed Molly's cheek, then knelt in front of Justice. "I brought these for you." He handed her the cake pops. "They're made of cake." Justice grinned.

"What do you say to Ian, Justice," Molly said.

"Thank you, Ian." She gazed up at Molly. "Can I eat one?"

"After dinner. We'll put them in the kitchen for later."

"Let's move to the deck for cocktails," Alyene urged.

Ian surveyed the surroundings, a beautiful home, the perfect mix of modern simplicity and antiques, comfortable, cozy even, a place that exuded well-earned tranquility.

"Ian, this is my father, Howard."

Ian handed the wine to Howard, shaking his hand in greeting. "It's my father's favorite."

Mr. Masterson studied the label. "Well, your father has excellent taste. Thank you."

"What would you like to drink?" Mr. Masterson said. "We usually have a cocktail, then wine with dinner. After that, everyone is on their own."

"Whatever you're having is fine."

Howard said, "Well the girls are drinking Vodka Gimlets, but I'm having a Tanqueray Martini on the rocks, with a twist of lemon."

"Martini it is."

Drinks made, appetizers munched, the conversation flowed easily in the cozy wicker circle. Justice sipped a juice box and nibbled lobster and pâté along with the adults. "She's a pretty good eater," Ian said.

"Tell me," Molly said. "I don't think we've discovered anything she doesn't like."

"Lucky, most kids I've meet don't eat anything except boxed mac and cheese."

Justice came near and wedged herself between his legs. "Still my coach?" she said.

"You bet."

Justice turned to Molly. "When can Ian come swimming with me?"

Molly hadn't considered the ramifications of this absurd arrangement, one she thought Justice might eventually forget. Where would this happen? There was a pool at the Montauk club, one at the YMCA near her SOHO brownstone, probably one in the vicinity of Ian's condo, none of which proved convenient. There was Alyx's house, where the ill-conceived commitment had been concocted. Plus, they both had full-time jobs sixty miles apart.

Molly frowned. "I'm not sure, sweetheart. I'll have to think about it."

Justice crawled into Ian's lap and he wrapped his arm around her waist. "You look like a Disney princess tonight."

"Thank you," Justice said. "Mommy looks pretty too."

Ian raked her with his piercing blue eyes. "She most certainly does."

Molly's heart swelled at his affection for Justice... and maybe for another reason. Justice grabbed Ian's cheeks and forced him to look at her. "Daddy likes you," she said.

Molly held her breath, her eyes shut tight. Oh God.

Chapter 30

D inner on the table, wine decanted and poured, Ian sat beside Molly, Justice on a booster seat between her grandparents. Thankfully, Ian had dismissed Justice's disconcerting remark with 'I'm glad' and no one offered additional commentary.

Her mother said, "So, Molly mentioned you're the chief assistant district attorney for Suffolk County. Must be a very demanding job. An important one too."

"Yes, ma'am, it is, and I love it. I feel like I'm doing some good in the world."

Her father added, "And she said you're from Detroit. Did you grow up there?"

"Actually, I grew up on Long Island. Went to Bayport High School, but my father took a job in Royal Oaks, Michigan after I graduated. Coincidently, I was going to college there. Saved them a bunch of money because the in-state tuition rates apply after six months residency."

"Quite fortunate," her father said.

"Do you still have family there?" her mother asked.

"I do. My parents, three married sisters, lots of aunts, uncles, and cousins."

"You must miss them," her mother said.

Molly realized she hadn't told her parents much about Ian's personal life, not that she knew a lot. She feared a discussion about the death of his fiancé would turn awkward.

"I do feel guilty, I haven't been home in a while. I need to make an effort soon."

"What do your parents do?" Howard said.

"They're both attorneys. My dad started out in the corporate world but my mom was a defense attorney, specializing in people who couldn't afford good legal defense."

"Must have made for some interesting discussions at home," Howard said.

"That's an understatement. Lots of arguing, but it never got personal and eventually my mother wore him down. They're very well off due to his years as an attorney for a big corporation and now they have a legal aid practice."

"But you work for the other side," Howard said.

"I do but I'm fully cognizant of their grievances. Minorities and the poor make up too large a segment of our prison population and I'm committed to helping change the tide."

"Good for you," Alyene said.

"Well, they must miss you," her father said. "I must say you're a very industrious and courteous young man. Your parents must be very proud of you."

"Thank you, sir. I firmly believe protocol and discipline to be my guiding principles."

Molly choked on her wine, sputtering, clearing her throat loudly. Ian patted her back as she attempted to catch her breath.

"Are you all right, dear?" her mother said.

"Yes," she cleared her throat again. "Just went down the wrong pipe." She glared at Ian but he smiled in return.

Bastard, he knew full well what he'd done. She placed a hand on her chest. Ian switched from patting to rubbing circles on her back. Her insides turned to mush, her pulse accelerated, heat creeped into her cheeks and between her legs. She sipped more wine, wine, wine.

Ian could hardly keep from laughing out loud. Molly gave him the evil eye and he knew he'd gotten under her skin. To the good parts. Her face flushed, the little blue vein in her neck pulsating. He wanted her badly, to ravage every inch of her, to bring her to many amazing climax crescendos.

He picked up his knife and fork and cut into his perfectly prepared steak, tender and mildly spicy. "Dinner is delicious," he said. "I'm privileged to sit at the table of a world-renowned chef. Not to mention an equally famous artist."

"You're very kind," Alyene said. "By the way, I'm having a show at the Met in a few weeks. You must come."

"I'd be honored."

"And next time you visit I'll give you a tour of my studio. It's in the barn."

Molly interjected, "My mother doesn't let anybody into her studio, Ian. Not anyone. I'm not exaggerating. Consider yourself a VIP."

Ian smiled. "Again, it's a privilege I won't take lightly."

Conversation turned to the state of world affairs, the business at Mr. Masterson's restaurant and plans for Ms. Bouchard's impending show.

"Dessert?" Alyene said.

They cleared the table and returned, red wine exchanged for white. Justice munched a cake pop while her grandmother cut wedges of blueberry pie. Molly added a dollop of cream atop each slice. They settled in the cozy wicker corner sipping wine and eating pie. "The pie is delicious," Ian said.

"I made it myself."

"My compliments to the baker then, and the chef." Ian held his glass high.

———

Darkness descended, and the fireworks display would erupt shortly, viewable from the beach. "Let's get you in your pajamas before the fireworks begin," Molly said. She rose and extended a hand to Justice. Her mother collected the dessert dishes and followed Molly inside. She laid the plates on the counter and turned to Molly. "Something's going on between you two."

Molly scooped Justice into her arms. "That's ridiculous. Why would you say that?"

"The way you look at each other. The word that comes to mind is *smoldering*."

Molly held her breath, unwilling to confess she'd slept with Ian, her mother unlikely to drop this line of questioning. "I need to get Justice in her pajamas." And she exited the kitchen.

Upon return she found the kitchen empty and proceeded out the back door where her parents and Ian sat atop a blanket on the beach. A red flare lit up the sky, exploding in shards of sparkling crimson and gold light. Justice squealed, pulled her hand loose from Molly's and ran toward the blanket. She pressed against Ian's back and wrapped her arms around his neck. Molly couldn't believe Justice had taken to Ian so quickly. She wasn't a shy child, and to Molly's dismay, never afraid of strangers, yet Justice's acceptance of Ian beguiled her.

Molly sat beside Ian on the blanket, who'd pulled Justice

onto his lap. He handed her a glass of wine, his smile brilliant as another flare illuminated the sky in red, white and blue splinters. Justice screamed, then covered her mouth with her hands.

Molly wanted to touch him. Slip her arm though his, hold his hand… take Justice's place on his lap. Good God. She wanted to kiss him, all over.

Ian smiled at Justice, the little imp squirmed on his lap with each burst, shrieking with delight. She screamed each time the white light popped, holding her ears and burying her head in his chest. He surveyed the beach where other families collected, nothing even close to a crowd as this was a private beach. "The fireworks are great and watching them in your backyard is pretty spectacular. No crowds, no parking nightmare. Awesome," he said.

"The best," Molly said. "We're spoiled."

Ian took a swallow of his wine. He desperately wanted to put his arm around Molly. He felt like he was with family and wondered, could this be his new, chosen family?

The finale set the sky on fire. Blast after blast, a plethora of vibrant colors, sparks twirling and sizzling like fishes on fire. Pop after pop, each firework exploded, sending Justice into a frenzy. The child's strangled hug took his breath away, not because it was too tight, because it melted his heart.

Howard and Alyene bid good night, offering to put Justice to bed. Ian stood. "Thank you for a lovely evening."

"Pleasure having you. Please come again," Alyene Bouchard said. "Very soon, hopefully."

"Yes, please do," Howard said, Justice in his arms, her head on his shoulder. "Night sweetheart," he said to Molly.

"*Bonne nuit, ma chérie*," Alyene said.

"Night, Mom, Dad."

Ian settled on the blanket next to Molly. "Finally, I have you all to myself. Permission to touch?"

Molly laughed. "Yes, Sir."

He surrounded her shoulders with his arm and pulled her into his chest. "I really like your parents."

"They are pretty amazing. I'm lucky."

"My mom called yesterday, they're anxious for me to come home for a visit."

"You should go, I'm sure it's torture having you so far away."

"I told them about you."

"You did? Why?"

"I'm not sure. My mother should work for the CIA, she has a talent for getting me to spill my guts. I wasn't planning on saying anything but before I knew it, I told her I'd met someone and I hoped to see her again."

Molly laughed. "She could be my mother's twin. If they both worked for the CIA no one would be safe. I said more about you than I intended to also."

Molly pulled out of his embrace and sat up. "There's something I want to ask you."

Ian grinned. "When will I have time to tie you up and do evil things to you again?"

Molly slapped his chest. "No. Well, yes, but that's not where I was going."

"Well, I want to go there. Right now. Unfortunately, this isn't the time or place."

"Will you be serious for one second?"

"I am being serious."

She slapped his chest again. "Alyx called me the other day and invited me to a party at the club."

All the breath whooshed out of his chest. Molly? At the club?

Chapter 31

"You want to come to the club?"

Molly considered his question carefully. In her wildest imagination she'd never entertained the idea of going to a sex venue. But… "Alyx said it was just a party because the club is closing down for renovations and there wouldn't be any play."

"She's right, it's kind of a sendoff, since it'll be closed for several months." There would be private rooms available to the Masters… dare he hope? "So they're going?"

"Apparently, Jamie and Colin and Laura and Steve too."

"I'd be thrilled if you come."

Molly's breath caught in her chest. She would love to play with Ian again, the memory of the night in his bedroom flamed her insides every time it came to mind.

And he wanted to make her come, hard and often.

"I am a little curious," Molly offered.

Ian's pulse spiked. He'd definitely gotten her attention the other night. "Well, it won't be the usual level of festivities but you can meet some of the people."

"I'm in, then."

And he wanted in... inside her... as deep and long as possible.

He couldn't control himself any longer and plundered her mouth. Coming up for air, he laid her back on the blanket and placed his hand on a breast, his head propped on his hand. "Can we have sex on the beach?"

The full moon cast her face in a shimmering glow, her eyes glistened. She smiled. "Hell yes, please, Sir."

Conveniently, the dress had buttons down the front. He unfastened them to the waist and slipped a hand inside, she wasn't wearing a bra. Her hard nipples signaled her arousal and his intrepid fingers traveled down into her panties, her wetness welcoming him in. He pulled the silky garment off and down her legs, pushing her skirt up to her hips. He unzipped his fly, releasing his burgeoning erection. "This is going to be fast and furious, but you will come first."

"Yes, Sir," she mumbled.

He shoved a finger into her vagina and she moaned. Two fingers and a third. He pressed his thumb against her clit and she shuddered, her hips rising, demanding. More, more. She wrapped her arms around his back, pulling him closer. His fingers thrust in and out, the rhythm building, her hips matching the cadence of his assault on her moist flesh. She groaned her release, her thighs clutching his hand. "That was fast."

"Well, I've been thinking about you all day. I was primed."

"Have you now? Good to know. I want another one." He spread her legs wide and sunk into the cradle of her legs. His cock plunged in, then withdrew, then in... all the way in. He growled. He wasn't going to last long either. He hammered her hard, flesh slapping flesh, her pelvis rocking up and down, taking him to the hilt, filling her swollen folds, a desperate frenzy. "Come now," he said. She clutched him to her chest, her tissues clenched around him as she bore down on his throbbing cock. He ravaged her mouth, their tongues dancing, twirling toward culmination. This union of souls.

They lay like that for an extended interlude, their breaths slowing in a syncopated rhythm. He whispered, "Maybe you'll let me make it up to you tomorrow night when I can take my time and we'll have more privacy."

"You're not getting any complaints from me, Mister."

He laughed, nibbling her ear. She giggled.

They settled back on the blanket, Molly's head on his shoulder, her arm wrapped around his waist. The stars twinkled in the dark sky, a haze forming a glittering corona around the moon.

———

Molly closed her eyes, the warmth of Ian's body infusing her with contentment, peace, as if she'd finally exhaled after holding her breath for nearly three months. She wanted to stay on this beach forever, in his embrace, encircling him as if holding on for a new life.

And true, she felt alive again, Ian had resuscitated her with his... dare she say it? Love.

"It's getting late," he said. "I should go." He kissed the top of her head and pulled her in close, both arms around her, then released her. He stood and extended a hand. Molly buttoned her dress and slipped into her panties before accepting his offer. They walked hand-in-hand into the house, lingering at the front door.

"Thanks for inviting me to dinner. I had a great time."

"You're welcome. I'm glad you came."

He kissed her lips tenderly and began to exit, yet suddenly stopped and pivoted. "By the way, I heard from Alicia Lopez earlier. Judge Smoot somehow wound up at Rikers and got the crap beat out of her."

Molly gasped, her hand over her mouth. "How in hell did that happen? I thought she'd be held locally and in protective custody."

"All true but no beds were available so they sent her to Rikers. I did order protective custody but someone dropped the ball."

"How extensive were her injuries?"

"Broken collar bone and two ribs, facial lacerations. I'm not happy and plan to launch a full investigation when I get back on Monday."

"How horrible. Paying for her crimes shouldn't include getting beat up. She's like fresh meat to the prison population."

"Agreed. I'm going to look into getting her moved to the Federal Prison Camp in Alderson, West Virginia. Where Martha Stewart went."

"That's very generous of you."

"I'm all for taking away her liberties but I'm not into adding physical abuse on top of it. Maybe she can do some good while she's there. Use her law degree to help some of the inmates. Teach a class or something."

"That would be excellent use of her time. Does she know about her cousin yet?"

"No idea. I guess I'll find out more Monday."

"Keep me updated, please. I've got an update also. Lily said they sent agents from the Massachusetts office to interview the owner of the juvenile facility. No sign of him, cashed out all his bank accounts."

"That's not good."

"It's not. Still on the hunt for him. Issued a BOLO."

"Good. Anyway, pick you up at six tomorrow night?"

"Thanks. What should I wear?"

He'd like to say it didn't matter since he fully intended on getting her naked, but he refrained. "It's casual, anything you want."

He took her in his arms and kissed her once more, hard and long. And he wanted to make love to her all over again. Did he really just say that in his head? Yeah, he did. They'd made *love*.

He wasn't afraid of that word.

Chapter 32

Ian held the massive medieval-style door open for Molly. A stocky, well-built man dressed in a white polo shirt and jeans greeted them. His face looked like he'd played goalie for a dart team. He smiled with his eyes, making him less intimidating, welcoming even.

"This is Zach," Ian said. "He's our gatekeeper. Zach, this is my friend Molly Masterson."

"Welcome, miss," Zach said. "Sign in on the guest registry." He pointed to a clipboard on the antique desk.

"Have her sign the paperwork, just as a formality," Ian told Zach.

"Sure thing, Master Ian." He pulled a multi-page document from a cabinet adjacent to the desk and handed it to Molly. "Even though it's just a formality, please read it carefully so we avoid trouble."

Trouble? Molly read the particulars, signed and dated it and returned the paperwork to Zach. Some items had caught her attention and she got the distinct feeling she better keep a low profile. Sounded like they meant business, if she fucked up.

"Thank you, Ms. Masterson," he said, stowing the form in the desk drawer. "Have an enjoyable evening, Sir."

Ian escorted Molly inside as other guests entered, a jovial atmosphere punctuated with light conversation and a sea of smiles. A handsome man, with salt and pepper hair, a close-cropped white beard and spectacular body for an older guy, intercepted them immediately. "Ian, welcome. And who's this lovely lady?"

"Molly Masterson, this is Jack Branford. He's the owner."

"Pleasure to make your acquaintance," Jack said. He kissed the back of her hand in an old-fashioned gesture of greeting. Molly smiled. "Are you Ian's guest tonight?"

"Actually, Alyx Cameron invited me."

Jack's eyebrows knit together. "You're friends with Alyx, and... don't tell me..." He put up both hands. "Perhaps Laura and Jamie also?"

"I am."

Jack crossed his arms over his massive chest. "Then you work for the FBI?"

"I do."

"Great," Jack said. "And you're dating Ian?"

Molly glanced at Ian, wondering why the interrogation? Jack should work for the FBI. "Not exactly, we just met."

Jack glared at Ian. "Again?"

Molly frowned, why had this classy, handsome, gracious man suddenly turned surly? "Did I say something wrong?"

Ian laughed. "Well, Jack has had a bad string of luck with Masters who date FBI agents."

Lightbulb moment. Of course, her fellow agents had all married – or would soon marry – Masters at the club, who'd all *left* the club. Jack must assume Ian was soon to follow suit. Molly furthered her line of thinking... IF she was to pursue a relationship with Ian, she certainly wouldn't want him having sex with women at the club—even if it was *his job*—or any other woman for that matter.

"Well, that is unfortunate," Molly said. A petite young woman lingered behind Ian, apparently waiting her turn to talk with him. Molly worried she'd stepped into a world she didn't really want to know about. She should never have come.

"Well," Jack said, "looks like there's nothing to be done about it at this point. I assume you're armed?"

"I am." She had her 9 mm in her purse, her service revolver locked in the gun safe at her parents' house.

"Normally I don't allow guns on the floor but since this is just a friendly get-together I'm making an exception for law enforcement types."

Molly didn't respond. Thank you seemed inappropriate as she was required to be armed at all times.

Jack's lips morphed into a grin. "Well, then I hope you enjoy yourselves." And he turned to greet new attendees.

"Master Ian," the petite woman said. "I'm so glad you're here tonight."

"Kelly, nice to see you too."

"I had a really amazing time the other night. I know play is restricted tonight but maybe you could find a little time for me?"

"Not tonight, Kelly. I have other plans."

Kelly's smile vanished. "Oh, sure, Sir, next time."

"The club will be closed for months, so I don't know when I will see you again. Not until the other side of the renovation."

"I understand, Sir. Until then." And she disappeared into the expanding crowd.

Molly's cheeks flamed. Had Ian had sex with her? When? Friday night? She was pretty sure he was at the club and yet she'd blocked out the idea that he was having sex with other women. And yet, she had no hold on him. No right to be jealous and chided herself… *keep your goddamned mouth shut.*

———

Thankful Kelly hadn't revealed the details of their time together, Ian steered Molly forward hoping she wouldn't interrogate him about his involvement with Kelly. Alyx and Daniel were engaged in conversation at the bar and he ushered Molly to their side. Alyx sat on a stool sipping a cocktail, Daniel with a beer in hand.

"Hey," Alyx said when she saw Molly. "So glad you came." She whispered in Molly's ear, "You came with Ian?" She pulled back, her eyebrows arched.

Molly whispered, "I did. He came by the house for dinner and I told him you'd invited me and I was thinking about coming. He insisted, so here I am."

"Excellent. You two hitting it off?"

"You could say that. In some ways, hitting it out of the ball park." Molly smirked.

"I do believe that's a rather satisfied smile on your face."

"Trying not to jinx it."

"What are you two whispering about?" Daniel said.

"Nothing," Alyx said. "Just girl talk."

"Molls!" He snuck up behind her and surrounded her in a bear hug, then turned her to face him, gripping her upper arms. "What are you doing here?"

Jax stood alongside Shadow and said, "Hey Molly. Good to see you again."

"You too," she said. Molly blanched. Apparently the club Shadow had been referring to was *this* club. Good God. "Uh, a friend invited me." She turned to Alyx. "This is my friend, Alyx."

Shadow extended his hand. "Pleasure." His gaze shifted

back to Molly, a devilish smile capturing his lips. "Didn't know you were in the lifestyle, Molls. Have to say I didn't see this coming after seeing you the other day."

"Well, John, you really don't know me at all. It's been a long time."

He slung an arm around her neck. "And I fully expect that to change. I think we could have a great time together."

She gazed past John Shadow to see Ian attentively observing. The realization that Ian and John Shadow knew each other threw her off-kilter and didn't bode well for the remainder of the evening. Ian continued conversing with Daniel, leaving her to fend off Shadow on her own.

A flurry of hellos, hugs and kisses, broke the tension as Jamie and Colin, and Laura and Steve made their entrance. Shadow and Jax excused themselves to get a drink, with a, "Catch you later."

Molly fully expected Ian to interrogate her but instead he walked to where Shadow and Jax sat at the bar. She'd give anything to hear their conversation.

"Ian, man, good to see you," Shadow said.

"Hey," Jax said.

"So you know Molly?" Ian asked.

"Yeah, we went to high school together. She was my study buddy in AP Bio. Smart as a whip, that chick."

"High school? Is that the last time you saw her?"

"Yeah, until Friday. I heard she was in town and her mother invited me over. Great to see her again. Just as gorgeous as she was in high school." Shadow laughed, then accepted his beer from the bartender. "She was kind of a plain Jane back in the day, had no idea she was drop-dead gorgeous. All the guys had a thing for her but she had blinders on. Grades were the only thing important to her. And then, she came back from college for Thanksgiving and… boom." Shadow splayed his fingers in the air. "It was like she'd landed on the super-model runway. Her roommate was a New York City rich bitch and taught her how to dress, do makeup, hair, all that jazz. She was a stunner before but now… Jesus." Shadow shook his head. "I took a shot in high school but she wasn't into it. Pretty sure she was a virgin."

Ian's teeth clenched so tight he feared he'd crack a molar.

"Terrible news about her husband." Shadow sighed. "She's got a cute kid."

Ian wanted to claim his territory, like a wild cat pissing in the jungle, but he had no right. Molly hadn't offered anything in the way of commitment and was free to date anyone she wanted, or have sex with anyone. And no woman could resist Shadow. Firefighters had their own unrivaled brand of sex appeal. Yet he couldn't hold ill-will against Shadow. He was one of the good guys. Damn. Maybe Molly would be happy with Shadow. He pinched his eyebrows wondering what to do. He should back off. He sorely wanted to tell Shadow that Molly had come with him. But it wasn't really a date. Alyx had invited Molly and he'd offered transportation, essentially her Uber driver.

Ian excused himself and positioned himself behind Molly who was engaged in conversation with Laura. "We need to talk," he whispered in her ear.

She gazed over her shoulder, her brown eyes serious. "What's wrong?"

He grabbed her wrist and pulled. "Excuse us," he said to Laura.

He tugged Molly toward the back, near the stairs and cornered her against the wall. "Are you interested in Shadow?"

"What? No. Why would you think so?"

"You hung out with him Friday?"

"What? No, not really. He stopped by my mother's house. She bumped into his mother in town and invited him over to say hi. He didn't stay very long and he had that guy Jax with him."

"Did you two have a thing in high school?"

"No we didn't have *a thing*. He tried to kiss me once, but I wasn't interested. He was a big deal in high school, way out of my league."

"Not in his mind."

"You talked about me?" She shoved his chest. "You're an ass."

Ian sighed, his hands at his sides, fists clenched. "If you're into Shadow just tell me and I'll be gone."

"You're giving me the third degree? I haven't done anything, and what about you? Did you have sex with that Kelly girl?"

Jack came up behind him. "Take this upstairs."

Chapter 33

Jack put a key in Ian's hand. "My private dungeon. No one will bother you."

Ian seized Molly's hand and led her behind the stairs to an elevator. He inserted the key in the panel and it opened immediately. He pulled Molly inside and pressed the arrow up button.

Molly yanked her hand out of Ian's grip and crossed her arms over her chest. "You're really pissing me off. You're making something out of nothing."

"I'm really frustrated here, Molly."

"You're frustrated? *I* didn't have sex with someone."

"It's my job."

"Don't give me that crap. You fucked that woman, then you fucked me the next night." She was being a jerk except she didn't care. She knew full well what he did at the club and hadn't given him any reason not to. She had no right to criticize him.

"Kelly is a sexual abuse victim. Jack asked me to work with her a few weeks back and I agreed. I'm helping her regain her sexuality."

"Oh, so you're a sex therapist now? That's your excuse?"

"I'm not making any excuses. But yes, I am. And you knew full well what goes on at the club and what my role is."

Molly didn't respond because she had no defense. He'd offered her a relationship and she rebuffed him. If she'd agreed maybe this wouldn't have happened. Maybe he'd have walked away from the club. But she couldn't ask that.

The elevator door opened and he grabbed her wrist again and pulled her inside the ominous chamber. Her heart pounded as she surveyed the equipment: a massive bed, restraining bench, St. Andrew's cross, a rack of leather floggers, buckles, ropes hanging from the ceiling. Her blood simmered in her veins. A medieval torture chamber or a hot sex dungeon. She went with the latter.

Ian sighed, dropping his chin. "Let's take this down a notch." He placed both hands on her shoulders. "I didn't mean to make you angry. I guess the green-eyed monster got the best of me."

Molly could barely breathe, overcome by his incredibly good looks. The blue eyes, ablaze with desire, his sable brown hair, his broad shoulders… made it hard to think rationally. She'd been captivated the moment she first saw him. His relentless energy and power, coupled with a heart that could be tender. A flicker of something danced across his eyes as he traced the line of her mouth with his thumb.

She regarded his crotch, a noticeable bulge straining the tight confines of his jeans.

"I bet you really want to spank me right now."

Ian never spanked a woman out of anger. But he wanted to spank Molly now. And yet, he wasn't angry, he was incredibly turned on.

Molly slid her hands under his blue button-down shirt and slipped them into his waistband. "I say the opposite. Let's take it up a notch."

"Are you serious? If you unleash the monster I can't guarantee what will happen."

"I have a safe word."

"You're in for it now, little subbie."

Molly unbuttoned his shirt and pulled it off him. Then his belt, stripping it all away until he was completely naked. She ran her fingers through his hair then pulled him into a kiss, his hands moving to the small of her back. He let her take the lead as his erection grew harder, pressing against her belly.

She stepped back to admire him, then took his cock in her palm, moving her hand up and down. He closed his eyes and let the sensation soothe him like a warm bath. She let go and raised her hands to his shoulders, then gave him a gentle push and he fell back on the bed. She crawled between his legs and took him into her mouth. Her tongue eager to please, swirling around the sensitive head, she nipped with her lip-covered teeth. A rumbling growl surfaced from somewhere deep inside his chest. She sucked gently on the head, moving her fingers down the shaft.

He moaned and fisted her hair guiding her with his hands. Her tongue traveled down the length of his cock, one inch at a time, painfully slowly, her fingers gently stroking as her mouth journeyed down and back up again. The pace deliciously torturous. She increased the speed and he groaned. She gazed into his eyes as she continued to suck. "Oh yes," he said, his loins contracting, his climax close. Too close to the fire.

He sat up, pulling her off him, forcing her onto her back. "As much as I love your perfect pink lips wrapped around my cock, I've let you have enough control for now."

He stood and dragged her to the foot of the bed by her ankles, unzipped her jeans and yanked them off. Her panties followed. He sat her up and pulled the black cami over her head and tossed it, then released the clasp on her lacy black bra and threw it on the ground.

Molly closed her eyes, barely able to breathe. He lay atop her, crushing her into the mattress, kissing her passionately, as they melded into one another. Their emotions fusing into the physical act of love-making. Two people head over heels, desperately. *Oh God.*

His fingers fanned out through her hair, his hand stiffening at the back of her neck. His grip tightened. His hand tensed, pulling on her hair. It hurt a little yet she wanted him to do it again, again, again.

"Touch yourself," he whispered. "I want you to touch yourself."

He pushed her hand between her legs and guided her finger against her wet clit. She moaned, their joined hands rubbing, taking her higher. He spread her thighs wide and forced himself inside as she continued to explore with her fingers, playing with his shaft, feeling the physical connection, the oneness.

He grabbed her hips and sank in deep, moving her up and down his cock, slowly, tenderly, controlled. His tongue teased her lips, then he took her hand and lifted it to his lips, licking her fingers. She tilted her hips and rolled with each thrust. He pressed in further, shifting the angle, each stroke rubbing her clit as he cradled her ass, shoving her onto him.

"Don't you dare come," he said.

"Ian, I can't hold out much longer." She pressed her lips together, stifling a moan.

"You will."

He raised a leg over his shoulder and plunged in deep, deeper. He bit down on her shoulder, as her hips rose as if to challenge him, the scent of their mingled desire over-whelming.

He flipped her onto her stomach and spread her legs, then got up and grabbed her thighs, dragging her down the mattress, toward the edge of the bed. Standing between her legs, supported by nothing but his hands, her hips and torso still on the bed, he entered her again and she felt every inch of him. Weightless, grounded only by him, his pace aggres-sive, as if he couldn't get enough. Each thrust shook her world. She grabbed the sheets to keep from floating away as the wave of her orgasm crested.

"Now, darling. Come for me."

A starry nebula of white erupted behind her eyelids. "Oh God, oh Jesuuss."

"Nicely, done, darling."

But he wasn't done.

So, she wasn't done.

Molly climbed on top of him, her body still reeling from the heights of passion. She straddled his cock and reset the rhythm, throwing her head back as she rode him home, his hands massaging her thighs. The trembling began anew and she moved faster. The fire inside raging, the lovemaking erupting in spectacular triumph as he joined her in this climax. Molly gasped, her whole body quivered.

A tender explosion of—

His shaft throbbed inside her and she collapsed on his torso, her breathing erratic, gasping like a runner finishing a sprint. Her cheek against his chest, she lay listening to his heartbeat. They stayed like that for a long time, a series of gentle moments sheltered in a warm embrace.

"Molly," he whispered. "I'm toast and utterly in love with you."

"I know," she said. They sank into silence again. Molly couldn't think of the right words to say and so she said nothing.

Ian broke the tension. "That was pretty fucking amazing and we didn't even use any of the equipment."

She smiled against his chest. "Next time."

He laughed, a low rumbling in his chest, always so sexy. He caressed her face, pulling her close and breathed into her ear. "I love you, Molly."

Should she, could she, would she... leap into the void?

Chapter 34

"It's going to be pretty difficult to look like we haven't just fucked our brains out," Molly said. Redressed, she washed her hands, checked her makeup in the bathroom mirror and ran her fingers through her habitually tousled hair.

Ian stood behind her, buttoning his shirt. "We'll just deny, deny, deny. Nobody will believe us, but who cares."

She turned and wrapped her arms around his waist, then pecked his lips. "Thanks, that was amazing."

"Thank *you*. I gotta admit you rocked my world, darling. I've never really let a woman take control before. It was a first for me."

"Hmm… well there's more where that came from."

"Lucky me."

At the bar, they ordered beers, then moved to the buffet area. "I'm famished," Molly said, putting fried chicken and potato salad on her plate.

"I guess we worked up an appetite," Ian said.

"Where did you two disappear to?" They turned to face Alyx. Her eyes flicked back and forth between them. "Never mind…" she said, with a wave of her hand. "Come on, we saved you seats."

They followed Alyx and joined a cozy circle of chairs where the discussion had turned to talk of Jamie and Colin's upcoming nuptials. "This is working out so well," Jamie said to Molly. "Isn't it a strange coincidence that I'd already planned on you and Ian walking down the aisle together and now I won't have to introduce you two?"

"I say it's kismet," Colin said. He wagged his eyebrows and everyone laughed.

"Am I interrupting something?" Shadow pulled up a chair next to Molly and sat backward, his arms perched on the chair back.

"Hi John," Molly said. "Yes, you're interrupting. I'm here with Ian."

Shadow peered at Ian. "Sorry, man. Why didn't you say something before? I didn't know you two were together."

Ian swallowed a mouthful of potato salad and sipped his beer, unsure of how to respond. Molly rescued him. "It's not for him to say, it's for me to say." She smiled, placing a hand on Shadow's arm. "It's been great to see you again, John."

"Likewise," he said. "You're a lucky dude, Master Ian." He took Molly's hand and kissed the back. "Struck out twice. Damn." He grinned slyly and rose, returning the chair to the corner before walking away.

Relieved, Ian let out the breath he'd been holding. Molly had pretty much stated in front of everyone that they were kinda, sorta, a *thing*.

"Justice still talking to Sam?" Alyx blurted.

"Sometimes. I'm still not sure what to make of it."

Ian arrived at his office shortly after eight Monday morning. His phone rang. "Hi, Mom."

"Are you at work? I hope I'm not interrupting anything important."

"You caught me just before an arraignment. What's up?"

"We're coming to New York City Wednesday and want to see you."

"Oh… really? What's the occasion?"

"Your father and I plan to open a new office and we're scouting out locations. We're meeting the realtor on Thursday."

"When did you decide this?"

"Just recently. We figured if you won't come back to see us, we'll move closer to you."

"You're moving?"

"Well, not right away. We'll see how it goes. But I do miss Long Island."

Ian rubbed his forehead. He loved his parents but he wasn't sure he wanted them that close. "That's great, but don't do it just for me. I promise I'll visit more often."

"I'm half-kidding except you never know. Anyway, we can come out to you for dinner one night or you can come into the city, whatever is best."

"How long are you staying?"

"Our flight leaves late Sunday afternoon."

"Okay. I'll have to check my work schedule. Let's tentatively say I'll meet you in the city Wednesday evening."

"Fabulous. Can't wait. Can you recommend a restaurant?"

"How about the Millstone, on Park Avenue South?"

"Great, I'll make reservations. Figure dinner at seven. I'll text to confirm."

"See you then."

Ian returned his phone to his pocket then popped a pod into the coffee maker. He stood and watched it drip into his cup, then added milk and sugar and sat at his desk leafing through paperwork, but he couldn't concentrate. The evening at the club had convinced him he and Molly were meant for each other. The sex incredibly hot and immensely satisfying. He still couldn't believe he'd let her top him. The images flooding his brain made his dick hard, his heart soft.

He was hopelessly, madly, in love with her.

Molly snuck out of her parents' house shortly after sunrise, arriving home in record time. Way too early for the cidiots traveling back to the city after the holiday weekend. She showered and dressed for work, missing Justice's usual morning enthusiasm for each new day. Brushing her teeth, a sinking feeling swarmed her. She returned the toothbrush to its holder, then sought out her duffle. Where the fuck were they?

The plastic packet had somehow wedged itself into a sneaker. She pulled it out and stared at the vacant spaces. Damn. She'd forgotten to take her birth control pills this weekend. Two days missed. Shit. And at the worst possible time. Shit. Shit. Shit. She downed the two overlooked pills, hoping the double dose might work some magic. Just in case.

She drove to the office, banishing the thought of an unplanned pregnancy from her psyche. She dialed her mother from the car, needing to hear her daughter's voice.

Her mother answered on the first ring. "*Ma chèrie*, how are you?"

"Hi Mom, good. How's Justice?"

"She's fine."

"Can I talk to her?"

"Sure… Justice, Mama's on the phone."

"Hi Mommy."

"Hi sweetie. How are you?"

"Grand-mère said I can eat pancakes for dinner, and she made ice pops. They're pink and taste like lemonade."

"That's wonderful. Make sure you tell Grand-mère *merci*."

"I did, I did."

"Good girl, now behave for Grand-mère and Grand-père and I'll call you tomorrow."

"Okay, Mommy. Love you."

"Love you more, sweetheart."

"So, how was your evening with Ian?" her mother asked. "You got home late and left at the crack of dawn."

Molly was glad her mother hadn't seen her when she arrived home last night. No way would she have been able to hide the fact she'd had sex with Ian. "I don't know, Mom. I really like him, but I'm thinking about Justice. She's my primary concern."

"I don't see what that has to do with anything. He's a natural around Justice. And the man obviously loves you."

"I don't know, Mom. It's just too soon." Her mother sighed. "I'm pulling into work. I'll talk to you later."

Alyx burst into Molly's office and plopped into the chair in front of her desk. "Did you hear about Jenny?"

"Is she the one you worked with on that sex trafficking case, when you were undercover?"

"Yeah. She's in the hospital. Drug overdose. She's been working a highly secret undercover assignment. We think they were onto her and tried to kill her."

"Doesn't she have two kids?"

"She does. Three-year-old twins."

"She gonna pull through?"

"It's touch and go. She's in a coma. We hope to hear something soon."

Molly spiraled into a dark abyss. What if something happened to *her*? Justice would be an orphan. Terror knotted her gut.

Alyx bit a nail. "I never really thought about it much before, but once you've got a kid it hits you differently. Perils of the job, I know, but it gives you pause."

I'll say, Molly thought.

"Anyway, how's it going with you and Ian? Seemed like you had a great time with him at the club. A damn good time. Am I reading it right?"

Molly's cheeks flushed and she twiddled her thumbs on the table top. "I really like him."

"That's an understatement if I ever heard one. You two are downright combustible when you're within ten feet of each other."

"The sex is incredible."

"Told ya."

"And he's a really great guy. Kind, generous."

"And damn easy on the eyes." Alyx laughed. "Don't tell my husband I said that."

"Daniel's incredibly good looking, I don't think he has to worry."

"You know, sometimes I think back to our days at Quantico, when we had no idea how our lives would turn out. Marriage was never on my to-do list. I don't think it was on any of our radars."

"Totally. I was dating Sam, but I still didn't think marriage was in my future."

"How are you doing in that regard? I know it's only been a few months. And I'd never presume to ask if you've gotten past it, or gotten closure. Those thoughts seem so trite. I don't think anyone ever gets over losing a husband, the father of their child."

"No doubt I've been conflicted. Ian swears he's in love with me, but I can't imagine that. We barely know each other. I keep pushing him away. It just seems too soon. However, I can't deny my attraction to him. I never thought I'd meet another man who made me feel this way." She plopped her chin in her hands, elbows on her desk. She was falling for the handsome Dominant.

Chapter 35

Wednesday morning, Ian reviewed current cases on the docket and assigned personnel to new ones. He had several meetings but needed to leave work early to meet his parents for dinner in the city. His mother texted: *7 at Millstone. Can't wait to see you.* She added the kissy face emoji.

Alicia Lopez entered his office just as he was about to exit. "I have bad news."

"Great." Just what he needed when trying to bolt early.

"Judge Smoot is dead."

His jaw dropped. "What the fuck? Wasn't she still in the infirmary?"

"She was. They said it was a heart attack but I'm suspicious. She'd agreed to testify against the cousin, something about him blackmailing her. We've launched an investigation."

"This whole situation is spiraling out of control fast."

Ian stood, pulled his keys from his desk and headed for the door. "I'm on my way out. If you need me, text." He called Molly from the car.

"Ian, hi."

Her tone alarmed him. "What's the matter?"

"Alyx just told me that one of our agents was targeted while undercover on a drug case. She's on life support. They made it look like a suicide. She's got two little kids."

"That's awful."

"It's got me upside-down. What if that happened to me? Justice would be an orphan. I can't live with that."

"I hear you. I understand how that makes you feel."

"Well, it's really got me thinking. So, what's up with you?"

"I hate to be the bearer of more bad news but Judge Smoot is dead." Silence, the kind that made him tap his foot, thankfully the car was in cruise control mode. "Did you hear me?"

"I heard, I'm just shocked. I thought she was in the infirmary."

"She was, under protective custody. They said it was a heart attack but Lopez and I are suspicious. The judge had agreed to testify against her cousin, you know, the guy who runs the detention center? Something about blackmail and since he's on the run, I'm wondering if there's any way he could've gotten to her."

"Well, it is a prison facility and he works in the prison system, I'm sure he has guys who'd do him a favor."

"That's what I'm thinking."

"Damn. I feel bad, and I don't. She was despicable."

"Yeah, I'm conflicted too. Anyway, I'm on my way to have dinner with my parents. I'll call you on my way home." He'd considered asking if he could stop by for some lascivious festivities but worried he might be coming on too strong. How did that old adage go? Absence makes the heart grow fonder? Maybe he should try that tack.

"Sounds good. Enjoy dinner."

Ian entered the well-appointed eatery, all chandeliers, dark wood and cozy nooks. He sighted his parents and the hostess escorted him to their table. His father rose and gave him a man hug, then he circled around and kissed and embraced his mother. The waitress was on him in an instant.

"Can I get you something to drink, sir?" She paused. "Oh, Mr. Turner. Good to see you again." His parents were imbibing their usual: a Cosmo for his mother and a vodka martini straight up with an olive for his dad. "The usual?"

"Yes, thank you, Maria."

"Right away, sir." And she disappeared into the subdued recesses of the restaurant.

"How's work?" his mother asked.

"Tough day. We recently arrested one of our own judges. It was that FBI case where I met Molly. Somehow the judge wound up at Riker's, got beat up and I just heard she died while in the infirmary. But I'm skeptical since she was going to testify against someone who might not want her to. The whole thing stinks."

"How horrible," his mother said.

The waitress returned with Ian's drink, Tanqueray on the rocks with a twist. "Thank you."

"Are you interested in any appetizers?" the waitress said, finger poised over the tablet.

"Not for us," his father said, "but my son hasn't had a chance to look at the menu."

"Obviously, I eat here a lot," Ian said. "I'll have the salmon."

"Excellent choice," the waitress said. "And for you?" she said to Ian's mother.

"The same."

"I'll have the rib eye, rare," Mr. Turner said.

"I'll put those orders in right away."

His mother sipped her drink, then asked, "So, are you and Molly officially dating?"

"Honestly, Mom, I'm not sure. We have a great time together. At first she was sketchy about the fact that it's only been three months since her husband died. I think she's finally past that, but one of her colleagues nearly got killed on the job and now she's freaking out about the idea of making her daughter an orphan."

"She has a daughter?" his father said.

"Yeah, she's four and friggin' adorable." Ian smiled. "She wants me to coach her for the Olympics. Swimming, she wants to win a gold medal like her Aunt Jamie."

"Her aunt won a gold medal?"

"She did, for the biathlon: skiing and shooting. It's not a biological aunt. Her name's Jamie Gallagher and she's also an FBI agent. She and Molly went to Quantico together. She's marrying a friend of mine, Colin MacKenzie, next month. I'm in the wedding." He sipped his drink. "And in a weird coincidence, Molly and I are walking down the aisle together." He chuckled.

So did his mother. "Downright portentous," she said. "We'd love to meet Molly. Do you think that could happen?"

Ian considered the possibility. Meeting one's parents was usually a big step, but he managed to wheedle an invitation to meet hers, so maybe he could side-step the enormity of such a proposition. "When are you going back again?"

"Our flight leaves Sunday evening."

"I don't know. I'll see what I can do." He took another swig. "So how's the search coming for the new office?"

"We meet with the realtor tomorrow. We'll be evaluating several properties. The prelims look promising," his father said.

"What made you decide to open another office, and why New York City?"

229

His mother smirked. "I was half kidding about being closer to you, but I do hope it would be an excuse to see you more." His parents exchanged furtive looks.

"What?" Ian said. "You two are up to something."

"Well," his dad began, "I know you haven't been in your job long, but we wondered if perhaps you'd like to run the office." His father spun his martini glass on the white table cloth a few times, then downed the last swallow and popped the olive into his mouth.

Ian frowned. "You want me to switch sides?"

His mother folded her arms on the table. "Your father did it. And knowing how the other side plays the game is an added advantage." She winked.

Ian's eyes narrowed. "I agree with your assessment but…" He took another drink. "It's an intriguing proposition, but the money's not great and after Rebecca's death I felt my obligation was to bring the bad guys to justice. Not the other way around."

"Understood," his father said. "But there's good work to be done on both sides. It took me a long time to realize that. And it's not all about money."

"I know. Money isn't the mitigating factor by any means." If he took the job he'd have to move into Manhattan and he wasn't sure he wanted that. He'd miss the beach. But he would be closer to Molly. A lightning bolt struck his gray matter. If Molly was having second thoughts about working for the FBI, then maybe… she might consider joining the practice.

The waitress arrived and served their entrees. "Can I get you anything else? Another drink?"

"We'll have a bottle of cabernet, you know the one," Ian said.

Molly returned home from work around seven-thirty, Jenny still on her mind. If Jenny died it would be a hard pill to swallow not only for Molly but the entire office. They hadn't had a single fatality since Molly worked there.

She poured a glass of chardonnay and rummaged through the freezer for something for dinner, settling on a low-cal entrée. She popped the cellophane and put it in the microwave then climbed the stairs to change her clothes.

Her phone rang. She settled on the edge of the bed and kicked off her shoes. "Hi Mom."

"*Bonsoir, Ma chèrie.* How are you?"

"Fine. You? I hope Justice isn't running you ragged."

"Well, I try not to get down on the floor too often to play with her because it's harder to get up these days. I'm becoming an old woman."

Molly chuckled. "Never, Mom. You look at least twenty years younger than your age. How is Justice?"

"She's wonderful. Enjoying the beach. I took her shopping and to the pool a few times and she found some children to play with. I think she's particularly enamored of a young boy named Ethan."

"No kidding. Attracted to boys already?"

"*Loves aime sa jeunesse.*"

"Yeah, well *this youth* is too young for love."

"The heart wants what the heart wants."

"Oh God, Mother. You're a hopeless romantic. And she's *four.*"

"Then let's talk about you. How is that scrumptious young man you're dating?"

"Mom!"

"Well, if I was you, I'd jump him. Don't tell your father I said that."

Did she dare tell her mother she already had? Her mother was probably the most open-minded person she knew when it came to sex. Perhaps, because she grew up in Paris, the French are notoriously amorous. Her mother's life philosophy being if people spent more time making love the world would be a happier place. Her solution to world peace. Molly smiled. Maybe she should take a page out of her mother's playbook.

"Honestly, Mom, I have other priorities at the moment. I need to do what's best for Justice and I'm genuinely considering a career change."

"You're leaving the FBI?"

"One of our agents is on life-support after an injury on the job. She's got two small kids and the idea of making Justice an orphan has me in a tailspin. I have plenty of money after the settlement from the accident, so financially I have no worries. I know I can't stay home and do nothing, but I'm not sure what I want. I should spend more time with Justice. My current job requires me to work crazy and sometimes long hours. It was fine when Sam was around because he could pick up the slack. I don't feel comfortable leaving her with the nanny so much, even though Colleen is great, and I wouldn't have gotten through the last few months without her."

"I understand. I know you'll do what is right. And since money isn't a problem you can take some time to decide. There's no rush."

"Thanks, Mom."

"Justice wants to say good night." Molly heard her mother call out, "*Ma chèrie*, Mama's on the phone."

"Hi Mommy."

"Hi sweetheart. Are you having fun with Grand-mère and Grand-père?"

"I got three new dresses and red shoes, and went to the pool and met Ethan."

"Sounds like you're having a lot of fun. Who's Ethan?"

"He's my boyfriend."

Molly shook her head, pinching the bridge of her nose. "Aren't you too young to have a boyfriend?"

"Grand-mère says to love everybody."

Of course she did. "I think Grand-mère is right." Molly smiled. "Well, sleep tight and I'll see you next week."

"Night, Mommy. Sleep tight."

And she was gone.

"Night, *Ma chèrie*."

"Night, Mom."

Molly fell back on the bed with the phone on her chest, missing her sweet daughter.

Chapter 36

Ian called Molly from the car on his return trip home. "I didn't wake you, did I?"

"Nope. Just watching TV in bed."

"What are you wearing?"

"Seriously? You're a slut."

"Guilty."

Molly laughed. "How was dinner with your parents?"

"Good. They're thinking of opening an office in the city. They want me to run it."

"Really? You'd leave the DA's office?"

"I don't know. There's a lot to consider. I'd take a pay cut, at least initially, and I'd have to live in the city. But there's something about defending people who don't have the financial means to secure proper defense that's appealing."

"I agree. Kudos, it's very philanthropic of you."

"Listen, my parents are here until late Sunday and they'd love to meet you. I know meeting parents is kind of a big deal but since I met yours, I thought maybe we could put it in the no-biggie category."

Molly considered Ian's invitation carefully. It shouldn't be a big deal, right? Except it kinda was. Ian's invite had been because he was a fan of her mother's work, right? Hmm. "Why don't you bring them here for brunch on Sunday?"

"You sure that's not too much trouble? I could bring food."

"Not at all. I can manage brunch."

"That would be great. What time?"

"Noon?"

"Great. I'll let them know."

"You driving home?"

"Yeah, another half hour."

"Well, drive carefully. Stay safe."

"I will. Get some sleep."

Several days passed. Ian called each day and they chatted aimlessly, effortlessly, to the point Molly anticipated hearing his voice. New cases flooded her office, they worked long hours to keep up and Molly had requested for additional agents to be assigned to the task force. She rehearsed her conversation with Rob ad nauseum, explaining why she needed to quit the Bureau. Should she call him ahead of time and not return at all? Or work the task force for a few more weeks before revealing her intentions? A conundrum. Each option making her anxious.

Sunday morning arrived and she headed out to the neighborhood bakery for croissants and donuts. All the ingredients for a frittata were nestled in the fridge, she just had to whip it up and put it in the oven. Next she stopped at the farmer's market and bought assorted berries, pineapple, and melons for a fruit salad. The makings for mimosas and Bloody Marys were arranged on the bar at home, champagne chilling in the wine fridge.

Returning with her purchased sundries, she finished her preparations, set the table with china, crystal glasses, sterling silverware, and cloth napkins. Hands on hips, she surveyed her work and smiled, satisfied, then trod upstairs to shower and dress.

Viewing her reflection in the mirror, her *former* self—from before the car accident—smiled back. Her appetite had returned and her face had filled out, her emaciated appearance had receded, sure she'd gained a few pounds. Even her boobs were bigger. She inhaled sharply and held it. Horrified by her supposition. Oh God. Could it be the early signs of pregnancy? Shit. *Please, God, no.* She closed her eyes tightly and slowly exhaled, forcing the terrifying thought from her psyche. *You're overthinking again.*

She slipped her hands into the pockets of her gauzy black pants and turned sideways to look over her shoulder, checking to make sure her bra wasn't visible in the cutout of her pale blue chemise. She felt pretty. In fact, she always felt pretty when Ian was around. An unexpected response she couldn't explain. The man had an effect on her like no one she'd ever met and she planned on asking him to stay after his parents left. Nothing too kinky, maybe something slow, and easy like Sunday morning, as the song went.

Should she? Would she?

She stood at her dresser, her gaze falling on her wedding photo. She picked up the sterling silver frame and ran her fingers over Sam's smiling face. Her chest tightened. *Oh Sam, is it too soon to move on?* Of course, she didn't expect an answer. *If* Sam really was around she was convinced he was attached to Justice. A sudden thought invaded: should she have asked her mother if Justice had made any new proclamations from Sam? Did she want to know? Would her mother share if it happened again or spare Molly the angst?

Okay, she was overthinking everything all of a sudden.

She returned the photo to its place, opened her jewelry box, deciding on a pair of silver dangling earrings, but hesitated before picking them up. Her diamond engagement ring caught a ray from a nearby window, glinting into her eye. She withdrew the sparkling ring and kissed it. *I love you Sam and I always will.* She pulled up the velvet shelf and tucked the treasure underneath, hiding it from further view. She donned the earrings, closed the case and sighed, patting the top of the beige satin box. *Bye, Sam.*

Slipping her feet into black patent leather sandals, she surveyed her image in the full-length mirror. The sound of breaking glass turned her head. The picture frame lay on the floor, the glass cracked. She did a three-sixty, how? Who? Maybe Sam wasn't tied to Justice. Her heart thudded, her pulse echoing the rhythm. Maybe Sam had been reading her thoughts about a possible pregnancy. Did he know she'd had sex with Ian? More than once.

She pinched her eyes closed again. *Please, Sam, you have to let me go.*

She knelt to retrieve the frame, carefully collecting the glass shards from the floor but one pierced her fingertip. She studied the red droplet as it grew bigger and bigger. Her mind went to a bad place. Blood seeping from Sam's head, neck… everywhere. She screamed, shaking him, hysteria thwarting every bit of FBI training to stay calm in a crisis.

Her jaw locked, her teeth hurt. She rose slowly, depositing the broken glass in the trash bin. She tucked the unprotected picture in the top drawer of her dresser, then went to the bathroom and washed away the blood. A quick vacuum and she descended the stairs, tucking away thoughts of Sam into her secret mind vault.

The Westminster chimes of the living room clock announced noon. She lit a few scented candles, then selected a jazz station on her phone and hit the house speaker app. Diana Krall crooned *"The Look of Love."* A wave of happiness banished her negative thoughts. She hadn't entertained anyone in months. She felt renewed, rejuvenated, reborn.

Could she? Would she? Move on? Would Sam let her?

She opened the front door where Ian stood, dressed in a pink button-down shirt and white shorts. He handed her a gigantic bunch of pink roses. His smile lit her up like the fireworks they'd enjoyed on the 4th of July.

Ian arrived on Molly's street a little before noon. His parents would meet him here and then take a cab to the airport. He spied a flower shop on the corner and beelined toward it. Selecting the proper flowers for a woman proved challenging. All kinds of hidden messages and even booby traps were imbedded in the selection, as explained to him by his former fiancé after he inappropriately selected yellow roses. He thought them beautiful, signifying sunny days ahead, yet apparently they meant interest in friendship only. Big mistake. Red was too serious, like madly in love, which he was... but didn't feel confident enough to put it out there again until Molly gave him some encouragement.

He went with pink.

Nervous, which made absolutely no sense, he stared at her front door. They'd bridged the sexual barrier, seen every inch of each other's bodies.

Molly opened the door before he knocked. "I saw you coming up the steps. Come in."

"For you," he said, kissing her cheek. Then kissed her for real.

Molly accepted the bouquet of a dozen roses laced with baby's breath and buried her nose in the soft blossoms.

"Thank you, they're lovely." She walked to the far end of the kitchen and grabbed a vase from the cabinet over the fridge.

"Nice place," Ian said, leaning a hip against the kitchen counter.

"Thanks, it was my grandparents' and I inherited it."

He watched Molly artfully arrange the blossoms.

The doorbell rang. "I'll get it," Ian said.

His parents entered, his mother kissing his cheek. "This is my mother, Madeline Turner and my dad, Richard Turner."

Mr. Turner held two suitcases. "Don't worry, we're not moving in, just heading to the airport from here."

Molly laughed. "No worries. My home is your home."

Ian bore a striking resemblance to his father. The same sapphire-blue eyes, muscular build, and thick brown hair, although somewhat muted by wisps of gray. A striking man for his age. His mother's shoulder-length flaxen hair and perfectly applied make-up belied a woman who looked younger than her age.

"Maddy, please," his mother said, taking both Molly's hands. "It's so nice to meet you."

"Rich," Mr. Tuner said, offering his hand. "Thanks for having us." He handed her a bottle of chardonnay. "Something for your wine cellar."

"Thank you." She parked the wine in the kitchen's built-in wine cooler.

"Ian, I have the makings for Bloody Marys and Mimosas. Can you make drinks?" Molly slid the frittata into the oven.

"I'm up to the task, ma'am." He winked. "Can I take everyone's orders?"

"Bloody Mary for me," his father said and his mother concurred.

"I'll have a Mimosa," Molly said.

Ian handed everyone their cocktail. They dined and drank for well over an hour, the conversation friendly and light. "Coffee for anyone?" Molly finally asked.

"I've got my eye on that chocolate donut," Mr. Turner said. "And coffee would be like extra icing."

Ian helped Molly clear the table, returning with the coffee pot, cream, and sugar. Ian poured and each succumbed to the intoxicating lure of a fresh baked pastry.

"Where did you get these?" Mrs. Turner asked, holding an apple tart mid-air. "They're decadent."

"Little French bakery on the corner. Their baguettes are to live for. And they sell cheese and other gourmet nibbles as well. I spent the first ten years of my life in Paris and this is the closest I've found to the real deal."

"Oh?" Mrs. Turner said. "That must have been amazing."

"Her mother is Alyene Bouchard," Ian offered. "The famous sculptor. The one I ventured to New York City to see for my art class."

Mr. Turner sipped his coffee then returned the cup to its saucer. "Oh yes, I remember. You and your roommate went. I thought that a ruse and that you just went there to party."

Ian laughed. "Well, plenty of other times I went light on the truth, but that wasn't one of them."

After making sure to let Molly know what a delightful time they'd had, his parents bid their farewell, a waiting cab ready to take them to the airport. They'd managed to avoid conversation about Ian taking the new job and perhaps... maybe... he hoped... Molly might consent to join him.

"I like your parents," Molly said.

"Pretty sure they love you," Ian said, shutting the door behind him.

Molly circled his waist with her arms, gazing up with her big brown eyes. "Do you have to leave right away?"

"I don't. I left the rest of the day open in the hopes you might let me hang around for a while."

"Yes. Stay. Maybe stay the night?"

Chapter 37

Ian smiled. This was going way better than expected. Absence made the heart grow fonder? Had it worked?

Molly stood before the kitchen bay window gazing out at the street. "It's a magnificent day, let's go for a walk." Ian came up beside her, his arm pressed against her shoulder. "There's a lovely park two blocks away with a neighborhood garden and a farmer's market. It's a co-op and I belong so I can also pick up some produce while we're there."

"Well, it wouldn't hurt me to walk off the two jelly donuts I ate."

They exited the brownstone and turned left. Ian took her hand, lacing his fingers through hers. A warm breeze wafted around them, the tree-lined street softening the city landscape, a perfect summer afternoon. In more ways than one.

"So, are we officially dating or not?" he asked.

Her eyes avoided him, then slowly returned. She regarded him carefully and suddenly he worried she'd say no. But he was done pussy-footing around. He wanted—no, needed an answer.

"I've done a lot of thinking these past few days and I

know I want you in my life. I'm not looking for a husband, although I won't say never."

Okay… still heading in the right direction. "I fully understand your hesitancy about the timeline. But I think everyone who matters is already on board. Our friends, our parents, even Justice. I think she likes me."

"She adores you, and my parents do too."

"Then there's nothing to stand in our way. Let's *go steady* and we needn't discuss marriage right now. I'm just happy you're keeping the door cracked open."

She chuckled. "Go steady? Are you going to give me your varsity jacket?" She shoved her shoulder into his side.

"I don't have it anymore but if I did, I'd give it to you in a heartbeat."

"And I'd accept."

"Maybe I could give you something else?"

Uh-oh. Had she stumbled into the engagement ring discussion? Or maybe he meant something more innocent. A piece of jewelry without an agenda.

"You know, in the BDSM lifestyle a Dominant collars his submissive to signify he belongs to her."

"What?" Molly said, coming to a stop on the sidewalk. "You're kidding, right? Like ownership? A master and a pet?"

Ian smirked. "Well, not in my mind. I'm only the Master in the bedroom and based on our last encounter, apparently not as much as I thought."

Molly wrapped her arms around him and gazed upon his handsome face. "I like what's happened so far and I want to keep that going." She paused. "I'm not opposed to a token of your affection. What did you have in mind?"

"I'd really like to buy you a ring. It doesn't have to be a traditional engagement ring. Anything you like. Only *we'd know* what it meant and that's enough for me right now. Like a promise ring, although the meaning's perverted since neither of us are virgins." He smirked.

Molly snickered. "How dare you." She hesitated before saying, "Okay, I accept your offer for a promise ring. Maybe my birthstone. But it'll cost you, mister. My birthstone is a ruby."

"Your birthday is this month?" The only reason he knew that was because it was his oldest sister's birthstone.

"Yup. The 18th."

"Perfect. Then I'll buy it for your birthday. What size?"

"Six."

"Can I take you out for your birthday? Saturday, right?"

"I'd like that."

They arrived at the community garden. "Wow," Ian said. "This is incredible. It really brings a touch of country life into the city landscape. In fact, your neighborhood is quite homey, tranquil, quiet."

"I do love it here. I used to come as a child and spend time with my grandparents. The house originally belonged to my dad's grandparents. My great grandmother was a dress-maker in the thirties. Made evening gowns for an upscale fashion house, lots of big-name movie stars like Loretta Young, Katherine Hepburn and Claudette Colbert. She had autographed pics from all of them. I think we still have them. My great grandfather was a waiter at Mama Leone's restau-rant. A pretty big deal, back in the day. A lot of famous people ate there. And he was a fantastic cook, which is where I guess my father gets it from."

"That's so cool. I bet they had some great stories."

"I've heard a few over the years. I bet I could pry more out of my dad after a couple martinis."

They roamed the garden, relaxing on the slatted wood and wrought-iron bench where a contingent of children played tag as their parents chatted nearby. Ian draped an arm over her shoulders and tucked her into his side. To the left, two young children played catch with a big red rubber ball. It came toward Ian and he caught it with one hand and tossed it back. They sat for a while, enjoying the sultry summer afternoon in the bucolic park.

"Let's see what the garden has for me to take home tonight. The tomatoes have been amazing this summer. Maybe I can make a pasta tossed with fresh tomatoes, garlic, basil and olive oil for dinner. You're staying, right?"

"No chance of getting rid of me today. Were you serious about me spending the night? I'll have to leave early in the morning for work."

"I am. I'm sans child for the night. But when she returns I'd like you to come over as much as you can. I want Justice to get to know you better."

And he was in. Almost all the way in. His pulse quickened, his heart swelled. And he blurted, "I love you, Molly."

"I love you too." Yup. In. It. To. Win. It.

They supped on fresh-made pasta, a crusty baguette from the French bakery, along with their special herb butter, and an excellent bottle of Merlot he found in the makeshift wine cabinet he was pretty sure was meant for something else.

Hanging out with Molly was easy, no pretenses, no drama, and he allowed himself the fantasy of them growing old together. Like both their parents, totally mad about each other after thirty-some years. He had forgotten how much he wanted that, and how he thought he'd lost it. But now, he had hope again. Hope for a family, a safe place to fall, to celebrate holidays with, to usher in each new year with happiness and love. Jesus. He was scaring himself. When had he become the sappy male lead in a Lifetime movie? But he couldn't deny his need for a family of his own.

60 Minutes ended and they surfed channels for a while, settling on Friends, watching two episodes until Molly finally said, "Ready for bed? We both have work in the morning and need our beauty sleep."

"Yes, ma'am. But I need some exercise before I fall asleep. I plan to roll you around on those sheets for a while first. You up for that?"

"Challenge accepted, Sir."

Ian watched as Molly turned out the lights and set the alarm on the keypad near the front door. She took his hand and led him up the stairs and into her bedroom, turning the lights on with a dimmer switch. No frills or ruffles in the Masterson boudoir, no curtains, only white wooden blinds covering the windows. The beechwood furniture had sleek lines, the king-sized bed covered with a beige waffle-textured quilt with double pillows on each side and the required throw pillows in between.

Molly couldn't believe she'd actually blurted out the L-word. Had it escaped merely as a reflex? When someone said it to you the *polite* response was to return it. But she didn't think that was the case. She'd meant it at the time, felt it, and it felt right.

"Be careful with your bare feet. I broke some glass earlier. I think I got it all but you never know." Should she tell him the truth? That her wedding picture had mysteriously leapt off her dresser and smashed to smithereens? Now that she thought about it, with Ian in her bedroom, would other items become airborne? Was Ian in danger?

"What's the matter?" Ian asked. "You look uncomfortable all of a sudden?"

"Ah…" Molly nibbled a fingernail. "The broken glass I mentioned, um, my wedding picture somehow fell off the dresser and broke. I was nowhere near it."

Ian studied her, his eyes narrowed. "What are you saying? You think it was some supernatural phenomenon?"

Molly shook her head. "No, of course not. I don't know why I went there. Justice is rubbing off on me. Forget I said anything."

Ian didn't respond.

Molly tossed the unnecessary pillows on a cream-colored bench under the window, then pulled down the quilt, exposing coffee-hued sheets.

"You can use the hallway bathroom. There are new toothbrushes in the drawer. Towels as needed. If you need anything let me know."

"Thanks."

———

Ian returned to find Molly under the sheets, her hands behind her head. He stripped out of his clothes and slid in beside her, turning on his side, his head cradled in his hand, elbow on the pillow. His hand found her belly and he slid it upwards, touching a breast. She winced.

"Sorry, my breasts are tender."

"You getting your period?"

"No. But even if I was, with the pill, I don't usually get sore anymore."

She touched her breast and massaged it. "It's okay. Don't worry about it."

"I'll just have to distract you with other dastardly deeds."

She leaned in and kissed him, their tongues stroking, caressing, an unhurried ballet of warm sloppy flesh. She inhaled his breath, the air she needed to live, to be alive. He pulled her into him, her breasts tight against his chest. A hand slid down her back, he clasped a buttock and squeezed. He couldn't get close enough, not until he was inside her. Even then, it would end all too soon.

Chapter 38

Their lips separated and Ian nibbled her ear, her head dipped down and she giggled. She wrapped an arm around his waist, her mouth on his shoulder. She sucked and he wondered if he'd return to work with a hickey. A prize he'd cherish because it reminded him of her, even if just for a few days.

He caressed her stomach, rubbing the taut flesh, his intrepid fingers traveling downward, slowly, until they reached their destination. He slipped a finger into her wetness, the slick warmth welcoming him in. Molly moaned, thrusting her pelvis up into his hand. He added another finger and pushed inward, then out and in again in rapid succession, building the rhythm. "I want you to come first. Always first," he whispered in her ear.

"Mmm," she mumbled, "is that an order, Sir?"

"It most definitely is, little subbie."

She snuggled his neck, landing sweet kisses on his overheated flesh, trailing over his collarbone then down his chest. She sucked on his nipple and his balls pulled up into his groin. Thankfully skin wasn't combustible, because every inch was on fire.

She got on top, straddling his thighs, then bent down and kissed him. Her scent surrounded him, the musky aroma he loved and would never get enough of. She took him in her hand, circling the head in her wetness, then guided it in. Her hand caressed his balls, a knuckle kneading the sensitive spot behind them. He groaned, his chin reaching for the ceiling, and he grabbed the headboard, holding on for the ride. The rhythm, the urge. Hungry beats and pulses. She started rocking, which brought the rubbing, the hurry, a promise of blinding bliss. The roller coaster of her ministrations took him higher and higher. Hurtling him toward the crest. He sucked in air, swallowed it. She lifted up and bore down again, fast and hard, in as deep as he could go. He growled as the overwhelming wave hit him. *No!*

Too late. His cock throbbed and jerked, his release intense. She slipped a finger between them, rubbing her clit until her vagina quivered around him, squeezing out the last of his essence.

"Shit. I broke my own rule." He circled her back with his arms and she settled atop him, her legs on either side of him, her head nestled against his collarbone.

"I'm not complaining," she whispered against his nipple, her hands tucked under his neck.

"You came, right?" He always knew when a woman climaxed yet somehow this had all been about him. Something he wasn't used to.

"You betcha."

All his BDSM tricks had gone out the window tonight, along with his ego, and he understood that tonight he'd only made love. Love, love, love. *They'd made love.* No apparatus, no bondage or blindfold, no toys, just unrestrained lovemaking, tenderness, a sacred communion.

They slumbered deeply, peacefully, never severing their connection, skin-to-skin until the alarm snatched them from dreamland.

They woke wrapped around each other like ivy on a tree. The sense of oneness made Molly smile. She slipped from under his weighty arm, turning on her back, focusing on the white stucco ceiling. She sighed. Having someone in her bed again made her feel whole, and not just anyone… Ian.

Ian roused and grabbed his phone, silencing the alarm. He groaned. "I think we should take the day off."

He nuzzled her neck, a hand sliding over her belly, to her back, pulling her closer. "I could stay in bed with you all day… all week. Forever."

"Well, that would be totally decadent." She caressed his cheek and kissed his nose. "Maybe this relationship is dangerous. We might become slugs."

He rubbed her shoulder, squeezing before running his warm hand down her arm. "I'm sorry about last night. You should have come first. You should always come first. And not just in bed."

She rolled onto her back and tucked an arm under the pillow. "I don't think there should be rules. I'm sure that goes against the Dom handbook and no doubt I find the Dom/sub interaction thrilling, but something simpler can be just as satisfying."

"You're definitely fucking up my rulebook. But I agree, it's all good with you."

She laughed. He put a hand on her breast and a bolt of pain shot through it. She held her breath. He noticed.

"Still sore?"

"A little."

"That seemed like more than a little. Is it anything to worry about?"

"No, don't worry your pretty little head. It's nothing." But she *was* concerned and the thought terrified her. She couldn't be, could she? Good God.

"I have something I want to talk to you about." He took her hand. "I'm seriously thinking about taking the job running my parents' new firm."

"You're switching sides?" She blinked several times, letting the thought settle. "You're serious?"

"Deadly."

"Wow, good for you."

"And, since you're having doubts about the FBI I wondered if you might consider joining me at the firm. You could run the investigation arm and try cases as you see fit."

She sat up alongside him. "You sure? People in relationships shouldn't necessarily work together."

"My parents pulled it off and I think we'd make a great team."

Molly considered his proposition carefully. *If* they married, Ian would move in, they could work together, be a team at work, home, and play. Talk about a turnaround in just a few weeks when she'd been lamenting about sleeping alone and now... a total commitment, immersion into each other's professional and personal lives. All the way... *in*.

She settled back on the pillow and faced him, her hands tucked under her chin. They were nearly nose-to-nose. "It's a lot to consider, but I'll give it serious thought. We might get sick of each other if we're together twenty-four-seven."

"I'm already sick—lovesick—for you."

Molly grimaced. "You're turning into a cornball."

Ian frowned. "I fear you may be right. You've topped me twice now, which is something I intend to correct immediately. I'm reclaiming my turf." He pushed her down on the sheets and shoved her hands over her head. "I intend to ravage you and you will call me Sir and submit. Understand?"

Molly chuckled, heat creeped into her cheeks. She loved it when he bossed her around in bed. "Yes, Sir."

"Where do you keep your scarves?"

"In the second drawer of the double dresser." He exited the bed, his erection proud and strong, and rummaged through the drawer returning with three silky scarves. "Why three?"

"That's for me to know and you to find out." He tied her wrists to the headboard, then straddled her hips, wrapping the final scarf around his hands several times and snapping it taut. "I'm going to blindfold you. Taking your sight will enhance your other senses. It will keep you off balance because you won't be able to see what I'm doing."

Her eyebrows shot up. Never had she experienced sex, sight-deprived. Her vagina clenched, butterflies swirling her belly. Her pulse throbbed, her breathing suddenly shallow.

He tied the silky swath around her eyes, creating a knot to one side. "Remember your safe words if you need them."

But she knew she wouldn't, she'd never need them with Ian, willing to take all he could give. His breath tickled her neck, her own breath quickening in anticipation. He made her wait. She felt lightheaded by the time he touched her. His hand reached between her legs. She sighed as he stroked. His hand was on her neck, then sliding down and over her shoulder.

"You're in for it now, little subbie."

Good God. "Fine. Whatever. Just do it."

"Molly, we're effectively doing a scene and you need to be back in protocol. Only speak when I ask you a question and address me as Sir. You do not have permission to speak otherwise. Is that clear?"

His weight remained on her thighs, his cock brushing against her warm flesh. He'd morphed her into a wriggling mass of molten jelly inside of a minute. "Yes, Sir," she mumbled.

"Good girl." He moved down farther on the bed and grabbed her ankles, spreading her legs wide. Exposed, vulnerable, fastened to the bed, blindfolded, unable to experience anything other than the feel of him, the smell of his cologne, the prickle of his five o'clock shadow. Helpless, yearning, aching... for him. And in that moment, he was her universe, multiverse. Her shining star, her everything.

Chapter 39

Molly lay under the covers, Ian insisted on letting himself out. She offered to make him breakfast or at least coffee for the road but he declined, encouraging her to doze a while longer. The afterglow of more amazing sex made her thoughts hazy, her eyelids heavy, and she slipped into oblivion.

The bed began to rock and suddenly she was in a boat on a gently swaying sea. No motor, no oars, nothing she could use to guide the craft, she drifted aimlessly. The boat ran aground on an island and she went ashore. She came upon a trail, confused as to whether to take the left or right path. She turned and gazed back at the boat, except it was gone. Lights, too many to count, danced on an ocean too vast to envisage. Each one brilliant, unique, the light coming from within, pure gold, lighter than oxygen, each one a small piece of heaven. She reached out, who wouldn't want to touch something so pure? The lights recoiled in fear, and vanished. She turned toward the path again. A man, swathed in mist, or a cloud, walked toward her. She couldn't discern his features. Sam?

He smiled and beckoned her to come. "Follow me," he said with a sheepish grin. Molly wrapped her fingers into his loose cotton shirt. "I will be your guide." Her heart flooded with relief. Ian.

She woke with an intense feeling of contentment, as if she'd moored in a safe haven after a violent storm. The dream eerily prophetic. Her decision made. She'd take the job, maybe marry Ian, start her new life.

She glanced at the bedside clock. Shit, she needed to hustle to make it to work on time.

Sylvia snapped her fingers and Ian came to attention. "Earth to the Chief ADA," she said. "Where's your head?"

Ian laughed. He loved his relationship with Sylvia. His work mom. No pretenses, no fuss, no muss, no drama. She called it as she saw it. "Sorry. I am a bit distracted."

"It's probably none of my business but are you dating Special Agent Masterson?"

He narrowed one eye. "You're right. None of your business."

"You're in love. It's written all over you."

He frowned, which morphed into a broad grin. "That obvious?"

"Yes. I think that FBI agent is holding you prisoner. At least your heart."

"Yeah, I'm done for. Hook, line and sinker. It's pathetic, I know."

Sylvia laughed, a laugh that came from deep in her chest. "I'm so happy for you."

He should come all the way clean to Sylvia. "Sit down," he said. Sylvia settled into one of the chairs in front of his desk and crossed her sleek legs. "I've decided to leave the

DA's office. My parents are opening a legal aid firm in the city and asked me to take the helm. Molly is having serious reservations about continuing in her role at the FBI since a fellow agent met with life-threatening injuries. They're not sure she's going to make it. She decided she doesn't want her daughter growing up without a father and knowing her mother could die any day. I've asked Molly to join me in the firm."

Sylvia's eyes expanded, her brows high. "Wow, I didn't see that coming. You're defecting?"

"I am. My dad did and he's never been happier. He says it's good for the soul. There's too much injustice out there. Too many people who can't afford adequate representation. We see it every day."

Sylvia hung her head. "I can't argue with that."

Ian had a sudden thought. "Would that be something that interests you? We could use a pro like you."

Sylvia sat tall in her chair and seemed to consider his offer. "I'm honored you asked. I've lived my entire life on Long Island. The commute would be awful. On the other hand, I did picture myself eventually retiring in the city. I'd love to spend my time going to plays and concerts, museums and art galleries. It's been my dream since Al died."

"You don't need to decide this minute. We'd match your salary and benefits. Plus two extra weeks of paid vacation. And I'd be thrilled if you accepted."

"I'll give it some serious thought. It might take some time. I have to sell the house and find a place in the city." Sylvia stood. "Thank you for the offer, Ian. It's an exciting proposition." Returning to work, she said, "You have a meeting with Brian before the Town Council meeting. Are you planning on telling him today?"

"I have to call my parents and let them know I'm taking

the job. Once that's done, I'll talk with Brian. Probably by the end of the week. Let's keep it between us until then."

"Of course. Mum's the word."

Before leaving the office that evening, Ian phoned his parents. "Hello, darling," his mother said.

"Hi, Mom. How was your flight home?"

"Fine, no delays for a change. Seems like you can't fly anywhere these days without a delay or cancellation."

"I hear you. Have you decided on a location for the new office?"

"Yes, the paperwork is in motion. It's near the courthouse in Manhattan and the space is excellent."

"I'm interested in the job," Ian said.

"Really? Oh, honey, I'm just thrilled. I can't wait to tell your father. He's in court, but I'll be sure to tell him the minute I see him."

The task force's case load continued to grow exponentially and everyone worked long hours. Each day Molly had been tempted to tell Rob she planned to quit the FBI, but each time she chickened out. When had she turned into such a wimp?

Today was the day.

The nanny would return on Monday and Molly planned to leave work early to retrieve her daughter in order to beat the usual weekend traffic. She missed her terribly. Ian was coming tomorrow to take them out for her birthday.

Molly entered her office Friday morning and stowed her purse in the desk's bottom drawer. She pulled her holstered Glock from her trousers' waistband and laid it on her desk. She stared at it. Telling Rob she was resigning had her stressed. Guilt nudged her, Rob and the FBI had put their faith in her, trained her, assigned her important work, trusted her with this new task force, and now, she was about to walk out the door and never look back. Ungrateful. Yet she wasn't ungrateful, the complete opposite. And she would put her skills to good use. She smirked. What if she wound up defending a guy against FBI charges? Fighting her former colleagues in court? That would be weird. Very. She sighed. Best get it over with. The only way to pull off a band aid… fast, and it always hurt.

"Come," a gruff male voice said.

She opened the door slowly to see Merryl, Rob's boss, sitting across from him at his conference table. "Oh, I didn't mean to interrupt. Hi, Merryl."

"Agent Masterson, good to see you."

Rob rose immediately and came close. "The task force is kicking some pedophile ass. Nice work."

"The Director is very pleased," Merryl added.

"Thanks, but it's a joint effort, Matt and Lily are doing a spectacular job as are the techs." She decided to get right to the point. "I'm giving my two-week notice. I've decided to leave the FBI. I suggest you let Matt take over the task force as well as Lily's training."

"What?" Rob said, his eyebrows hiked up. "Why?"

"After what happened to Agent Robinson, I can't bear the thought of not returning home to my daughter on any given day."

Rob harrumphed, studying the floor, hands on his hips, his weight shifting in his shoes. "I'm speechless," he finally said, his eyes too serious.

"I don't want you to think me ungrateful. You've placed great faith in me over the years." She glanced at Merryl. "Both of you. And I appreciate every opportunity you've given me." She handed Rob an envelope and he reluctantly accepted it.

"What will you do?" Rob said.

"Well, I'm not exactly the stay-at-home-mom type. I'm thinking about taking a position with a legal aid firm. A friend of mine is opening a new office in mid-town. I can manage the investigative arm and also try cases."

"Commendable," Merryl said. "We need more of that in this world."

Surprised at Merryl's comment, Molly smiled. "Thank you for understanding. And again, I hope you don't think me ungrateful."

"Not in the slightest," Merryl said. "Family comes first. Always."

"It's been a privilege to work for you, both of you."

Rob faced her, way too far into her personal space. "I can't lie, Molly, I'll miss you and so will the Bureau. You're one hell of a kick-ass agent. I wish you greener pastures."

Chapter 40

J ustice crashed into Molly's knees, strangling them with the power of a four-year-old hug.

"Mommy! Mommy! I missed you so much!"

Molly lifted Justice into her arms and kissed her cheek like ten times. "I missed you too, sweetie." Justice squeezed her neck affectionately, holding on tight. "Did you have fun with Grand-mère and Grand-père?"

"Oh yes, Mommy. S*ooo* much fun."

"I'm glad," Molly said, returning her daughter to the ground. Her parents looked on, smiles stretching wide.

Howard Bouchard served fresh lobster over a bed of arugula dressed in a lime vinaigrette for dinner and Molly brought a baguette from her bakery. They ate on the back deck, sipping jasmine iced tea while Justice nattered on about her adventures with Grand-mère and Grand-père and her new-found affection for Ethan. She wore a baby blue sundress imprinted with tiny white starfish, compliments of her grandmother. Her hair was coiffed in a French braid, something Molly never had the patience or the proficiency to style, besides, she could never compete with her mother's expertise.

They cleared the table and settled into the comfy back porch furniture while Justice wandered the beach under Molly's watchful eyes, collecting shells in a red plastic pail.

"I've resigned from the FBI," Molly said. Her parents laser-focused on her, awaiting her announcement. "With Justice having no father and the possibility of her mother not returning home on any given day, it's too much to bear." Her parents remained silent, gazes intense, patience their forte. "I do feel guilty, the FBI has been very good to me."

"We understand perfectly," her father said. "Makes sense."

She inhaled deeply and exhaled slowly. "And I can't deny my feelings for Ian any longer. He's a wonderful man, smart and well… damn easy on the eyes, and he's good to me, good *for* me. And he adores Justice."

"Will you marry?" her mother said.

"I'm seriously considering it."

"Has he asked you?"

"Yes, but I've been evasive. He's coming to take me out for my birthday tomorrow. I think he's buying a ring. Not a diamond, something less official."

Molly changed the subject. "Justice behaved for you?"

"Perfectly," her mother said. "She's such a sweet child, a kind child. A little beyond her years, as were you."

"Only child syndrome?"

Her mother grinned, her eyebrows arched. "Perhaps. But there's still time, she could have a sibling."

Molly swallowed hard. Yeah, maybe like in nine months. Her period was late and with the pill she was *never* late. She'd stop at the drugstore on her way home and purchase a pregnancy test. Maybe two. One as backup… just to be sure.

Molly hadn't truly considered how she felt about an unplanned pregnancy. She was a planner in every aspect of her life. No surprises on her watch. Sam had often commented on her lack of spontaneity and it usually resulted in an argument. She reflected on the last few weeks of her life, with Ian. She'd done things she never imagined. They'd not even known each other a month and she was going to marry him. By most people's standards that would be spontaneity, right? Maybe she had changed.

"Any mentions of messages from Sam?" she asked, narrowing one eye in a half-grimace.

"Not a peep," her mother said.

"Good. Maybe this creepy fascination has passed." And yet Molly wasn't completely sure it had been merely Justice's imagination, especially after the picture incident. She prayed Sam was done with them and had moved on to wherever dead people go.

———

Ian arrived home late Friday night, a load of new cases hit after they cracked a sizeable drug ring this week. Over thirty arraignments, bail hearings, statements and depositions overwhelming his entire staff. He wouldn't miss this shit.

He poured himself a scotch and scrounged leftovers from the fridge. He studied the congealed linguine with clam sauce and soggy garlic bread from his last pickup at Fred's place. A pathetic excuse for dinner. But then he smiled, tomorrow was Molly's birthday and he'd be spending it with his *maybe* soon-to-be new family. He was wearing Molly down, he was sure of it.

He stripped out of his clothes and grabbed a hot shower, the powerful jets pummeling his tight muscles. Entering his bedroom, he toweled dry and slipped on a pair of gym shorts and a tee-shirt. The tiny turquoise package sat on his dresser and he couldn't wait to give Molly her present. Tomorrow couldn't come soon enough.

His phone rang. Molly. "Hey."

"Hey. Driving home from my parents. Daughter retrieved."

He sunk onto his bed and collapsed against the comforter. "Was she glad to see you?"

"For sure. Nothing like the love and adoration of a four-year-old."

"I get it."

"How was your day?"

"Brutal. I'll be glad to leave. I think we broke our own arrest record this week. Ton of work."

"Getting lots of bad guys off the street is a good thing. Kudos."

"Thanks. Did you tell Rob today?"

"I did. Gave my two weeks' notice. He was gracious and understanding. Coincidentally, his boss, Merryl was there. She was very complementary. They made it easy. Have you told Brian?"

"Actually, I just told him before I left work. Now, it's just a matter of cleaning up loose ends. Did I tell you Sylvia has agreed to join us?"

"No way. I didn't know you asked her."

"Well, things have been moving so fast I forgot to mention it."

"That's great, she seems like a real gem."

"Yeah, she's the best. So, psyched for your birthday celebration tomorrow?"

"I am. Can't wait to see you."

"Well, I've got lots of surprises for you?"

"Surprises? We only agreed on one."

"Well, I'm bringing toys. Grown-up toys."

Toys? Her imagination ran wild. What was he planning? What kind of toys?

Chapter 41

Her birthday morning arrived and she awoke excited. Ian had included Justice in their celebration and so 'out on the town' would be activities appropriate for a four-year-old. Molly was looking forward to experiencing a family dynamic again and Justice expressed sheer delight at a visit from Ian.

They would have lunch in midtown, go to MOMA and then see Trolls in the nearby movie theatre. Dinner would be at Molly's favorite Italian restaurant, in walking distance from her home.

Her thirty-fourth birthday never portended anything eventful, not an important birthday in anyone's mind, yet this one seemed to mark a rebirth. A new job, a new man and, eek, maybe a new baby. The pregnancy tests sat on the medicine cabinet shelf, waiting, waiting, waiting. And she worried, springing an unplanned pregnancy on a guy was about the worst thing imaginable. And a guy marrying you for that reason even worse. She'd assured him she had birth control covered and felt responsible, even though a guy should probably share equal responsibility. But she knew Ian wanted to marry her without the nudge of a pregnancy, yet it still held a negative connotation in her mind. Trapping a guy, forcing him to marry you. Guilt. Guilt. Guilt. Maybe he'd freak. Most guys would. That sinking feeling morphed into a giant pit in her stomach. Maybe it was a bad idea to wed. They could just go on like this, even live together, without making it official. Give him time to see if this was really what he wanted.

She donned a mint-green sundress with spaghetti straps and a pair of white ballerina flats, then opened her jewelry box. Her old engagement ring taunted her. Maybe she should sell it. Donate the money to a food bank, or better yet to Laura's foundation to help children in need along with that $90 million dollars idling in her savings account. Or perhaps she should save the ring for Justice. When she was old enough, she could do whatever she wanted with it. Hmm.

She selected the green emerald studs Sam had given her last Christmas. A giant lump formed in her throat. She leaned her hands on the dresser and hung her head. Oh, Sam, I'm sorry your life ended so suddenly. That you will never get a chance to see your daughter grow up. See her graduate. Walk her down the aisle. See the woman she will become. A tear threatened her makeup and she sniffed, touching her knuckle to her eye to sop up the salty droplet. A shiver ran down her spine. The last time she thought of Sam in this exact spot her wedding photo mysteriously levitated. Although she hadn't actually seen the aberration, she had no other explanation. She searched the room wondering if her husband's spirit was near. Was it an angry spirit?

"Mommy, can I wear this? I think Ian will like it."

Molly frowned. *Dressing for a man already?* She squared her shoulders and sucked in a breath, then turned.

Justice held up a pink confection, all satin and toile, obviously one of her mother's typical selections. Odd, since her mother favored a sleek, no frills, Vogue-ish style herself yet she'd always dressed Molly in more frou-frou than Molly would ever consider now, and Justice would apparently suffer the same fate. And yet it suited Justice. "Of course, sweetie. You'll look very pretty."

"Yay!" And she ran from the room, literally.

Ian arrived at the appointed time clad in a blue and white striped button down and black shorts, his feet sporting black topsiders. More flowers, red roses this time, and a tiny gift bag in his other hand. He kissed her cheek, pulled back, then ravaged her mouth. Damn, he smelled good enough to eat. The kind of meal she could savor as an appetizer, dessert, and the main course.

"Happy birthday."

"Thank you."

"For you," he said, handing her the flowers and the tiny turquoise bag. Unmistakably, Tiffany's. "A small token of my love and affection." He pecked her cheek again.

She shut the door and placed the bouquet on the kitchen counter, then studied the diminutive package. "This is what we agreed on, right? No surprises?"

"I can take direction. As long as it's not in the bedroom."

Molly chuckled. Just the mention of being in bed with Ian spiked her pulse. Would it always be like this? As much as she loved Sam, she had to admit it was *never* like this with him.

Sorry, Sam. And he better not be eavesdropping.

Ian's anticipation for a perfect day had him stoked. Out with his two favorite girls for a birthday celebration. He hoped Molly liked the ring, he'd even risked buying red roses to express his love. "Should I open it now?" Molly asked, bag in hand.

"Definitely, I can't wait to see it on you." He had spent nearly an hour at the famed jewelry store agonizing over nearly a dozen rings. He'd finally settled on a two-karat emerald-cut ruby, highlighted by a dazzling halo of white diamond accents, set in 14K white gold.

She pulled out the tissue paper to reveal the turquoise box and opened it, the ring wedged into the black velvet lining. She gasped, covering her mouth. She peered at Ian. "Oh my God. Ian, it's spectacular."

"I'm willing to get down on one knee?" he offered. "But I know you don't want to make this a big deal."

Molly studied his handsome face. He looked so happy and her heart swelled. She wanted this man badly, in her life, in her bed, even in her work. And she wanted to make him happy. Every day of her life. "That won't be necessary and besides we don't need to talk about this with Justice today. Soon, but not today."

"At least let me put it on you."

He pulled the jewel from its resting place and took Molly's hand. He slipped it on her finger, then clasped her hand with both of his. He coaxed their joined hands to his lips and kissed the back of hers. "I can't wait to make you my wife."

Justice bolted into the room, a fluffy pink cloud of childish enthusiasm. "Hi, Ian." He released Molly's hand but kept it tethered at their sides.

"Well, hello cutie. My, you look beautiful."

Justice twirled on her pink-patent leather toes, her hands

over her head. A perfect little ballerina, complete with curtsy at the end. "Thank you, sir."

Molly blanched. Ian stared at Molly. "Ah, um, as in Prince Charming."

"Okay. Good. Threw me off for a second."

Ya think? The salutation spiraled Molly right into the kinky world of Ian's domain. One she'd embraced with more enthusiasm than she ever imagined. Her face heated at the memory of him restraining her, blindfolding her, playing her body like a fine instrument. And now… she was wet. Jesus. He'd only been here like five minutes.

Ian picked Justice up and held her in his arms. "I'm so happy to see you again," he said. "Are you ready for some fun?"

Well, Molly was, but not that kind of fun. Maybe her hormones were running amok. She was pretty horny when pregnant last time. And there it was again, a cloud hanging over her head, which in the last few seconds had turned gray. How would Ian react? Would he be pissed? Happy? Stoic?

Maybe he'd run the other way. The entire array of emotions abraded her mind, a flash, like lightning hitting water. But she didn't even know for sure. She should have taken the test. Maybe all this angst was unwarranted.

Molly's gorgeous face had suddenly turned serious. "You okay?"

"Yes, why?"

"Because you look like someone just walked over your grave."

"That's a horrible expression."

"Sorry, you just looked troubled all of a sudden."

Justice placed her tiny hands on Ian's cheeks, forcing him

to look at her. "Daddy says you can be my new daddy." She smiled.

Ian stared at Molly again. Nobody said anything.

"I thought she was over this," Molly finally said. "It's been a week and nothing."

Ian was secretly elated. Whether it was actually Sam or not, Justice had accepted him into her life. He'd take it. He decided to just accept it and move on. "I'm so glad," he said to Justice. "And I would love to be your daddy."

"Oh goody," Justice said. Ian lowered her to the ground and Justice smoothed out her skirt.

Justice kept at it. "And Daddy says, happy birthday, Mommy."

"Okay, now I'm freaking out. She didn't know it was my birthday. I never mentioned it and even if my mother did, she's not old enough to keep track of the days."

"I hear you," Ian said.

"This is getting too weird for my liking. I can't live with a ghost, especially not my dead husband's."

Chapter 42

They returned home from the perfect birthday celebration, Justice asleep, her head resting on Ian's shoulder. Molly prayed Sam would find peace soon and move on. The thought of his tortured soul following them around tugged at her heart. Was there something she could do to help him move on? Only time would tell. Still hard to wrap her mind around the reality that Sam might be communicating with them.

Together they tucked the sleeping child into bed then returned to the bedroom.

Molly slipped out of the green sundress. Ian unbuttoned his shirt, then shrugged it off, exposing his well-toned pecs and rock-hard shoulders.

"My period is a week late," she blurted.

Ian blanched. "Aren't you on the pill?" He threw his shirt on the chair and came close.

"Yes, but I somehow forgot to take them the weekend at my parents' house. That's two days missed at the worst possible time."

"You think you might be pregnant?"

"I bought a test but I've been too chicken to take it." Ian grabbed her by the shoulders, his blue eyes dark, tight. *Oh God. This is not going to end well.* "I'm sorry. I know it's a terrible thing to do to a man. I can handle it by myself. You're not obligated in any way." He frowned and a stab of pain pierced her chest, the thrust so forceful it knifed her guts.

"You're not considering abortion?"

"What? No, of course not."

"And you're sure it's mine?"

She laid her hands on his chest and pushed him back. "You're an ass. Like I've been with anyone else. I barely convinced myself to sleep with you."

Ian actually smiled. "It didn't take that much convincing, but you did spend the afternoon with Shadow."

"Seriously, we're back to that again? I saw him for like ten minutes at my mother's house. There wasn't time to fuck." She crossed her arms over her breasts and turned her back on him.

"Did you want to fuck him?"

She whirled on him. "Oh my God, Ian! Don't be an ass. No, I didn't want to fuck him. You heard me tell him I was with you."

"Good." He pulled her into his chest, wrapping his arms around her. "Then take the test right now. I hope it's positive. Nothing would make me happier."

Molly couldn't breathe. Her throat constricted. *Do not cry,* she warned herself. She'd never been much of a crier until Sam died. Who was this woman? Perhaps, a woman flooded with a megaton of unpredictable hormones, that's who.

"You don't have to say that. I fully understand if you're not on board with this. The thought of trapping a man with an unplanned pregnancy is a despicable act. You don't have to marry me."

Ian laughed. "Now, who's being an ass? Remember when you suggested we just be fuck buddies and I questioned why it was okay for me to fuck you but not love you?"

Molly grimaced. "It sounds terrible when you say it like that."

"Well, here we are again. You'll have my child but marriage isn't necessary, even though I've made it no secret I want to marry you, practically from the first day we met. That I love you with all my heart. That I love Justice and I want a family of my own. I guess we never actually discussed it, but I want kids, more than one. And I'm anxious to get started."

"We've known each other for less than a month. How can you be so sure? Ten years from now you might wind up resenting me. I think that's pretty common in a situation like this."

He wrapped his hands around her upper arms, his grip tight. "Let's take this down a notch. You're overthinking. Just like you do in bed."

"What? I do not."

"Yes, you do. And I think a blindfold is in order again tonight. I need to shut that brain down. And I fully intend to pillage every inch of you. I think fucking a pregnant woman is incredibly hot."

"What?"

"Where's the test?"

"In the medicine cabinet."

He marched into the bathroom and returned with two packages. "Two?"

"Just to be sure."

"Okay, let's go. I want you to pee on this stick right now."

He removed the items from their packages and ripped off the wrappers. He glanced at the directions. "Doesn't look very complicated. Do you need help?"

Molly snatched the devices from Ian's hands and walked toward the bathroom. "I can manage, thank you."

Ian sat on the bed, his hands in his lap. His heart pounded like he'd sprinted three laps around a track. He couldn't believe his luck. A child of his own? Would it be a boy or a girl? Either would elate him. Molly was right, it had barely been a month and his entire life had changed. Would continue to evolve. He still couldn't believe it. After Rebecca died, he thought his life was over. He tried to think logically, telling himself he might find someone new, someday, maybe. But his grief never really waned, never allowed him to move on until he met Molly. Then, somehow a window had opened and he breathed fresh air for the first time in the longest, then he'd kicked in a door, and now… he was all the way in. Inside her heart. At least he hoped.

The door opened. Molly clutched something to her chest. He couldn't read her expression. Anger? Terror? Acceptance? "Well?"

She walked toward him and wedged her legs between his knees. "Are you sure you're ready for this?"

"You're killing me, woman. Show it to me." She handed him the sticks. He held his breath, afraid to look, his eyes focused on Molly's face. Stoic, no clue as to the outcome.

"Go ahead, tough guy. Look."

His eyes dragged over her body, her white lacy bra and matching panties, he really wanted to rip them off. And he fully intended to, whatever the test revealed.

He slowly loosened his grip on the plastic sticks and lowered his eyes. A pink plus sign. Both of them. His heart leapt and he followed it, onto his feet, he surrounded Molly with his arms, squeezing her tight, unwilling to let go.

"I can't breathe," she whispered.

"Oh, sorry." He released her, holding her at arm's length. "Now you have to marry me."

"What? No. We need time to let this settle. Be sure we're both okay."

"Absolutely not."

"You're out of your mind." Molly bit a fingernail, tight lines between her eyebrows.

"Yes, insane with pure joy."

"We're moving too fast and honestly, I'm terrified."

"Of what?"

She pulled from his grip and walked toward the window, gazing out into the dark sky. "The idea of falling in love with you terrifies me."

He came near, his chest against her back. "Why would you say that?"

"Because, what if something happened to you? I'd never survive if I lost you. I barely survived this time."

He shifted her toward him. "I won't leave you. Never. I'll always be here."

"You can't know that. Sam didn't know he'd leave me. He had no control over his own death."

"Molly, no one knows what tomorrow will bring. But I know I will be with you forever. We'll be okay. We both have to keep the faith."

His lips captured hers and every rational thought flew out of her head. Just like always. His kiss the salve to heal every laceration, each wound.

Chapter 43

"So, let's stop being so serious and have some fun. I brought a toy."

Yikes. Her blood pressure spiked into the stratosphere, her heart pounded like a jackhammer, her mouth dry.

Ian stood in front of her, close enough to touch, the heat radiating off his body scorching her skin. "I plan to take my time, little subbie."

Good God.

"Your tits still sore?"

"Some, a massage helps."

"That, I can deliver."

He stripped off her bra and panties and threw her on the bed. "I normally aim for a noisy woman but you'll have to be quiet so we don't wake a sleeping child."

"Agreed," Molly said. "Turn the video on the baby monitor off. I don't need a child visual during sex. We'll hear her if she wakes."

"Good plan." He stared at the miniature TV, hands on his hips. "I don't know how to work one of these things."

"Well, you better learn. Give it to me."

"Not tonight." He handed it to her.

She flicked off the video, leaving the audio on and Ian returned it to the nightstand.

He grasped her shoulders and centered her on the bed, reaching underneath and pulling back the quilt and top sheet. A flush ran through her, her heart thudded. His ability to keep her off-center, never the mundane, trilled her veins. And he was hers, forever.

"Remember when I asked you if you had a vibrator?"

"Yea, but I told you I haven't used one since college. I always thought of it as solo sex. Why would I want a vibrator when I have you?"

"Because a vibrator in the hand of a man is an entirely different experience."

Desire rushed through her as violent heat. Her voice shrank to a whisper. She might orgasm before the first touch. And *that* would definitely get her spanked. "Yes, Sir."

He pulled out a tissue-wrapped parcel from his duffle. He approached the bed, opening it as he walked. The plastic dick was giant—and *thick*. She had the urge to comment on its size yet refrained, remaining silent and obedient. She did trust him, right?

"Don't worry, little subbie, it'll fit," he said, reading her mind.

She pressed her lips together, no comment, and held her breath.

"Good girl. Now close your eyes and stay perfectly still."

Her eyelids shut tightly, she waited with unbearable antic-ipation. "Breathe, sweetheart," he commanded.

Damn, why did she keep holding her breath? Well, duh, because her primal mating instincts overrode the mundane urge to breathe. She forced out a long slow breath.

Ian couldn't take his eyes off his adorable little subbie. Jesus, she was beautiful. Her lips pressed together in an effort to keep silent and her eyes squinting like a little girl waiting for a surprise. And a surprise she would get. Something delectable.

He grasped her feet and pushed her heels to either side of her ass. "Lift your hips." He slid a pillow underneath her bottom. Placing his hands on the inside of her thighs, he ran his fingers up and down their length, gently stroking the soft tender skin. She sighed and mumbled, "Oh, God."

"Silence." Yet his lips quirked upward with satisfaction at her words. She trembled under his touch. She was close to coming. What? He'd barely touched her. "You do not have permission to come, Molly."

He sat between her legs and flipped the switch on the phallic-shaped vibrator. Probably his favorite toy, the Rabbit–named for the tickler arm shaped like an actual bunny–could do the trick in no time at all. The combination of internal and external stimulation can make for a quick orgasm, he needed to go slowly. He fully intended to bring her close to the edge several times before he let her orgasm. He wanted her frustrated until he determined she'd reached the height he wanted, and then, well, she'd be one satisfied lady.

His finger entered her, so wet, soft, hot, no need for lube. "You're so wet, darling. I like that very much." He added another finger, stretching her already swollen tissues. He slid the vibrator into her vagina and flipped the switch, her back arched. The bunny twitched against her clit and she moaned. He pushed it in deep, the twirling motion drilling into her as the bunny ratcheted her higher. He shifted it into second gear, the frenzied bunny working her hard. She moaned again, writhing on the pillow.

"Quiet," he murmured, gripping a hip to pin her against the mattress. "Do. Not. Move." He held the toy against her opening, letting it take her higher. He knew she couldn't last much longer and pulled it out, letting her catch her breath. Molly opened her eyes, lifting her head off the pillow. "What the fuck?" He slapped the outside of her thigh.

"Uh-uh, little subbie. You were too close to coming. You will wait until I allow it."

"But…" She dropped her head back onto the pillow and groaned.

"Quiet." He snuggled against her side, vibrator poised for a second round. "I want you good and frustrated before you come. Trust me, it will be spectacular," he whispered near her ear. "Stay statue-still and just let me pleasure you."

———

The vibrations from his words tingled her flesh. Too much like a threat. His hot breath ignited her skin. She shut her eyes and kept her lips tight, being quiet more difficult than keeping still. He slid the pulsating contraption into her again. The fluttering in her belly grew as he probed a spot inside that made her clit throb. His tongue tickled her ear, momentarily distracting her from the toy's trembling pulsations.

He shoved it in as far as it could go, then pulled it out, in and out, building the rhythm. Her thighs quivered, her muscles taut, the quake near. Suddenly, the intensity increased, a frantic tempo making her dance on the pillow.

"Come now, baby," he finally cried. Her hips rose higher and pressed against the thrashing mechanical cock. "That's it, baby. Look at me. Let me see you fly." She sank into the blue abyss of his eyes, so deep, as deep as the pulsing toy inside her. She yelped and he pulled the gadget out and placed his hand over her mouth. "Shush," he said. "We don't want to wake the dead."

"My God, you're going to kill me."

"Not tonight, I won't."

———

He knelt between her thighs and his tongue swept through her throbbing flesh. She tasted so salty-sweet and he nipped and teased her clit. Adding two fingers, he pushed into her forcefully, rotating them back and forth. He pulled them out and probed her with his tongue again.

He moved a hand to her ass, urging her toward his erection. Sliding his hand under her right knee, he threw her leg over his shoulder. He sank in deep. Their hips moved in a gentle tempo but quickly built to a feverish thrashing. Flesh against flesh. His orgasm seconds away and he wanted her to climax with him.

A tense coil built at the center of his body, tightening with each forceful stroke. The pressure reached its apex, ecstasy filled him, flooding his body with fire and ice. "Come again, baby," he said, his lips crushing her mouth. The moorings broke loose, his climax hurling him into the eddying riptide of carnal bliss.

Her body trembled beneath him as the shockwave hit, arms clutching him to her chest as he collapsed onto her. Their breathing slowed and he kissed her lightly, lingering, inhaling her musk. He retreated and gazed into the deep brown pools of her eyes, brimming with tears. "You okay?"

She buried her face in his neck, strangling him with her embrace. "All good," she whispered. "No, not good, excellent."

Chapter 44

Ian wrapped his arms around Molly's waist as she flipped silver dollar-sized pancakes. "Now that it's morning and we can see more clearly in the daylight I wonder if you've given marrying me any more thought."

She lay the spatula on the spoon rest and turned in his arms. She tapped her chin several times. "Hmm, let me think…" She made him wait. Tap. Tap. Tap. "I've thought of nothing else. I have let go of the panic and all of my other terrifying thoughts." She made him wait again. Tap. Tap. Tap.

"You're killing me, woman."

She broke into a smile. "Yes, Ian Turner. I will marry you."

"Thank, God." He kissed her, because he couldn't think of anything else to say.

Molly caressed his cheek, her thumb stroking his chin. "I love you," she said.

"How about tomorrow?"

She chuckled. "You've got to give a girl a little more notice. How about two weeks, on Saturday? It's a week before Jamie and Colin's wedding and I don't want to rain on their parade. We could just invite our parents. Simple, at City Hall. No fuss, no muss."

"Done."

"Justice skipped into the kitchen, Sparkle dangling from her hand. "I'm hungry."

"Well good because we're making pancakes. Your fave."

"The little baby ones?"

"Yup."

"Goody gum drops."

Ian helped Justice set out plates, napkins and silverware, Justice instructing Ian how to fold the napkins into pretty triangles. They sat around the kitchen table and Ian poured orange juice into three glasses.

"Sweetheart, there's something I need to tell you," Molly said to Justice.

"Okay, Mommy."

"Ian and I are getting married."

Justice clapped her hands. "Really? Just like a prince and a princess?"

Ian laughed and Molly smiled. "Well, not exactly, but we love each other as much as a prince and a princess."

"Yay," Justice said. "Can I wear a pretty dress? Like the one for Aunt Jamie's wedding?"

"Let's save that one for Aunt Jamie. We'll buy a new one."

"Yay," Justice said again. "So, Ian will have a sleepover like last night, every night?"

"Yes, he will."

"Can I call him daddy?"

"If you want to."

"Yes! And now I have a daddy and a coach." Justice kneeled up on her chair and faced Ian. She leaned in. "I love you, Daddy."

Molly covered her mouth with both hands. Tears welled.

Ian pulled his new daughter into his chest, kissing the top of her head. He closed his eyes, savoring this moment for eternity. "I love you too, sweetheart," he mumbled into her hair. They lingered for the amount of time a four-year-old would allow.

Justice pulled away. "I'm going to eat ten pancakes," she said. "How many can you eat, Daddy?"

"Ten sounds good." Ian forked more pancakes onto his plate and smothered them in butter and syrup. He sipped his coffee, smiling over the rim at his soon-to-be wife.

Molly's phone rang. "Hi, Mom," she mumbled through a mouthful of pancake. "He's right here, I'll ask him. My mother wants to know if you'd like to see her new work. It's getting shipped out in two weeks but the exhibit isn't for another month."

"Are you serious? She's going to let me preview it?"

"Apparently. Consider it a great honor. Even I haven't seen her latest stuff."

"I'm in!"

"He'd be delighted," she told her mother. "We'll figure out something for next weekend."

"And we can tell them about the wedding," Ian whispered.

Breakfast over, they began to clear the table. "Daddy, come to my room. I want to show you something." Justice tugged on his index finger urging him forward. Ian looked to Molly for explanation but none was forthcoming.

"Get dressed while you're up there," Molly said.

They returned, Justice wearing a pale blue sundress and her white Nike kicks, courtesy of her Uncle Jesse. Molly wiped her wet hands on the kitchen towel and turned away from the sink.

"What did she want to…? She stopped mid-sentence. "You braided her hair… a *French* braid?"

"She asked me to."

"I have no words."

"What? I told you I had three older sisters and when the first two went off two college they said I had to pinch hit if needed since my mother was always in court."

"Again, no words."

"It's not that hard."

Colleen returned to work Monday morning and Justice was just as excited to see her as she'd been when Molly retrieved her from the care of her grandparents. Molly almost felt jealous, but then she smiled. Justice was lucky to have so many people who loved her.

Even though she only had two more weeks left working on the task force, she threw herself into it, putting in the usual long hours and required tenacity.

Molly's phone rang. Ian, the lock screen announced. She picked up. "Hey."

"I've got great news."

"What?"

"I made a few calls and the mayor will marry us."

"You're kidding?"

"Nope. Two o'clock, a week from Saturday."

"Holy shit. You're serious?"

"Deadly. I'm calling my parents as soon as I hang up. I'm not inviting my sisters because it's too much to manage in such a short time, I don't want them to feel obligated. So you get a reprieve from the full Turner onslaught." Molly laughed. "Oh, and can I move my things in before the wedding? Maybe the Thursday before. I don't have much, just personal stuff since I've been renting. That okay?"

"Yes, of course."

"Great. Oh, and I made a reservation at the Millstone for after the ceremony."

"That sounds lovely."

"Morning!" Matt said, filling the doorframe.

"Ian, I have to go, talk to you later." Molly put the phone down.

"Am I interrupting something?"

"Not at all."

He seated himself in front of her desk and plopped his coffee cup atop. "Got ten new cases."

"Incredible."

"The word is out and local law enforcement is calling nearly every day. Feels good to be helping them."

"Yes it does. Listen, Matt, I have something to tell you."

Lily entered. "Morning, boss."

"Hi, Lily." She took the seat next to Matt and reiterated Matt's assessment of the task force's importance. "Ton of new cases. We can barely keep up. The tech guys are doing an amazing job. We arrested four perps last week and two warrants issued today."

Molly inhaled and exhaled slowly. Lily's unbridled enthusiasm reminded her of herself when she was assigned her first big case. Leaving the task force wrenched her gut. But she was doing the right thing, the right thing for her daughter and she needed to stay strong, move on. She'd still be doing good in the world, just not with the FBI.

"What did you want to tell me," Matt asked.

"I'm leaving the FBI. I gave my notice on Friday and Rob accepted."

Matt's eyes narrowed, the lines on his forehead furrowed. Lily actually gasped. "Did I hear that right?" Matt said.

"You're joking?" Lily added.

"I'm not. After Agent Robinson's near-death experience I had a come-to-Jesus moment. I can't risk making my daughter an orphan. I can't live with the fact that her father is dead and on any given day her mother might not come home."

Matt leaned back in his chair. Lily's shoulders deflated.

"Matt, I recommended you take over the task force. You've been practically running it anyway. And you can take over Lily's training."

"Molly, I think you're making a rash decision. You're one of the best agents I know. We need you. Maybe give it some time."

"I've given it a good deal of thought but the decision is made."

Matt shook his head. "Wow, I didn't see this coming. What will you do?"

"Actually, I'm thinking about taking a position with a legal aid firm. Heading investigations and trying cases as needed."

"You're switching sides?"

Why did everyone keep saying that? Even she'd said it to Ian when he first told her he was leaving the DA's office.

"Aren't we all on the same side?" Molly said. "The side of justice?"

Matt sighed. "Sounds like there's no talking you out of your decision. I'll miss you and I wish you the best." He stood. "And don't be a stranger."

"Thanks, I won't. And just as an aside, I'm getting married a week from Saturday."

"To that hot ADA?" Lily said.

Molly laughed. "Yes, to that hot ADA."

"That was fast," Matt said.

"I know, but when you know it's right, there's no need to waste time. I'm starting a whole new life and I'm anxious to get on with it."

"Good for you," Matt said. "You deserve to be happy again." He walked around her desk and hugged her. "Go get 'em, girl."

Chapter 45

I an dialed his mother's number.

"Hi darling, what's new?" No matter how old he got, her voice always brought comfort.

"I'm getting married. A week from Saturday at City Hall. Nothing fancy and we'll have dinner after at the Millstone."

The silence on the other end of the phone lingered. Then she screamed. He'd never heard his mother make such a noise. Never-ever. "Are you serious?" his mother finally said. "Richard! Come here! Ian's getting married!"

"Give me the phone," his father's booming voice said. "Jesus, Mary, and Joseph, son, I'm so happy I could jump out a window."

"Well, that would be ill-advised. I need you here this weekend. It's a small ceremony at City Hall. Just our parents."

"Your sisters will be pissed," his father said.

"I know but it's last minute and it's too much to get everyone on a plane in just a few days."

"Give *me* the phone," his mother said. Hadn't they ever heard of speaker phone?

"Ian, why can't your sisters come?"

"It's too much, Mom. In a few months, we'll do a big splash for family. They'll meet Molly soon enough."

"Fine, but you're going to get a ration of shit."

"I can handle it. So, you guys can make it?"

"Of course. I'll make plane reservations as soon as I hang up. And Ian, I'm so damned thrilled. For you."

"Thanks, Mom. Me too."

Friday afternoon they both managed to leave work early. Molly picked him up at his condo and he insisted she come in for a minute. Justice and Molly walked toward his front door, Justice breaking free from Molly's grasp and jumping into his outstretched arms.

"Hey, beautiful. How are you? I missed you."

"Hi Daddy. I missed you too." She kissed his cheek, three times, with a certain deliberateness. He returned her to the floor and she ran to the sliding glass doors. "Oh, the beach! Can I go outside and look at the water?"

Molly stood beside her and opened the door. "Yes, but stay on the deck."

"I will, Mommy," and she plopped onto the green cushioned lounger looking like she expected someone to serve her lemonade and a cookie with her name on it. She was just missing the floppy hat and Jackie O sunglasses.

Ian came up behind Molly, his arms surrounding her waist. "I have a present for you." He held out a long white envelope in front of her.

"What's this?" She turned and gazed into his eyes, then slid the flap open slowly. She gasped, clutching the paper to her chest. "Oh, Ian. Two tickets to Paris?"

"Our honeymoon, or maybe a baby moon. The week

before Christmas. I thought it would be the perfect time to visit your birthplace. And I've never been, so I'm hoping you'll show me a good time."

"I couldn't be more excited. I've often considered going back for a visit but never seem to get around to it." She kissed him tenderly. "Ian, you're so thoughtful. Thank you."

"Don't worry. You'll make it up to me."

"What I can promise is to make it a week we'll both never, ever be able to write home about." She bit her lip, before continuing, then whispered into his ear, "Can you take a vibrator on a plane?"

Ian laughed loudly. "I guess you liked it the other night?"

"You couldn't tell?"

Yeah, he could tell. "I'll research that but if not, I'm sure France has toy stores for adults."

Molly smiled. "I can't wait."

They traveled the rest of the way in Molly's government-issued Escalade which she'd relinquish at the end of the week. Along with her badge, credentials and service revolver.

Entering her parents' seaside abode, they found her parents in the kitchen preparing dinner. Justice ran to her grandmother and wrapped her arms around her knees. She looked up and said, "Guess what?"

"What?" Alyene said.

"Mommy and Ian are getting married. And I'm getting a new dress. And Daddy says Ian can be my *new* daddy."

Ian and Molly remained silent. Molly had no more words for this ludicrous scenario. This *Sam thing* had to be over soon and she filed the idea of his ghost into the furthest corner of her mind, unsure any of it had the slightest shred of reality. Why she'd let it have any sway over her made no sense. She'd let her emotions overrule logic.

Her mother clapped her hands together. "*Finalement! Avec soulagement!* I am so happy for you both," ignoring the reference to Sam.

Her father grinned. "Me too. I couldn't be happier."

Howard and Alyene levied hugs and Molly basked in the warm glow of their love for Ian.

Alyene escorted them toward her hallowed temple, Justice attached to her grandfather's hand. Alyene tugged on the groaning, oversized barn doors, and Ian peered into the darkened chamber. He held his breath.

Alyene flicked a switch and an otherworldly golden hue bathed the giant chamber. Six ten-foot figures were arranged in a circle with one larger piece in the center. "It's my Dancer Collection." She strode toward the first statue. "This is the Red Dancer. A woman in full flight, defying gravity, determined through precise movements to convey the hidden language of the soul. Emotion."

She moved to the next figure. "And this is the White Dancer. She struggles to rise against the massive weight of her hair, the symbol of the burdens of femininity. The hair is a crown of thorns, a dynamo of energy tying her to the earth. The costume is a binding wrap, constraining and at the same time exposing her body." Her fingers caressed the cool marble affectionately, as if she touched a treasured child. "Next, is the African Dancer, inspired by the African-turned-Canadian dancer Zelma Badu. The dancer turns her face to the blazing sun while her feet are rooted in her native soil. The ebony hair, made from billiard cue blanks, heavy—

visually and physically—strikes the earth in a gesture of defiance."

Throughout the *tour* Alyene avoided eye contact, she spoke in a dreamlike tone, and Ian imagined the untold hours she spent immersed in this fantasy world. Sculpting cold stone into vibrant, animated beings.

"And the Black Dancer. This came to me in a dream. The sleeping figure is imbedded in the mundane, a platform constructed exactly like a cheap kitchen table. The wings, rising from either side, begin with the Old Testament story of Jacob's ladder and lead through the tale of Daedalus to our own obsession with flight.

"The Japanese Dancer depicts the force and strength of another dancer in flight. The raven hair is designed to be seen from the back, a spiral pattern of an unfolding flower, a powerful part of Japanese iconography.

"And Persephone's Dance. Inspired by the goddess of the seasons, and the underworld. The crossed wrists signify her abduction and captivity as a common female fate. The circular structure reflects the cycle of the seasons, the dress being the dark night of winter, the energy of the dance itself manifesting the seasons of renewal and growth, and the golden hair the reward of the harvest."

She faced the enormous form in the center of the circle, crossing her arms over her chest, then landing a finger on her lips. She tapped it several times. "This is my favorite."

"Mommy, that lady looks like you," Justice said.

Alyene ruffled her granddaughter's hair. "Very astute, *ma petite chérie*. This is titled the Dance of Generations. I made this piece as a tribute to my mother who studied dance but never made it professionally. The double dance bar symbolizes her death, the barricade over which she passed. Her left hand is held before her eye as a shield from what she must eventually look upon. While carving the face, the spirit of my daughter emerged from the marble, giving the piece its title."

She clasped her hands behind her back and asked Ian, "So, Number One Fan, give us your critique." Her serious eyes found his. She sucked in a quick breath. "Oh, *mon cher garçon*, are you okay?"

Ian pinched his eyes to suppress the tears. Alyene put her arms around him and he mumbled into her hair, "I've never seen anything so transcendent."

She released him, holding his elbows. "I'm very moved."

"You put the old masters to shame."

"Damn, daughter, if you don't marry this man, I will. Sorry my sweet," she said to Howard.

Molly encircled her mother's shoulders with an arm and pulled her close. "Too late. And one more thing." Molly hesitated, then announced, "We're having a baby."

Alyene raised her hand to her mouth, smothering a gasp. "*Vous attendez un bébé?*" she mumbled through her fingers. "*Magnifique! Je suis si heureuse!*"

"We're happy too."

"Congratulations," her father said. "Two new members to our family. I couldn't be more delighted."

"I'm getting a baby sister?" Justice said, pumping up and down on her toes, hands prayer-like under her chin.

"Oops," Molly said. She knelt in front of her daughter. "You could get a brother."

"That's okay. Boys are nice too. I'll teach him how to play Barbie dolls!"

They sunned themselves and swam in the ocean, and generally enjoyed the perfect summer afternoon. Dinner was scrumptious of course, and Ian basked in the limelight of his newfound family.

They decided to leave for home a little late hoping the traffic would thin out. "Mom, would you mind putting Justice to bed while Ian and I go for a walk on the beach?"

"Of course."

"Sweetie," Molly said, "time for bed. I'll bring you home later."

"Okay, Mommy. Is Ian sleeping over?"

Molly studied her parents faces for signs of disapproval yet knew it wouldn't be forthcoming. "Not tonight. He has to work tomorrow, but he's moving into our house next week."

"Oh goody," Justice exclaimed.

"It's breezy, maybe you want a sweatshirt," Ian suggested.

"Good idea." She borrowed a white zippered sweatshirt jacket from her mother's closet and they sauntered out the back door.

The evening wind fluttered Molly's hair and she brushed it off her face as they strolled toward the water's edge, the briny air filling her nostrils. The full moon cast a shimmering conduit on the water, toward the horizon. Eerily beautiful. Like a path beckoning her to a mystical destination. The surf crawled gently to the shore, the flowing tide languorous, comforting, the lapping waves mesmerizing.

Ian put his arm around Molly's shoulders, pulling her into him. He kissed the top of her head. "Your parents seemed overjoyed about the wedding and the baby," he said facing the ocean.

KENDRA GREENWOOD

Molly placed a hand on his cheek, shifting him toward her, and kissed him. "As happy as I am." She slipped her arm around his waist and leaned her head on his shoulder. "I wasn't planning on telling them about the baby. It just slipped out."

"Well, I'm thrilled they know. If I could, I'd shout it from the top of the Empire State Building."

"You're insane."

"Love breeds insanity." He squeezed her shoulder.

A chilly spider-like sensation crawled down Molly's spine. Dread prickled her nerve endings.

From nowhere, a sizzling discharge. Ian's body jerked violently and he fell to his knees. The silver glint of two coiled wires protruded from his back. He groaned and collapsed in a heap. "Ian," she screamed, stooping to grab him. A man stood behind them. No, two men.

The bolt hit her back, like she'd gotten slammed with a metal baseball bat. Prickling mutated into painful spasms wracking her body. Her teeth clamped down on her lip. Her muscles froze, her mind went rigid. An intense cramp seized her limbs, followed by the stab of a thousand pitchforks.

Then, then.

The light of consciousness.

Slipping.

Into a malevolent darkness.

Chapter 46

Molly's eyelids fluttered open, her chin lolling on her chest. Sitting on wooden planking, her hands tied in her lap, her shoulders secured to a… pole? She ran her tongue over her swollen, bloody lip, her mouth gritty with sand from what she assumed was a full faceplant on the beach. She spat out the contents on the grimy timber. Every inch of her ached, her mind fuzzy, her thoughts jumbled. A memory from Quantico surfaced: Tased. Part of her training.

But who? Why? And Ian? Where was he? Was he okay?

She lifted her head, leaning back against the cold metal and swallowed back the bile seeping into her throat. Her eyes roamed the surroundings, soaking up every detail. The hum of an engine vibrated beneath her. The thump, thump of a hull slapping waves. She turned her head slowly, dizziness roiling her gut, struggling against the cable lashing her to the stanchion, her ankles secured with thick mooring rope.

A groan. She strained to peer over her shoulder. Ian. They were tied back-to-back around a white metal pillar, near the stern of a small fishing boat. "Ian? Are you all right?"

Ian moaned. "Fuck. Not sure. What the hell?"

"Bastards tased us." She tried to slip her hands from the bindings on her wrists, tugging and writhing, to no avail.

"Shit, that's not fun. I had no idea how much it hurt."

"Yeah, shouldn't render you unconscious unless you have a heart attack. Pretty sure they drugged us."

"Where are we?"

"On a boat."

"Why?"

"No idea. But I doubt it'll be a luxury cruise."

A bald man entered the cabin, an AK-47 in hand, his black mustache too large for his face, his lips invisible. "Well, well, Princess Bitch is awake. And Asshole Charming too."

He cocked the rifle and pointed it at her. Her eyes fixed on his face, not wavering. "Who the hell are you?"

"That's for me to know and you never to find out." He lowered the rifle and grinned.

"What are you like, four? Are we playing some kind of game?"

"Feisty little Feeb, I like that."

He approached and the heel of his knee-high rubber boot stomped her thigh. He laughed. Molly yelped in pain, her stomach heaved. *Don't throw up. Don't do it.*

He knew she was a federal agent. That ruled out robbery or a random kidnapping. "What do you want?"

He didn't answer. "Hey, Boss," he yelled through the doorway. "She's awake. And the dude too."

Another man entered the cabin. He stood taller than the first, wearing a dirty white tee-shirt tucked into tattered jeans, a protruding belly hanging over his belt. Boss came close, gazing down at his prisoners.

Rifle Guy said, "How much longer?"

"About a half-hour, still too shallow. I want them deep, deep."

"We gonna shoot 'em first?"

"Nah, we'll just dump them in the ocean and let the sharks do the dirty work."

"Weigh 'em down, right? Don't want them getting rescued." Rifle Guy laughed.

"Not likely, we'll be twenty miles off shore. Nothing but fishes to keep them company."

"What's this about?" Molly said.

"Like you don't know," Boss said.

"I don't."

Boss squatted, alcohol on his breath. The smell of sweat. He stunk nasty. This couldn't be her last inhaled scent, Goddamnit.

"You took everything from me, now I'm taking everything from you two."

"I don't understand. I have no idea who you are."

"You know my cousin, Judge Vera Smoot? We had a sweet deal until you and your buddy here stuck your nose in our business. And then you go and get her fucking killed."

He stood, circling around to Ian. Molly wrenched her body sideways, struggling against the ropes. She heard a thump and Ian grunted. Molly grimaced. This was the cousin on the run. The one who owned the juvenile detention facility and he was here to get his pound of flesh.

Boss kicked Ian in the gut, sending his head tottering forward. He tried not to give the guy the satisfaction of showing pain yet a strangled scream crossed his lips.

Ian sucked in a breath slowly, raising his head, his eyes

narrowed. "What about all the kids she railroaded? She broke the law."

"That's debatable," Boss said.

"Then take it up in the courts."

"You and your whore *are* the law. Even though you hang out at that sadomasochistic brothel."

Ian frowned. They'd been following them? He leaned his head against the hard metal and measured his inhalations. *Stay calm.* "Look, I believe in the system. Justice is served in the courts, not by vigilantes. They have appeal courts for grievances."

Boss guffawed. "We'd never get a fair trial. And besides, you sent her to Riker's and she got the shit kicked out of her and then you got her murdered. Same would happen to us. What kind of justice is that?"

"It's not," Ian said. "I didn't send her there. Someone else did. And I'm investigating what happened. You're right, something went wrong and someone will have to answer for it." Ian's ire escalated. He should keep his mouth shut, but— "Are you going to stand there and tell me you had nothing to do with it?"

"Why would I kill her?"

"Because I have it on good authority that she was about to turn State's evidence against you. Something about you blackmailing her."

Boss's jaw tightened, his lips pressed into a thin line. Ian was pretty sure he'd hit on the truth.

"It really doesn't matter who killed her, she's dead and you'll be joining her any minute now."

Molly said, "You do realize I'm a federal agent and the FBI will hunt you down until they find you. There's no escape for you, no normal life after this."

Boss orbited around again, out of Ian's view. "I got enough money to disappear. You'll never find us." He snorted. "And they'll never find you. Maybe they'll think you two ran off together. You've been playing enough kissy face."

A pain stabbed Ian's chest. The prospect of escaping… thin, the probability of getting thrown in the ocean… drowning… likely. His throat choked. He closed his eyes and steadied his breathing again, keeping panic at bay, barely.

The slap of flesh and Molly yelped, thrashing at his back. Ian tightened his fists, flailing against the ropes, his teeth clenched. "Don't hurt her, you bastard."

"Shut up, tough guy. I'll do with her as I please."

"Rifle Guy rested the gun butt on the floor, his hands covering the muzzle. "She's a beauty. Can't we have some fun before we feed her to the fishes?"

"Tempting. But she's a Feeb, probably got skills. Too risky."

Boss kicked his steel-toed boot into Molly's thigh for good measure. She gritted her teeth so as not to shriek.

"Hey, Boss," a voice from outside. "Get out here."

Boss swiveled, a 9 mm shoved into his waistband at his back, and disappeared through the hatch.

Molly considered her options. Defenseless, no weapon, not even her lock pick or pen knife. Inhaling deeply, she exhaled slowly and studied the surroundings again, searching for anything to use to defend herself. Rifle Guy had a knife strapped to his side. A crowbar leaned precariously under a portal window. Several cinderblocks were stacked next to a mound of thick rope.

Rifle Guy pulled a rickety wooden stool from under a small cabinet and took up guard duty, his rifle between his knees. He leaned his age-spotted hands on the muzzle and perched his chin atop his knuckles. Molly whispered to Ian.

"I'm sorry. Both my guns are back at the house. I've got nothing. Any chance you've got something to use as a weapon?"

"I wish, Molly. I love you so much."

"Good. That's extra motivation to survive. Our only option is to make a move once they try to move us."

"I hope you have a kickass strategy because I only know brute force."

"That'll do." She hoped.

"Shut up, you two," Rifle Guy said as his sidekick returned. "Problem, Boss?"

"Just a whale-watching boat, a good distance away and it moved on. Don't need the Coast Guard surprising us." Rifle Guy remained silent. "I'll let you know when we're ready to dump them. They each get a cinderblock tied around the waist."

"Gotcha."

Boss exited again.

Time moved sluggishly. If they threw them over the gunwale, tied up and weighted, it'd be impossible to pull a Houdini. The ropes binding her limbs were tight, nearly cutting off her circulation. Trepidation cramped her stomach, the muscles in her shoulders objecting against the strain of bondage. She'd never overcome the two of them and was running out of time. If she could only get her hand on the knife or better yet, a gun.

And she had to pee like a motherfucker. Fuck!

The smacking of the bow on the water slowed, the engine hum diminishing. Boss entered through the hatch. "It's time."

Chapter 47

Rifle Guy squatted and severed the ropes around Molly's ankles with his Bowie knife, firearm slung across his back. The sweat slathering his bald head reflected the overhead cabin lights. If Molly could get her hands on that knife… He was big, over six feet, at least 220 pounds.

He pressed the knife point into her breast, eyes squinted on his smug face. His lipless mouth morphed into a sinister grin. The dagger's tip lingered, pressure slowly increasing. She held her breath in anticipation of the blade piercing her flesh, cutting her heart out, like in some B horror mess. Provoking her a few seconds longer, they remained in a staring contest yet she wouldn't blink first.

He snickered, then slid the blade under the rope binding her chest and yanked it forward. It took two slices before the strands released, hands still bound in front of her. He stowed the knife in the sheath on his belt and yanked her to her feet by one arm.

Boss dragged two cinderblocks over, ropes tied through the holes. "I'll take the guy, you do her."

Now or never. Jesus, if you're real! Never or now.

Rifle Guy bent to grab the cinderblock's tether and Molly kneed him in the chin. He fell backward and she grabbed the knife from its sheath with both hands. Stunned, rifle guy silently writhed on the floor. She held the knife out in front of her, ready to attack.

On his feet again, he lunged for the dagger but she feinted, he swung his fist and missed, nearly falling forward. Ire exploded in her gut. Her face burned, an animal snarl clawed its way up her throat. She planted her feet several feet apart, brandishing the knife, he wouldn't get close enough. He scrambled upward, eyes bulging with rage.

She took a lurching step forward. He sidestepped, landing a blow to her ribs, sending fresh zigzags of pain through her torso. She didn't fall, she made absolutely sure she didn't, but damn was it close.

The guy went in for another shot. Molly slashed his arm with the blade. He knocked it out of her joined hands, then recoiled, clutching the wound. She kicked him in the groin and he crumpled. She jumped on his chest. They smashed onto the floor together.

She slammed his head into the planking until he stopped moving.

Boss crouched and slashed the ropes binding Ian's ankles, then stood and snaked the rope around Ian's waist. Ian swallowed hard. Of all the ways he'd ever imagined dying, being chum wasn't one of them.

Would Molly give him a signal or should he take his own initiative?

He heard a whack and turned to see Molly knee her captor in the face. She had the knife. Boss stopped tying Ian's waist to the block when he witnessed Molly pummeling his partner-in-crime. Molly straddled her captor's chest, pounding his skull into the floorboards.

Ian might not get another chance.

He slammed his bound wrists into Boss's jaw, sending him reeling. Boss stumbled and fell, but clambered to his feet and charged. Ian maneuvered right and Boss hit the sidewall. He quickly pivoted, landing a punch to Ian's gut. Ian doubled over, expelling his last bit of choked air. He struggled to stand, glowering at his attacker.

Boss's eyes glinted, wild. Ian advanced, pinning Boss against the cabin wall, his forearm crushing his attacker's neck. He shoved all his weight into it. Boss sputtered and grabbed Ian's arm, pulling downward, gasping.

Boss's blow glanced his chin, then he buried his fist in Ian's gut, again and again. Ian fell to his knees, the wind knocked out of him. Boss yanked him up by the collar, the rasp of material ripping. Dragging him to his feet, he slammed Ian against the wall. Then bashed him in the stomach again. Ian's legs gave out, his back sliding down the wall until his ass hit the ground. He closed his eyes, trying to catch his breath.

A single deafening roar from an assault rifle punctuated the air like an exclamation point, the bullet piercing the ceiling of the tiny cabin.

Everyone froze.

Ian turned and stared down the rifle barrel of the third kidnapper. *Shit.*

"Over against the wall," Third Man said. "Both of you." He pointed the rifle to the left several times and Ian and Molly haltingly complied, managing to stand shoulder-to-shoulder.

Rifle Guy groaned, blood poured from his lips and nose. His face ashen. "Motherfucker," he said, struggling to sit up. He wiped the gore from his face with his sleeve and clambered upward. He glared at Molly, their eyes locked in battle. He picked up the knife and held it to her throat. "You bitch, I should have cut your heart out while I had the chance."

"That's enough," Third Man said.

Rifle Guy studied Molly's face for a too-long moment before returning the knife to its sheath. He continued to stare at her then slammed his fist into her jaw. Her head snapped back and she tasted coppery blood, surging. He struck again, hitting her in the midsection then backhanded her, knocking her off her feet. Felt like she'd never stop seeing stars. Blood pounded in her ears. He towered over her and kicked her for good measure. She rolled onto her side, pulling her knees into her chest.

"Enough," Third Man said again. "Let's get this over with."

Boss yanked Molly to her feet and pinned her back against his chest, her upper arms caught in his vice-like grip. "Tie it on," he said to Rifle Guy.

Rifle Guy cinched the rope around Molly's waist while Third Man grabbed Ian so Boss could secure the cinderblock around his waist. Ian's eyes fixated on Molly, his jaw tight, sweat beading his forehead.

"I'm sorry," she said.

"Don't be. It's okay."

Rifle Guy spat a bloody wad on the floor, wiping his mouth with the back of his hand. "Aww, Romeo and Juliet are having a moment."

"No banter," Third Man said. "You two almost fucked it up. Let's get this done."

Rifle Guy picked up the cinderblock and marched Molly

through the hatch like a dog on a leash, while Boss escorted Ian in similar mode.

The ocean breeze fanned Molly's skin, her hair swirling every which way. So cold suddenly. All around her—bone-chill. As if the Reaper himself hovered over the grisly scene. Only the constellations bore witness. She gazed into the night sky, the North Star bright. If only it could guide them to safety.

They forced Molly and Ian to sit on the gunwale. Molly glanced over her shoulder at the onyx water. Three guys, all armed and they were weaponless again. Done. Death imminent. They'd be thrown overboard and drown. Molly despaired. She'd never get the chance to love Ian. Or the new baby, who wouldn't even get to be born. And Justice… her worst fears had breached reality. The idea of her daughter growing up without her father and now her mother spiraled her into a hopeless abyss.

Third Man slung his rifle across his back, switched off the engine, and perched his buttocks on the console. He withdrew an open whiskey bottle from the cupholder and took a long draught, then crossed his arms over his chest. The deck diminutive, they were compressed in a tight circle, just inches apart. The boat swayed gently to the rhythm of the waves, the night suddenly too quiet.

The full moon's rays beckoned her down its gloomy pathway. She imagined hitting the freezing salt water, the cement block dragging her downward, down. Past sleeping barracudas, goblin sharks, slithery eels and spiny sea cucumbers.

Unable to breathe. She'd heard dying by drowning wasn't painful and the ice-cold water would numb her into oblivion. And Justice, oh God. Soon to be an orphan.

Her psyche fractured into shards.

She closed her eyes and inhaled the salty air. Her chest

hurt, probably busted a few ribs. She'd made her move and failed.

"Wait!" Ian yelled. "She's pregnant. Let her go. What happened to Judge Smoot was my fault. She had nothing to do with it."

Boss studied him. "A bun in the oven? Well, ain't that a hoot."

Rifle Guy snickered. "Looks like I got it wrong. We got Prince Valiant here, not Asshole Charming."

"Boss," Third Man said. "I'm all for killing the dude but I'm not on board for killing no baby."

Molly didn't think being pregnant would save her, even with Third Man's reluctance. This was the end. *Or*, maybe.

"Listen," she said, "I have money. A lot."

Chapter 48

Boss focused on Molly, his unblinking eyes tight.

"I can get you enough money so you'd be set for ten lifetimes."

Boss flicked his eyes back and forth between her and Ian. "Feebs don't make that much money. How much we talking?"

"Ninety-one million."

"How does a Feeb have that kinda dough? You dirty?"

"My husband was killed. Hit by a truck that belonged to a major corporation. They gave me ninety million dollars without even going to court. Don't take my word. Go online, it was a record settlement and made the news. Plus we had a million-dollar insurance policy."

Rifle Guy rested his gun against the console and seemed to consider her offer. "That's a lotta moola," he said, "we could disappear and live the high-life."

Molly kept up the momentum. Even if they didn't go for it, distraction changed the equation. "Let us both go. Please, I have a young daughter. I can't leave her alone in this world.

And a new baby coming. I promise I won't pursue you. Nobody has to know this even happened."

Third Man interjected, "This was supposed to be about revenge but I say we cut the chick loose and take her money."

Molly said, "I can put the money in your account in sixty seconds. I know how to hide transfers."

"Do it," Rifle Guy said to Boss.

Boss rubbed the back of his neck. "I don't trust her. This might be a trap."

"Then we kill her. Just like we planned," Rifle Guy said.

An argument broke out as the nefarious trio debated the pros and cons of taking Molly up on her offer. She focused on the unattended rifle leaning against the console. She intended to live up to her reputation as one of the Four Horsemen and this would *not* be her Apocalypse.

With tied hands, she snatched the rope attached to the cinderblock and swung it, hitting both Rifle Guy and Boss in the gut. They tumbled onto the deck, the 9 mm dislodging from Boss's waistband, sliding sideways, crashing into the transom, about ten feet away. Molly plucked the knife from its sheath once more and slit the rope secured to her waist, then pointed it at both men.

Boss stood again. Rifle Guy remained prone, holding his knee, writhing in pain.

Surreal. The aching in her belly and ribs, the confusion of being punch-drunk. The thought of facing off against Boss again.

He lunged and managed to seize her wrist, jerking the knife from her grip, slicing her palm. She winced, squeezing her hand to stifle blood flow. He threw a haymaker. She ducked and responded via an upper-cut with bound fists. The snap of his teeth fueled her. He charged again, shoving her shoulders backward.

Falling down was not an option.

Whipping around, she karate-chopped the hell out of his throat. He dropped, choking, sputtering. "Cunt."

Panting, she pulled him to his feet, ready to claw his larynx out. He stumbled forward, reeling from the hit, swinging blindly. She kicked him in the back, flattening him.

Click. "That was entertaining," Third Man said. She spun, facing an AK-47.

Behind Third Man, like a vengeful angel, Ian slammed his tethered fists against the perp's temple, knocking him to the ground. His adversary struggled to right himself. Ian landed another blow, smashing his fists into his chin, reeling him backward, then grabbed one leg and flipped him over the gunwale. Third Man hit the water, taking the rifle with him.

Boss ran to secure the lone rifle but Ian beat him to it. He pointed the weapon at Boss—standing a foot away. "Don't," Ian said. "I'll kill you if I have to."

Molly stood over Rifle Guy, knife in hand.

Boss grabbed the gun barrel and yanked it from Ian's grip. "Big mistake, Mr. ADA. Don't ever stand that close to your target." He pointed the weapon at Ian. "Over there, next to your baby momma."

Damn. The 9 mm, still behind Boss. No way Molly could get to it.

The back of Rifle Guy's hand hit the side of her head and she plummeted sideways, landing on her back. Pain seared her insides, a witch's brew of sharp and dull daggers, her brain signaling a red alert to her injured tissues and bones.

Done. Over. No strength left to fight.

How many seconds of precious life left? *I love you, Justice.*

A gust of gale-force wind lashed her face. *So cold.* A wailing, high-pitched sound all around her. Alien, other. As if the Reaper himself hovered over the grisly scene.

A jolt against the boat's hull jerked the bow up, tilting it at a nauseating forty-five-degree angle, then slamming down against the ocean surface. A torrent of freezing seawater washed over the starboard side, the ocean's fury once again threatening their lives, thrusting Molly against the deck and slamming her into the gunwale. She grabbed the rail, hanging on for dear life, swallowing saltwater, choking and sputtering, barely able to breathe.

Something small and silver glinted. Hurtling toward her, as if seeking her out.

The object smacked into her knee, a sharp stab.

The 9 mm.

She would never remember reaching for it. Focusing on the eerie wailing, she watched Rifle Guy and Boss rush toward her, faces gnarled in pure hatred.

The first shot pierced Rifle Guy's forehead. The second hit Boss in the identical spot. Just like she'd done a thousand times on paper targets at the gun range. The bodies crumpled to the deck and Molly collapsed back against the gunwale, every inch of her body *whimpered*.

Standing directly behind the two dead men, Ian groaned. "Oh shit," he said, then clutched his chest and sunk to the ground.

Time slowed—halted.

She staggered toward Ian, who lay prone on the deck, his eyes closed, his body disturbingly still. So much blood. Oh God. He couldn't be.

"Ian?" Her knees buckled. "You're hit!" A bullet must've exited one of her targets and struck him.

She searched out the knife, severing the ropes binding her wrists, the one around Ian's waist and those around his hands. She ripped open his shirt. Fresh blood everywhere.

No, please. Please, no. Why did every man she love end up dead?

Chapter 49

Molly shrugged out of her sweatshirt jacket and used it to wipe away the blood so she could assess the damage. An obvious bullet hole. She peeked under his shoulder. *Thank God.* An exit wound. If not, the danger would be great, the shell could migrate anywhere, even piercing a vital organ. She'd seen that happen.

"Stay with me, Ian." She put two fingers against his carotid. A pulse. "Don't you dare leave. We have two kids to raise."

Using the cloth as a make-shift bandage, she pressed down hard, putting her weight into it. After a minute, she released the pressure and watched to see if blood soaked through. She'd staunched the bleeding.

Ian's face twisted in pain and he drew his knees up and moaned. His eyes fluttered open.

"Thank God," she said, then jumped up and plucked the whiskey bottle from the holder and knelt beside him. "This is gonna hurt." She doused the wound.

"Fuck!" Ian said, pounding the deck with a fist. "Motherfucker. You weren't kidding."

"I rarely kid about stuff like this." She cut off the jacket sleeve of her sweatshirt and fashioned it into a binding, then positioned his arm over his head and tied the makeshift tourniquet tight around his shoulder, knotting it under his armpit. She exhaled the breath she'd been holding, her gore-covered hands resting on his chest.

"I—I think you're gonna be okay," she said. "You got lucky. The bullet didn't stay in your body."

"I think I'm in shock," he whispered.

"No doubt."

"Nice save, Special Agent Masterson. On both counts."

"Yeah, after *I shot* you."

"Help me up," he urged.

She put an arm around his back and eased him up, settling him against the gunwale. Water dripped off his nose and Molly laughed. "You're soaked."

"Ya think?" He ran a hand through his wet hair and wiped it on his pant leg. One eye slitted. "Your nipples are hard."

"Seriously?"

"I'm shot, not dead." Somehow, he simultaneously smiled and winced.

She regarded his face in the bright moonlight, his eye nearly swollen shut. "Nice eye, by the way."

"Sexy black eye?" he suggested.

"Yeah, builds character."

Ian laughed. "I haven't been in a fight since I was like ten and it wasn't much of one. It was a dare and I think we were both scaredy cats."

He wrapped an arm around her and snuggled her into his chest.

She embraced him in return, her head on his uninjured shoulder. Their hearts beating in grateful rhythm. "I thought we were goners," he mumbled into her hair.

She peered up at him. "We kicked their asses." Hesitating, she added, "Let's drive this mother-fucking boat to shore."

Facing the console, she turned the key. Another whining noise, the sound du jour or rather *nuit*. Again. A click. No power. "Fuck. Engine flooded. This night just won't end."

"We need a phone," Ian said.

She rummaged through pockets, finding one in Boss's jeans. "It's wet, hope it works." Molly dialed Matt. *Pick up, pick up,* she prayed.

"Hello?"

"Matt, this is Molly. I need an extraction."

"Where the hell are you? Your mother alerted us you were missing. What happened?"

"Long story, but I found the guy who ran the detention center. Or rather he found us. Ian Turner is with me. We're on a boat about twenty miles offshore of Montauk Point. Send the Coast Guard."

"Are you safe, hurt?"

"Ian's been shot but I've stopped the bleeding. I'm banged up pretty good. Three guys dead, one in the drink, two onboard."

"We'll track the phone. Keep it on. Lily and I are at your parents' house. We'll meet you at the hospital."

Molly and Ian sat on the gunwale in silence, her body hollering in agony.

"You definitely got the worst of it," Ian said.

"What? You took a bullet."

"Sorry I wasn't more help."

"Are you kidding? You were a worthy combatant. I'd go into battle with you any day."

Ian grasped her good hand, slipping his fingers through hers. "Are we gonna talk about the elephant on this godforsaken boat?"

Molly sighed. She touched a finger to her split lip and flinched. "Elephant?"

"It's probably shock..." He grabbed her hand. "But, listen. I-I... saw something... scary, weird."

"What do you mean?"

"That gun found its way to you." Molly didn't answer. "And... I swear... time went screwy. I-I could see the bullet coming for my heart. Then something shimmery. A hand, maybe. It flicked the bullet sideways, changed its trajectory just enough."

"A near-death experience can trigger a hallucination," she offered as a lame excuse.

"Maybe, but I didn't hallucinate everything: totally calm seas, then something hits the boat from underneath, a freaking tornado erupts, a wave swamps us, and that gun magically finds its way into your hands?"

Molly stared at Ian but again didn't respond.

"...and then something deflects that bullet, saving me."

"I don't believe in ghosts. I can't," she said.

"I didn't think I could either, not until now."

"Maybe a whale crashed into the hull."

"You should've seen your own expression when you just said that."

Molly slid a hand down her wet face and exhaled force-fully, almost a sigh. "There are whales this time of year. Easiest explanation. Mother Nature." She paused then added, "And I'm not reporting some bullet-deflecting ghost. Jesus."

Ian frowned. "I'm not that imaginative, or prone to fantasy."

"Then Occam's razor."

Ian narrowed one eye. "Well, either way, it's a miracle. And we need to get our story straight."

Three beats elapsed, as a certain understanding passed between them.

Molly gazed up to the distant heavens, then at her immediate surroundings. An unmistakable iciness caressed her face, ever so gently.

Chapter 50

T he chop-chop of helicopter rotors recalibrated her focus. A bright beam in the dark sky searched the water's surface. From the other direction fast-moving red and white blinking lights approached, a far-away siren heralding salvation.

Molly tried to stand, but doubled over, holding her side. She gasped for breath.

"Easy," Ian said. "Sit back down. Wait for medical help before you make it worse."

The search light from above lit up the tiny fishing boat like a Broadway stage. The force of the rotors churned the seas. Three Coast Guard skiffs surrounded them. Men and women barking orders, tying ropes to cleats to stabilize the bobbing boat.

"Agent Masterson?" a uniformed woman in a cap asked, climbing aboard with a male companion.

"Yes," Molly said.

"Lieutenant Austin, at your service, ma'am."

"I don't have my credentials."

"No problem, ma'am. We're here to take you to the

hospital on Agent Holloway's orders. Lieutenant Briggs here is a certified PA and will assess your injuries. Your companion incurred a bullet wound?"

"Yes, but there's an exit wound and I was able to stop the bleeding."

Lt. Austin scanned the deck where Boss and Rifle Guy lay crumpled in the pose of corpses, then leaned over and checked for pulses. "These the perps?"

"Yes," Molly said, surrendering the 9 mm. "Another went overboard."

Lieutenant Austin accepted the firearm, secured the lone AK-47, put the safety on, then handed them off to another officer on the skiff. "We'll order a search immediately."

"I hit him pretty hard," Ian said. "I assume he was unconscious when he went over."

Lieutenant Austin gave Ian the once-over. "You FBI too?"

"Nope. Suffolk County Chief ADA and I don't have any credentials that matter."

Vitals were taken, wounds triaged, and bandaged.

Lieutenant Briggs informed Lieutenant Austin, "Could be internal injuries on the female but nothing life-threatening. No need to transport by helo. Probably some bruised ribs, I don't think they're broken. We'll take them aboard."

"Roger, that," Lieutenant Austin said.

Two ambulances waited at the dock. Ian was reticent to leave Molly's side as they were strapped onto gurneys and transferred to Southampton Hospital, lights flashing, sirens blaring. Entering the emergency room, Ian sighted Lily and a man he assumed was Matt, in the company of Mr. Masterson.

"Jesus," Matt said, "Molly, you took a hit." He turned to Ian, "Special Agent Matt Holloway." He extended his hand.

"Ian Turner." They shook. "Hello, Agent Blakely."

"Lily, please."

Mr. Masterson grabbed Molly's uninjured hand. "You scared the crap out of us, sweetheart."

"Sorry, Dad. But it's all okay now. Other than the fact I shot Ian."

Mr. Masterson's eyes knit together as he studied Ian. "I don't understand."

"Collateral damage," Ian offered.

"Jesus, man, you okay?" Mr. Masterson said.

"Apparently, I'll live. Molly proved to be an excellent EMT."

"Well that's a relief." He turned to Molly. "Your mother stayed back with Justice. Luckily, she slept through the whole thing."

"Glad about that." Molly wondered aloud, "What time is it?"

Her father checked his watch. "3:35."

"Jesus, what a fucking night."

A nurse motioned the EMTs to usher the gurneys forward, hitting the square silver button opening the doors to the treatment area.

"Molly." Ian turned to see Daniel Taylor, *Dr.* Daniel Taylor. He stopped the gurney and picked up Molly's gauze-wrapped hand by the wrist. He pulled back the bandage. "This will need stitches. Maybe we can get by with surgical glue."

"Daniel, how did you get here so fast?" she said.

"I was here to see a patient when I got the call from Alyx that they transported you guys to the ER."

"I called Alyx," Matt said.

Daniel faced Ian. "Nice eye. What happened to the shoulder?"

"Shot. I'm told I'll live. Honestly, Molly took the worst of it. I don't think I was much help."

Daniel peeled back the make-shift dressing and scrutinized the wound, checking the exit wound. "Hit in a good spot. Looks like it missed the bone. We'll get an x-ray."

Molly's eyebrows lifted. "Don't say that, Ian. We never would have gotten the upper hand without your intervention, your bravery. Not many everyday citizens would've stepped up like you did."

"I was fighting for my life, for *our* lives. That kinda makes you do things you never thought you'd do, and you don't think about repercussions until after the fact. I'm sure I'll have my *holy shit* moment in the near future."

Ian thought about the bizarre gun incident. Molly would never put that in her report, nor would he. They'd agreed to that already. Would they ever speak of it again?

"Nurse," Daniel said, "who's the ER doc on call tonight?"

"Ginny Mason."

He turned toward an ambulance EMT. "What are their vitals?" The tech rattled off a string of numbers and a general summary of observed wounds. To Molly, Daniel said, "I'm concerned about internal injuries. We'll do some tests. Nurse, tell Ginny I have to check on a patient but I'll be back shortly. I want a full report on both patients, stat."

"Of course. I'll let Dr. Mason know."

Daniel squeezed Molly's uninjured hand. "Are you in a lot of pain?"

"Not too bad, as long as I don't move."

"She's lying," Ian said. "She doubled over as soon as she tried to stand. And she wasn't quiet about it."

"We'll get you something for the pain. How about you?" he said to Ian.

"I'm fine. Kinda numb."

"Endorphins will do that. I'll check back with both of you in a bit."

The gurneys entered adjacent bays and Ian requested they pull back the curtain so he could keep his eyes on Molly. A short, round woman dressed in blue scrubs entered, a stethoscope around her neck. "What do we have?" She observed Molly. "Looks like you fought a good fight. How's the other guy?"

"Dead."

Dr. Mason blanched. "Okay, then. Busy night for the morgue too." She listened to Molly's heart and lungs, palpated her ribcage, and flashed a tiny white light in her eyes. Molly winced and groaned and Ian held his breath. Seeing Molly in pain squeezed his heart. "I don't think they're broken. How's the breathing?"

"Painful."

"We'll get a CT scan for confirmation and to rule out internal injuries. We'll know more after the scan." Dr. Mason placed a thumb on Molly's split lip. "Not too bad, should heal fine without stitches. Anything else hurt? Any numbness?" She studied the laceration on Molly's hand. "I'll use glue on this."

"She's pregnant," Ian said.

"How far along?"

Molly gave him the evil eye. "Not far. I just took the test."

"Good to know. We'll do a sonogram to be sure everything is okay."

Dr. Mason swapped out her gloves. "What about you?"

"Shot in the shoulder and popped in the eye." She came close and examined Ian's shoulder. "Nurse, let's get film." She opened his half-closed eyelid and stabbed his eyeball with a beam of glaring white light, flicking it back and forth several times. "Did you hit your head?"

"No, just punched in the face."

"I don't think you have a concussion. The eye looks okay, we'll get some ice on it. On and off every fifteen minutes for the next twenty-four hours."

A med-tech arrived to wheel Molly for her scan and Ian to radiology for his x-ray. Their gurneys side-by-side at the elevator doors, Ian leaned over and whispered, "You better be okay or I'll have to spank you."

"Careful mister. You've just seen what a fucking badass I am." Molly smiled then winced, touching her split lip. "Ouch."

Chapter 51

M olly donned her wedding dress, a gorgeous ivory lace, backless sheath, the hem midway down her calves.

"*Ma chérie, tu es si belle,*" her mother said.

"Thank you, Mother. Can't believe I'm doing this."

"Well, I couldn't be happier. Ian is a magnificent man, I couldn't have wished for anyone better for you, and for Justice."

As if on cue, Justice ran into the room, grandfather in tow, having been assigned the task of dressing his grand-daughter. "How do I look, Mommy?" By some miracle, Molly's mother had found nearly the identical dress for Justice, not backless, but other than that, pretty damn close.

Alyene Bouchard clapped her hands together. "*Ma petite chérie*, so beautiful. Turn around."

Justice did her usual ballerina twirl.

"Wow," Howard Masterson said. "Molly, you look lovely. And so happy. Does my heart good."

Ian fumbled with a cufflink and his new father-in-law came to his rescue. "I'm all thumbs for some reason."

"If a man isn't nervous on his wedding day then he's not human." Howard slipped the silver shaft through the double holes and fastened it shut, then helped Ian into his jacket. "How's the shoulder?"

"Healing fast."

Ian turned and Howard smoothed down his lapels. "Excellent, now you just need that shiner to catch up."

Yeah, Ian thought, his wedding picture would immortalize his black eye for eternity. But he considered it a badge of courage and a reminder that he and Molly had fought for their lives and won against all odds, which meant they could survive anything. Supernatural assist notwithstanding.

Howard stepped back and gave Ian the once over. "Looking quite dapper, my man."

Ian smiled.

1:45 p.m. City Hall. They waited in the vestibule of the mayor's office. Molly's mother presented Molly with a small bouquet of white roses interspersed with violet allium, and also one for Justice. "This is all happening so fast. Why isn't my stomach doing loops?"

Her mother grasped her upper arms, her eyes serious. "When it's right, it's right. You have no reservations. It was the same with your father and me. We eloped in Paris. No one attended. Our parents were totally caught off guard and it took them a while to understand. But my mother knew I'd made the right decision. She said, 'I can see there's no such thing as too much of this man, you want him when you're happy, sad, tired, sick. You, my daughter, are hopelessly in love'."

Wise words, and exactly how she felt about Ian.

"Never try to hide anything from trained detectives,"

came a voice over her shoulder. Molly faced Alyx and Daniel with their son in Daniel's arms, Laura and Steve with their baby, and Jamie and Colin too."

Molly's jaw dropped. "How?"

Laura explained, crossing her arms over her silky pink dress. "Colin and I were having lunch with the mayor to plan this year's fundraising gala for our Foundation and he accidentally spilled the beans. Of course, he thought we knew, with us being so close and all." One eyebrow hiked up.

"And don't think because you've quit the FBI, that you can quit us too," Alyx said.

"I just didn't want to rain on your parade," Molly said to Jamie and Colin.

"Well, you're not and we're here so let's get this show started," Jamie said.

Ian's mother rushed her next. She grasped Molly's hands and pulled her close. "This may easily be the happiest day of my life." A tear glistened. "I worried my son would never be happy again, but you've saved him."

"We saved each other," Molly said.

Ian's father added, "I'm thrilled to welcome you into our family. To merge our family with yours. I couldn't be happier."

Ushered into the mayor's inner sanctum, Molly was grateful there was no aisle to walk and fortified by her best friends, she threaded her arm through Ian's and faced the mayor. Justice wriggled free from her grandfather's arms and stood beside her, slipping her tiny hand in hers. She gazed at Justice's smiling mug and squeezed her hand. It felt as if Justice was older all of a sudden. A wiser, worldly woman who someday would be her best friend.

The mayor began, "May today be the beginning of a long, happy life together. I wish you a wonderful journey as you build your new life as one."

Molly's eyes met Ian's, his smile as wide as the new world they would soon enter.

"Repeat after me," the Mayor said. "I, Molly Masterson, call upon these persons present to witness that I take thee, Ian Turner, to be my lawfully wedded husband... to be loving, faithful and loyal to you all the days of our lives."

Ian repeated the declaration. They glided white gold bands on each other's fingers.

"I now pronounce you husband and wife. You may kiss the bride."

And he did, way too passionately for a public gathering. "I love you," Ian whispered.

"I love you too. More than I ever could have imagined."

Their lips touched again, their tongues entwined.

The extra attendees were invited to the small reception at the Millstone, toasts made, food eaten, conversation merry and light. Even a little dancing.

Justice wheedled her way in between Ian's legs as he conversed with Daniel, Colin and Steve. "Daddy, dance with me."

Ian scooped Justice into his arms, laying his glass on a nearby table. She wrapped an arm around his neck and announced, "Uncle Daniel, I'm getting a new sister. Or maybe a brother. I don't care, I like boys too." Daniel knew about the pregnancy after treating Molly at the hospital, but had vowed to file it under doctor-patient privilege for the time being.

The three men didn't respond, but Laura, nearby, did. "What? A baby?" as Alyx and Jamie looked on.

His mother chimed in, "Did I hear you right? I'm getting a new grandchild?"

Ian had grilled plenty of witnesses on the stand and he now understood exactly how that felt. "Ah… well…"

Molly wrapped both hands around Ian's bicep, holding tight, remaining silent.

Hands flew to mouths. "Oh my God," Jamie said. "Congratulations."

But Justice wasn't done. "Oh, and Daddy says you're welcome, Mommy."

Molly frowned. "For what?"

"For saving you guys. On the boat."

Molly's face grew ashen. Ian gulped. "I don't know what to say to that," he offered.

"Me either." Their friends studied them, waiting for clarification. "One of these days I'll explain, just not today," Molly said.

Not done yet, Justice added, "Don't worry, Mommy. Daddy said he has to go away."

Relief wormed its way into Molly's psyche. "Oh? Where's he going?"

Justice shrugged. "I don't know. He just says he's not worried anymore."

Thankfully, their cadre of friends politely ignored the bizarre colloquy, it would be a future discussion, one that included copious amount of alcohol.

The three female FBI agents, plus former Agent Molly Masterson, formed a tight circle. Alyx raised her champagne glass. "To the Four Horsemen of the Apocalypse. The four married horsemen. Back at Quantico, I never could've imagined us married with children. Still freaks me out."

The band of friends held up their glasses in tribute. "Here, here."

Ian nudged Colin, and whispered, "Apocalypse? Horse-what?"

"Their nickname at Quantico. They held almost all the records in their class and everyone claimed if the world was ending, they wanted them at their side."

Ian smiled. "Good to know."

"Daddy, dance with me," Justice pleaded again.

"It would be my pleasure." Ian carried her onto the shiny laminated floor, swaying in rhythm to the music.

Molly smiled, comforted by Ian's love for their daughter. And for her.

Whiff of premium liquor, floral perfume, Alyx whispered into Molly's ear, "I'm so, so, so happy for you. Seeing you sad nearly broke my heart."

Sadness? Molly thought. Undone.

Finally and forever.

Unsaddened.

The End

First Look!

Book Five in the Steel and Desire Series

Unburned

Shaking, the world. Aquiver. Blurred at the edges. She couldn't tell up from down. A claustrophobic light ensnared her synapses. Choking, ripped apart. A scream tore from her chest.

Shadows fell, washing away the sky's sharpened glare. A moment of silence. Shattered.

The smoke, the heat. Fire! She couldn't breathe.

Lily woke. A dream? But the alarm blared. Her nostrils burned, acrid air assailing her tiny bedroom.

Lily jumped out of bed, clad in a white tank-top and a pair of boy-shorts, unable to see past her nose. Darkness, fumes. She beelined to the bathroom and grabbed a towel from the rack, doused it with cold water, slapped it over her face and opened the door to the hallway. Flames!

Slamming the door shut, she sprinted back toward her

bedroom. She stood on her bed and peered out the double-hung window. Flashing red lights, firetrucks, one with a bucket moving skyward. Her apartment was on the fifteenth floor.

She slapped the window several times. *Help! Somebody help me!*

Unlatching the window, she tried to shove it up. Wouldn't budge. She'd been meaning to tell the super the window was stuck. Too late now, Goddamnit. Trapped.

She surveyed the small bedroom for something to smash the window with. The metal wastebasket, too flimsy. She had a hammer in the laundry room, in the toolbox. No way to get there. Flames crept toward her bedroom door.

Her gun. She pulled her Glock from the bedside drawer and double-checked to make sure the safety was on. Hopping back on the bed she heaved the gun's butt against the pane. Nothing. Three more times. The fucking glass had to be double-paned and break resistant. Damn it!

Her breathing labored, her pulse skyrocketed. She needed to calm down, shallow breaths, think, think.

Dense smoke surrounded her and she pressed the wet cloth against her face again, her forehead flush to the unyielding windowpane. She was dead. Consumed by smoke and flames. Her young life snuffed out before she had a chance to really live. She'd just begun her career at the FBI, a job she coveted. And she'd never loved anything this much, other than Sean, who'd left her at the altar.

Good Lord. She'd die today. Her tombstone announcing: Here's a girl who never got a chance to fly. Never accomplished anything. Never knew what true love was.

Heat scorched her back and she pivoted, the door on fire. She faced the window again. What? She blinked, coughing. A figure appeared, an honest-to-God superhero.

A firefighter dangled in front of her like a spider on a silken tether.

He signaled her to move back from the window. She read his lips. "Back up, I'm gonna break the window." He had a pointy metal bar in his hands. "Cover your face."

She moved off the bed, her back against the wall and hid her face in the towel. The shattering glass sounded like a miracle. She peeked out from behind the towel. He clambered inside the frame, his massive form standing on her bed. "Come on, I've got you." He beckoned her toward him.

A cold wind wafted in. A shiver wracked her nearly naked body. It had to be like thirty degrees, way too cold for an autumn night in New York City. She grabbed her service revolver and his expression crimped.

"I'm FBI and can't leave this behind."

"The safety on?"

"Yes."

He grabbed the barrel. "Give it to me."

"No. It's against regulations."

"I don't give a shit about protocol. This is my call." Seriously? Locked in a staring contest in the middle of a raging fire. She handed over her service revolver. "Good girl." He shoved the Glock into his side pocket and zipped it shut. "Put your arms around my neck and hold on tight."

He unbuckled his oversized black jacket and tucked her inside. "You're not wearing much clothing. You'll catch a cold."

His smile relaxed her. Safe. Saved. His body heat was something else… a fire of its own. She pressed her face into his neck, her chest against his. "Thank God for you," she mumbled.

He put one arm around her waist and hauled her onto the window frame, securing her against his chest. He barked into his radio and motioned thumbs up. "I've got her."

Barely rising one story, fire exploded from an adjacent window, igniting the line. If it burned through, they'd plummet to their deaths. Splattered on the macadam street. They swayed on the rope, precariously, at least two hundred feet off the ground.

He tightened his arm around her, and she held on for her future—all of it. Every single day, year, decade.

"JT," a voice over his radio said, "the roof collapsed, you'll have to lower yourself down."

"Not gonna happen," JT said. "The rope's on fire. We're going down fast."

"Roger that. We're in position."

"Hold on tight, darling, looks like we're landing on the jump cushion."

Lily peered down. A ring of rescue personnel surrounded a giant black air bag. *Oh God.*

The rope snapped. Falling! Time slowed. The night seemed to swallow her whole. Everything a haze, tumbling. Air pushed against her face and she closed her eyes, waiting for the inevitable smash.

They hit the cushion with considerable force, JT on his back and she sprawled on top of him. She pulled up and stared at his handsome face, his blue eyes bulging like someone who'd just met their Maker. He smiled. "Close one."

Tearful, she climbed off him and two firefighters grabbed her and lowered her to the ground. Lily nodded her thanks. He handed her the gun, garnering stares from his comrades. "Here you go, Miss Special Agent."

JT picked her up in his arms and carried her toward a waiting ambulance. "Let's get you checked out." He smelled alluring, not of smoke, of something more intoxicating. Pheromones?

He placed her into the open ambulance, sitting her on the edge. "You saved my life," Lily said.

"John T. Shadow, at your service, ma'am." He made a hat-tipping gesture, then like a guardian angel who'd completed his mission, vanished into the melee of flashing lights and mayhem.

Coming Soon!

Kendra Greenwood

Kendra Greenwood has always been a storyteller. She often told stories to her kids at bedtime in lieu of reading to them. A serious daydreamer, she used to think it the complete opposite of her education and work in the sciences, but now realizes scientists are the ultimate daydreamers. Fantasy has always been an escape for Kendra. Weaving a thrilling romantic tale around her favorite TV and film characters, her favorite way to fall asleep at night. Eventually she wrote them down and found a place to share her stories.

Kendra grew up on the beaches of Long Island's bucolic east end, but recently relocated to Virginia. When she's not writing you can find her in the kitchen whipping up something scrumptious or in the studio fusing glass into decorative dishes.

Follow her on:
Twitter @k51greenwood
Facebook Kendra Greenwood
Email kendra51greenwood@gmail.com

Don't miss these exciting titles by Kendra Greenwood and Blushing Books!

Steel and Desire Series
UnSub
UnBound
Unguarded

Unsaddened

Blushing Books

Blushing Books is the oldest eBook publisher on the web. We've been running websites that publish steamy romance and erotica since 1999, and we have been selling eBooks since 2003. We have free and promotional offerings that change weekly, so please do visit us at http://www.blushing-books.com/free.

Blushing Books Newsletter

Please join the Blushing Books newsletter
to receive updates & special promotional offers.
You can also join by using your mobile phone:
Just text **BLUSHING** to 22828.

Every month, one new sign up via text messaging will receive
a $25.00 Amazon gift card, so sign up today!